PRAISE FOR Ch__

Small Town Superhero

"Anyone who grew up in a small town or around motorcycles will love this! It has great characters and flows well with martial arts fighting and conflicts involved."

—Karen, Amazon Reviewer

"Cheree Alsop has written a great book for youth and adults alike. . . Small Town Superhero had me from the first sentence through the end. I felt every sorrow, every pain, and the delight of rushing through the dark on a motorcycle. Descriptions in Small Town Superhero are so well written the reader is immersed in the town and lives of its inhabitants."

—Rachel Andersen, Amazon Reviewer

The Silver Series

"Cheree Alsop has written Silver for the YA reader who enjoys both werewolves and coming-of-age tales. Although I don't fall into this demographic, I still found it an entertaining read on a long plane trip! The author has put a great deal of thought into balancing a tale that could apply to any teen (death of a parent, new school, trying to find one's place in the world) with the added spice of a youngster dealing with being exceptionally different from those around him, and knowing that puts him in danger."

—Robin Hobb, author of the Farseer Trilogy

"I honestly am amazed this isn't absolutely EVERYWHERE! Amazing book. Could NOT put it down! After reading this book, I purchased the entire series!"

—Josephine, Amazon Reviewer

"Great book, Cheree Alsop! The best of this kind I have read in a long time. I just hope there is more like this one."

—Tony Olsen

Thief Prince

"This book was a roller coaster of emotions: tears, laughter, anger, and happiness. I absolutely fell in love with all of the characters placed throughout this story. This author knows how to paint a picture with words."

—*Kathleen Vales*

"Awesome book! It was so action packed, I could not put it down, and it left me wanting more! It was very well written, leaving me feeling like I had a connection with the characters."

—*M. A., Amazon Reviewer*

"I am a Cheree Alsop junkie and I have to admit, hands down, this is my FAVORITE of anything she has published. In a world separated by race, fear and power are forced to collide in order to save them all. Who better to free them of the prejudice than the loyal heart of a Duskie? Adventure, incredible amounts of imagination, and description go into this world! It is a 'buy now and don't leave the couch until the last chapter has reached an end' kind of read!"

—*Malcay, Amazon Reviewer*

Stolen

"This book will take your heart, make it a little bit bigger, and then fill it with love. I would recommend this book to anyone from 10-100. To put this book in words is like trying to describe love. I had just gotten it and I finished it the next day because I couldn't put it down. If you like action, thrilling fights, and/or romance, then this is the perfect book for you."

—*Steven L. Jagerhorn*

SMALL TOWN SUPERHERO II

Small Town Superhero Series Book Two

Cheree L. Alsop

StoneHouse Ink 2014
Boise ID 83713
http://www.stonehouseink.net

First eBook Edition: 2014
First Paperback Edition: 2014
ISBN: 978-1-62482-117-2

Cover design by StoneHouse Ink
Layout design by Ross Burck – rossburck@gmail.com

This book was professionally edited by Tristi Pinkston
http://www.tristipinkstonediting.blogspot.com

The characters and events portrayed in this book are fictitious. Any similarity to a real person, living or dead is coincidental and not intended by the author.

Published in the United States of America

To my husband, Michael Alsop,
my hero and my true love.

To my family for each and every day.
No matter the ups and downs,
every moment is an adventure.

I love you!

SMALL TOWN
SUPERHERO
II

Chapter One

I MOTIONED TO MAGNUM and he darted to the right. I rolled the throttle of my motorcycle and took the left. The engine of the semitruck protested as the driver forced it up the steep mountain incline. According to the sheriff, if we had the right truck, it was loaded with stolen televisions and other electronics. The plates matched, so all we had to do was get the driver to pull over and check the cargo.

I rode on the yellow line, waited for a car to pass, and then widened the distance between me and the truck so the driver could see me. I motioned for him to pull over. He glanced at me, then turned his attention forward again. Frustrated at how far away from Sparrow our search for the truck had brought us, I decided to take a chance. I drove close to the truck's door and banged on it with my fist. He jerked the truck toward me. I backed off quickly so I could gesture for the driver to pull over again.

The truck driver glared at me, but his attention suddenly shifted to the other side where Magnum was no doubt running out of patience as well. The pavement hummed under my tires. The vehicle between us swiveled from side to side as the driver tried to force either of us off the road. The telephone poles that dotted the road flew past as the truck barreled up the road at speeds far faster than its safety or size could handle. The engine growled in protest as it was pushed even faster.

The truck again swiveled slightly, but the driver wouldn't look at me. I wondered what Magnum was doing to keep the driver's attention. We rode through a mountain pass that angled sharply upward. There was a turn to the left at the top of the incline. Two cars sped down the pass toward me. I fell back and tried to catch Magnum's attention. The cars rode by in a blur on my left side. Magnum glanced back once and I waved him down, but he turned back to the driver.

I gunned the motorcycle and raced to Magnum's side. He was shaking his fist at the driver and pointing ahead, trying to get him to stop before we reached the turn. I slapped him on the shoulder, a dangerous move with both of us riding at such speeds near the edge of the road, but it got his attention. I motioned quickly for him to fall back. There would be room to take the driver down after the turn. He nodded and I slowed, relieved.

Magnum didn't fall back with me. Instead, he grabbed something from his jacket pocket and threw it at the truck's window. The driver jerked the truck toward Magnum. I was forced to fall back or be crowded off the road to the ravine beyond. My heart leaped in my throat at the sight of Magnum fighting for room. I couldn't do anything when the truck driver jerked his vehicle all the way over.

A plume of dirt and grass signaled Magnum's crash. The truck shook like it had been hit by a massive fist. My breathing stopped entirely at the sight of sparks shooting from beneath the tires. The vehicle gave another massive shudder as it veered onto the shoulder, then lurched over something in its way. I darted to the left just in time to avoid the destroyed remains of Magnum's blue CBR motorcycle. I braked hard, desperately searching for any sign of Magnum. He wasn't with the wreckage. My blood ran cold at the thought that he was still somewhere under the truck.

The truck centered itself in the lane. I downshifted and surged ahead, speeding past the right side of the truck. I spotted Magnum underneath the trailer, holding on to the frame directly in front of the rear tires. My heartbeat pounded in my ears. If I couldn't get the truck to stop, he would be crushed for sure.

The truck jerked toward me in the same maneuver the driver had used to run over Magnum's motorcycle. I anticipated the move and braked so the truck passed, then gunned to the driver's door again. The need to save Magnum filled every thought. I gritted my teeth and grabbed the rail by the door, then pulled myself onto the step.

My motorcycle tipped and slid along the road. I yanked at the door, but the driver had it locked. Enraged, I pounded on the window. The driver grabbed something from beneath his seat. I cursed at the sight of a handgun. Before he had time to turn it on me, I slammed my head forward, hitting the window with my helmet as hard as I could. The glass shattered around me. Shards bounced off my riding gear.

I reached through and grabbed the gun with one hand and the steering wheel with the other. The driver braked, sending the truck careening back and forth across the road.

"Pull over!" I shouted.

When he failed to comply, I elbowed him in the nose. His head jerked back and he let out a yell of pain, dropping the gun. I grabbed it and pressed the barrel against the side of his head. "Pull over," I growled.

He nodded and slowed the truck. We stopped at the top of the incline just before it veered to the left. I could see the abyss of the ravine through the passenger window.

"Get out," I said.

He fumbled for the door handle and opened it. I pulled him to the ground and forced him on his face on the gravel.

"Magnum!" I shouted. "Are you okay?"

I jogged around to the other side in time to see Magnum slowly release his grip from the truck's frame. He set a leg shakily on the ground, then let go of the vehicle as if he would never touch another semi again. I grabbed his arm and steered him away from the ravine.

He pushed back the visor on his blue helmet. "Took you long enough to stop the thing," he grumbled, his voice shaky.

"Sorry, man. I tried." I checked him over quickly to make sure he was all right. Besides a few scrapes and some dirt on his helmet, he appeared to be unharmed.

"I'm fine," he snapped, pushing me away. "Where's the driver?"

"On the other side. Just try not to kill him," I said.

He ripped off his helmet and followed me around to the other side. A string of not-so-muffled curses told me exactly how he felt.

I let out a huff of air at the sight of the driver running down the road. Magnum glanced at the gun I still held, cupped his hands around his mouth, and shouted, "We have a gun. We'll shoot you if you don't get back here!"

The driver slowed, then stopped and threw up his hands in defeat. He turned and made his way back toward us.

Magnum lowered his voice and growled, "I should shoot him anyway. He tried to kill me."

"The sheriff will deal with him," I said, glad I was the one holding the gun.

"We could toss him over with the truck."

I rolled my eyes. "The bullet holes would be suspicious."

"Now you're getting technical."

I let out a slow breath, "That didn't go the way it was supposed to."

Magnum chuckled, surprising me. "The sheriff owes me a new bike."

I jerked my head back toward the truck. "We just recovered major evidence in a merchandise theft ring. I'm guessing he'll be glad to get you a new motorcycle."

He was about to reply when the truck's wheels turned slowly backwards.

"Uh, Kelson," Magnum said as the truck's back tires slipped off the road toward the ravine.

"Crap," was all I could think of to say.

I ran for the door, but Magnum grabbed my arm. "There's no time!"

He was right. Before I could touch the frame, the second set of tires was over the edge of the road. The vehicle paused, then slid into the ravine.

Magnum and I watched as the truck rolled over and over, smashing trees and bouncing down the side of the mountain with the sound of twisted metal and breaking glass. Smoke and dirt rose in a plume as the back doors flew open, sending boxes of merchandise flying. The vehicle carved a path like a giant bulldozer, leaving destruction and tattered boxes in its wake.

The driver stopped next to us and watched silently for a moment until the truck came to a stop near the bottom.

"That's not my fault," he said quietly.

I glared at him, even though he couldn't see me through my black visor. "This whole thing's your fault," I replied.

He shook his head and pointed at the truck. "Not that."

Magnum's mouth fell open and I could see him trying to maintain control. "You should have put on the brake!"

"Your comrade here pulled me out before I could," he protested.

"Everyone puts on the brake," I said, astonished.

"Not when they have a gun to their head," the truck driver argued.

Magnum's fists clenched. "You almost ran me over and left me hanging on the side of your truck, and you're the one who's mad? You'll be going in for attempted murder along with transportation of stolen merchandise."

The driver glared at him. "You'll have to prove it."

Rage showed in every line of Magnum's body. "It's our word against yours. Who do you think the sheriff will believe?"

"Two high schoolers on motorcycles who just sent my truck off the side of a cliff? You should be going in for destruction of property."

"The sheriff will take care of you," I said, trying to stay calm despite my urge to hit the guy. Silence followed my words. The three of us stared at the wrecked semitruck for a few minutes.

"Maybe not everything was destroyed," Magnum mused.

"It rolled about four hundred times," I countered.

Magnum shrugged. "Televisions are packaged pretty securely with all that Styrofoam. Some boxes might have stayed in the truck."

An explosion drowned out his last words. The valley below us washed in orange. Dirt and debris flew everywhere. The blast ricocheted off the peaks around us. We stood in silence as the sound faded away to leave the quiet pop and hiss of flames amid the wreckage.

"That's not my fault," the truck driver repeated as the three of us stared down at the burning mess that used to be a truck full of stolen merchandise.

"Shut up," I growled.

Magnum cleared his throat. "So, uh, how are we getting back?"

I glanced at him. "You didn't bring your cell phone?"

He shook his head. I thought of my phone sitting on the end table at the Ashbys' house. "Where's your cell?" I asked the trucker.

He gestured at the destroyed truck lying in the bottom of the ravine.

I fought back a wave of ironic laughter. "I guess we'll have to take my motorcycle."

"Let's see if it still works," Magnum muttered, obviously sore about his own pile of twisted metal down the road.

I kept the driver between us as we made our way to my motorcycle.

I righted the Er-6n, checking it over to make sure no vital fluids were leaking. It was pretty scratched up, but the sliders had prevented it from being too damaged in the fall. I pulled dirt and clumps of grass from the pegs and brushed what gravel I could from the paint. I slid the gun behind my belt and studied the limited seating options.

Chapter Two

WE PULLED UP TO the police station with the truck driver
sitting in front of me on the gas tank and Magnum behind me
perched on the very back of the bike. Needless to say, it was a very
uncomfortable ride, and Magnum's muttering wasn't quite shielded
by his helmet. The few cars that passed us on the road definitely
got a laugh out of the situation. I wouldn't be surprised to see the
picture in the next Bulldog Bulletin, if not on the local news.

A deputy spotted us as we pulled up to the sheriff's office. He
waved, then disappeared inside. "Just perfect," Magnum grumbled.
Before we could climb off and save what was left of our dignity,
half a dozen deputies and the sheriff came out.

"What do we have here, Black Rider?" Sheriff Bowley asked.
He rubbed a hand down his short-trimmed beard and mustache,
obviously trying to hide a smile of amusement at the situation.

I kept my voice level as I pulled the driver from the motorcycle.
"This is the driver of the truck of stolen merchandise."

The sheriff's smile faded completely and he gave the driver a
serious look. The man had spent the whole trip trying to convince
us to let him go because the merchandise had burned with the truck,

so there was no evidence against him. I wasn't sure what the sheriff could hold him on, but after everything Magnum had gone through, I wasn't about to see the man walk free.

"Well done," the sheriff said. He glanced at Magnum, surprised he was with me but willing to save his questions for later, given the circumstances and our audience. "Where's the merchandise?"

I fought the urge to drop my head and said, "In the truck."

Magnum stifled a laugh. Though we both wore helmets, the deputies probably recognized his riding gear and would definitely know the smashed-up CBR we left by the side of the road. That might be a problem for us.

Sheriff Bowley's gaze tightened. He looked at me. I let out a small breath. "The truck's at the bottom of a ravine."

"Is the merchandise destroyed?" he asked.

Magnum laughed flat-out. I punched him in the shoulder and he shut up. "The odds are fairly good that there's nothing much left," I said, picturing the giant explosion.

"You have to let me go," the truck driver said smugly. "You don't have anything to hold me on."

"Shut up," the sheriff and I told him at the same time.

"You tried to murder me," Magnum snapped. "He's got that on you."

"And there is evidence—it's just not very accessible," I pointed out, picturing the few boxes that flew out of the truck on its way down.

"They're trying to blackmail me!" the driver protested. "I didn't try to kill him. You can't prove anything!"

The sheriff's gaze tightened. "That's for the judge to decide. The Black Rider knows where your truck is; we can match the plates to the pick-up location, and I'm guessing both boys will be glad to provide a statement. You're not going anywhere."

Sheriff Bowley handed him off to his men. They grabbed the protesting driver and hauled him inside.

When we were alone, the sheriff gave me a searching look. "You were supposed to locate the truck and call for backup, not try to take him on single-handedly. Most drivers are armed these days."

I nodded. "I noticed." At his look, I shrugged. "I forgot my phone and didn't want him to get away, and then Magnum's bike got run over and he was hanging under the trailer. I had to pull it over to save his life."

Magnum was over surveying the damage my bike had taken during the fall. He glanced in our direction, then looked away.

The sheriff lowered his voice. "Why is Magnum with you?"

I could hear the caution in his voice. I watched the leader of the Bullet gang as I replied, "Better with me than against you."

He hesitated, and then nodded. "Just be careful. This town doesn't need to lose any more of its sons."

"I will."

"And start carrying your phone. I only got you involved because we couldn't patrol every road and keep an eye on the parade at the same time. I promised Dale in Herring we wouldn't let the thief slip through, but a truck isn't worth a life."

I rubbed my chest where my bruised ribs ached. "If they can link this truck to the runs, then track down who hired the driver, they'll have an in to stopping the merchandise thefts. That'll relieve the store owners cowering in fear that they'll be hit next."

The sheriff's eyebrows rose. "You've done your research. I didn't take you for the cautious type."

"I'm not," I admitted. "But Maddy was worried and did some searching."

A slight smile touched his lips at that. "You've got an interesting team."

I nodded. "They tell me there's a better way than jumping through windows."

He laughed. "They have a point. Take care of yourself."

I shook his hand. "Call me if you need anything."

"We'll need a report."

"It'll have to be from the Black Rider," I said.

He pushed his flat-rimmed brown hat up. "Of course, but when we pull the plates, we should have everything we need."

I fought back a wry smile even though he couldn't see it through my tinted visor. "Good luck on the plates, Sheriff. You may have to do some searching."

"That bad, huh?" he said. "One of these days, you'll have to tell me how it ended up in the ravine."

I raised my hands. "It was the driver's fault, and I'm sticking to it."

He laughed and turned to walk back up the stairs, then paused. "Kel—uh, Black Rider?" When I waited, he said quietly, "Keep your eyes peeled. I have word that some of the Verdos and Brown Hawk gang members who weren't involved in the shooting have been hanging around. I wouldn't be surprised if they're looking for revenge against you and Magnum for the failed drop."

The thought sent a surge of warning through me. "Why weren't they with the others?" I asked in as calm a voice as I could manage.

He shook his head. "I'm not sure, but they'll blame it on both of you, so be careful."

I nodded. "I will."

I walked back down the steps, not at all anxious to ride my motorcycle with Magnum on the back, but at least it was better than three of us.

Magnum looked up. "Hey, Sheriff?"

Sheriff Bowley paused with his hand on the door.

"I'm gonna be needin' a new ride," Magnum drawled. "You'll find mine back up the road."

The sheriff sighed and entered the building.

Magnum chuckled. "It'll be nice riding a CBR again after this hunk of junk."

"It's a good bike," I shot back.

"If you like secondhand wrecks from the junkyard."

"Maybe I do," I replied, then rolled my eyes at the stupidity of the statement.

Magnum grinned through his visor.

A thought occurred to me as I ran my hand over the scratches that marred the flat black paint. "What do you think about not getting a CBR?" I asked casually. "How about getting a bike to match mine?"

Magnum stared at me. "Why would I do something stupid like that?"

I blew out a slow breath and tried to keep my patience. "Look, Magnum, everyone knows your motorcycle. It doesn't matter if you keep your helmet on because the entire town knows it's you."

He shrugged. "So?"

I stifled a groan. "So the point of being the Black Rider, or the Black Rider's sidekick—"

"Partner," he snarled.

I ignored him and continued, "Is to work under the cover of our disguises in order to protect our families."

He thought about it for a minute. I knew he liked the town knowing who he was. Hiding his identity was a new concept entirely.

I was worried he would balk at the idea, but a grin spread across his face. "Yeah, and I could get a matching helmet and leathers." He paused and studied me. "Those look familiar."

I grinned. "I wondered when you would notice. Jeremy used them to keep pressure on my leg the day I wrecked your bike."

"Into my truck," Magnum reminded me. "I wanted to punch your face in."

I grinned under the helmet. "I remember."

He rolled his eyes at my tone. "At least I know where to get another one."

"You're going to match me completely?" I asked doubtfully.

He nodded, excitement growing in his expression. "That way, there can be two Black Riders. We'll be like a super team. No one will know who is who, and it'll be like we're everywhere at once!"

I smiled, warming to the idea. "We could help the sheriff deter a lot of the crime in Sparrow."

"I wonder what name Martin will give me in the *Bulldog Bulletin*," Magnum mused.

I shook my head. "The point is for no one to know that there's two of us, for least as long as we can keep them guessing. That way, we'll be more formidable."

Magnum sighed as though staying anonymous was a challenge. "Fine. But I think your bike needs a few modifications."

I STOPPED AT THE one stoplight in Sparrow. A truck across from me was the only other vehicle in sight. They definitely needed a motion sensor on the light. Around me, shops painted carefully by hand sat open amid the lull of the workday. Most farmers were busy clearing fields, plowing, irrigating, or tending to livestock. The shops would be full by evening, especially the two grocery stores and the three bars.

The air was touched with a scent of alfalfa and exhaust from the smoky engine of the green truck that continued to creep forward despite the stoplight. The farmer never truly stopped. By the time the light turned green, he was halfway across the intersection. I figured it was a good thing traffic was low, though as the farmer sped off, it was at a rate not much faster than his crawl through the light. I guessed someone could easily avoid hitting him.

The main street was four lanes, two in each direction. A few dilapidated buildings near the bridge were remnants of upstart businesses either too forward-thinking for the town or limited enough in their scope that after a few sales, they had saturated Sparrow with their products. Somehow, the sight of the town's main street was familiar and comforting. Sparrow hardly changed, a fact I used to despise but now found reassuring. Enough happened in my life that the stability of the small farming town gave me an anchor I never expected.

I drove fifteen miles from town and pulled down the dirt road to Jagger's junkyard. Though Uncle Rick felt the damage I did around the farm was enough to send me to work unpaid for his brother, the stacks of cars and organized parts showed the results of my labor. I felt like I was doing something, even if only Jagger and I could tell a difference.

I pulled the motorcycle around Jagger's wooden shack and stashed it in the lean-to before he could ask me about the shape it was in. I wasn't sure how to explain it. Frustrated fury at what had happened raced through my veins. I carried car parts and stacked them in piles in an effort to keep myself busy, but my mind refused to stop replaying what had happened.

I had almost seen Magnum get killed. The sheriff was right—it wasn't worth dying over a truck. I could put *myself* in danger, but if my actions threatened someone else, I wasn't ready to deal with the consequences. It was only through sheer luck that Magnum had escaped with his life.

I threw a car door onto a growing pile, then picked up a bumper and dragged it behind me toward the stack near Jagger's wooden shack. I could have used the four-wheeler, but the physical labor helped to chase the pent-up anger from my body. I wanted to hit something, anything. I threw the bumper into the pile. It landed with a satisfyingly loud crash. Two seconds later, the entire pile tumbled down. I let out a sigh and began to stack it again.

Maybe inviting Magnum to join me had been foolish. He was foolhardy and definitely was not in control of his temper. I wasn't sure what he would have done if he had been holding the gun. I didn't like entertaining the idea that he would have shot the driver, but given the circumstances, I was almost ready to shoot him myself. Between the two of us, self-control was going to be severely lacking.

A few days later, I was carrying steering wheels for Jagger's never-ending organization of the junkyard when the rumble of an engine caught my attention. I watched a rider pull into the junkyard and my heart slowed with recognition and a touch of trepidation.

The rider rode a flat black Er-6n and wore black gloves, black riding gear, and a black helmet with a tinted visor. The effect was daunting and a grin spread across my face. I had seen pictures of myself as the Black Rider, but I had never confronted the image head on. It was pretty intimidating.

Magnum pushed his visor up and a matching smile showed on his face. "Man, this feels awesome! Everyone waved at me in town, and kids even asked to take their picture with me."

The trepidation returned, but I tried to keep smiling. I didn't realize how much I had grown to associate myself with the Black Rider. Hearing someone else parading around and accepting the welcome meant for me smarted a little. I swallowed my pride and nodded. "It's a good look for you. How'd the sheriff find one so quick?"

"Apparently the sheriff has a buddy who owned one. They painted it black and called me. I gave them a few suggestions."

I walked around the bike. "What did you do to it?"

He grinned. "I asked them to put a fender eliminator kit and a new exhaust on it. It gets more power and that ugly mud flap is gone. I think it looks sleek." He got off and followed me around the bike. "What do you think?"

"They're supposed to be the same," I replied, but I had to admit it looked better.

He nodded. "The sheriff said he'd do the same to yours."

I stared at him. "Why?"

He shrugged, another smile stealing across his face. I had seen Magnum smile more times in the last two days than in my entire time at Sparrow combined. "Apparently he feels like the town owes you a thank you or something."

I rubbed the back of my neck. My bruised ribs ached with the movement, reminding me of the past behind Magnum's words. "They don't owe me anything," I said quietly.

Magnum glanced at me. "Yeah, they do. Everyone does, so accept it like a man and let the sheriff upgrade your bike a bit. It'll look better and give you more power. What's there to complain about?"

I didn't reply.

The door to the shack opened and Jagger came out with his little dog, Mick, at his side. At the sight of Magnum standing in his junkyard, Mick immediately started yapping. He charged down the single step and bounced around Magnum, growling and barking with all the ferocity the Chihuahua could muster. Jagger put up with it for a few seconds, then stomped his foot.

"Get o'er here," he commanded.

Mick barked one last time, then stalked slowly to the porch where he sat with his head on his paws, his eyes never leaving Magnum.

Jagger crossed to the motorcycle. He squinted, his eyes almost disappearing behind his red cheeks. He ran a hand down his long beard thoughtfully. "Hmph," he grunted noncommittally, his shrewd eyes shifting to me. "Looks a lot like your'n."

I shrugged.

"Looks better'n your'n," Jagger concluded with another grunt. I gritted my teeth and refused to comment. Jagger turned his attention to Magnum. He eyed the Bullet leader up and down. "You Fisher's boy?"

Magnum nodded and glanced at me, unsure how to respond to my uncle's eccentric brother.

Jagger tipped his head toward a large pile of random car parts. "I'll be need'n those sorted next."

The stack was a mess of rusted car hoods, fenders, axles, partially decayed seats, steering wheels, and what was once a nice little BMW that now better resembled a crushed soda can.

"Why that stack?" I asked. I usually wasn't obstinate with Jagger, because in Sparrow a job was a job and working in the junkyard was less hazardous to my health than farming, but that particular pile towered three times my height and my ribs were already aching.

"'Cause it's there," Jagger replied. He lifted the crowbar he used as a cane in a half wave and made his way back to the shack.

"Have fun," Magnum said with a smirk. He climbed on the motorcycle and slid his visor shut. "I'll be working on my name, since you don't like Magnum."

I rolled my eyes at his tone. "Magnum's a great name," I said with more than a little sarcasm. "It's just that I can't be calling you Magnum when we're supposed to be in disguise. It'll blow our cover."

He paused with his hand on the key. "I guess you're right. It would make sense to have something that works with the Black Rider." He started the engine, then lifted his visor and looked back at me. "How about Dark Wing?"

I fought back a laugh. "Like the duck?" He glowered and I put up a hand. "I have the perfect name." At his eager look, I grinned. "How about 'the Black Rider's sidekick'?"

He slammed his visor back down and gunned the motorcycle, leaving me in a cloud of dust and rocks. My smile faltered. I might have been witty, but I was the one stuck sorting through piles of junk while he rode away on a newly customized motorcycle. Somehow my victory didn't feel very sweet.

Chapter Three

I WADED THROUGH JUNK until the sun set completely—the end of the true farmer's workday, as my cousin Cassidy would say. I drove Jagger's four-wheeler to my aunt and uncle's house and waited just long enough for Jake to run out and join me. Somehow it felt right to have the black-and-white dog loping at my side as I made my way along the empty road to the house at the end.

I couldn't understand why anybody would live so far from the city, but I was grateful for the lack of streetlights as I parked at the edge of the Wests' lot and made my way across their lawn in the cover of darkness. Buck, Madelyn's big brown dog, raced through the grass and jumped around Jake. I smiled. If the dog was loose, Maddy was already outside waiting for me.

"Have fun at the junkyard?" she asked from the shadows of the tree.

A tremor ran through me at her soft voice and my heart raced at the thought of her so close. "Always," I replied. I ducked under a branch and found her watching me, the gold that outlined her hazel eyes bright in the moonlight. She lowered her gaze so her eyes were hidden beneath her lashes.

"I was hoping you'd come tonight."

I touched her chin, and a jolt of electricity raced down my arm at the feeling of her skin under my fingers. "I was counting down the seconds until I could get away."

A smile spread across her face and she looked up at me. "I'm hard on your work ethic."

I shrugged. "What work ethic?"

She laughed, then covered her mouth and glanced at the house. "Let's go," she whispered.

I led her back across the lawn. She climbed onto the four-wheeler behind me and wrapped her arms gently around my waist, mindful of my bruises. The dogs fell in as I drove slowly up the road, taking the path between the fields to the wash hidden beneath a grove of reaching, thorny trees.

I offered Madelyn my arm and led her down the wash to the small knoll of grass that offered a lookout over the still pond. The surface was unbroken, reflecting the light of the half-moon with all the grace and expectant silence of a mirror.

"Where are the geese?" I asked. There was no one around for miles, but the crickets chirruped quietly around us and the sound of the wind brushing softly through the tall reeds captured the night in a blissful harmony I was reluctant to break.

"They left this morning," Madelyn said. Her breath tickled my ear from where she leaned against me. "I heard them honking when I awoke and made it to the window in time to see them as little specks before they disappeared against the mountains."

The wistful tone in her voice made me pull her closer against my side. "You're not trapped here," I reminded her. "Your father's taking care of your mother. You can go when you're ready."

She let out a small sigh I barely heard, but didn't reply. Instead, she sat on the grass and pulled me down beside her. "How was your day?"

It was my turn to sigh. "Magnum showed up dressed as the Black Rider." I felt her head lift from my shoulder in surprise, but she kept silent, knowing I had more to say. I took my time trying to put into words how I felt. "I'm fine with the idea of a partner, especially if it gives him something to do and keeps the Bullets out of trouble."

"But *you're* the Black Rider," she said softly.

I nodded. "It was my idea, but now I'm not so sure."

She was silent for a few minutes and I waited, hoping she would say it was a crazy idea and Magnum shouldn't be riding with me. Instead, she surprised me by saying, "I think you should see where it goes."

I leaned back to look down at her. Maddy's eyes captured the starlight, the gold flecks bright amid the green. "Why is that?"

Her forehead creased slightly and my heart clenched at the concern in her eyes. "You could use a bit of help once in a while," she said, running a hand over my chest.

I breathed through my nose, willing my heartbeat to slow.

"You almost got killed, Kelson," she continued, her voice tight as though the words were hard for her to say. "If someone else had been there to help, you might have gotten off better."

My voice was thick when I replied, "It wasn't so bad."

Her lips pressed together to hide a smile. "Let me see how it's healing."

When I didn't move, she slipped her fingers under the hem of my white T-shirt and slid it up. I obliged by raising my arms as far as my ribs would let me. She eased the shirt over my head and off my arms.

I let out a breath at the feeling of the night breeze against my skin and lay back on our little knoll. The cool grass tickled my back.

Madelyn settled against my side, her head pillowed on my shoulder. Her long brown hair tickled my arm. I smiled at how good it felt to relax with the one person who knew everything about me.

Maddy's fingers trailed softly across my chest, touching the purple bruises that splayed out from where the bullets had hit the vest a week before. "Does it hurt?" she asked.

"Only when I breathe," I replied with a wry smile.

She turned her face toward mine. Her cheeks were rosy and highlighted by the moonlight that caressed her skin. I lifted a hand and gently brushed a strand of hair from her face. It meant so much to me that she wore it down now that her uncle wasn't a threat. A blush highlighted her cheeks, and the barest touch of light gold eye shadow accented her hazel eyes. She looked stunning. I felt a surge of gratitude that she no longer felt like she had to hide her beauty.

She tipped her head and her lips touched mine. My breath caught in my throat as I kissed her back. Her hand rested above my heart and I wondered if she could feel how it threatened to burst through my chest.

She smiled against my lips and then tipped her head down to kiss the four bullet bruises that made dark circles against my skin. The feeling of her lips on my chest made my heart pound even harder. I tipped my head back and let out a slow breath. Her lips brushed the healing gash across my shoulder Dr. Carrison had stitched up, and then she leaned back on one elbow to look down at me. "How about now?" she asked teasingly.

Her head blocked out the moonlight, her face a silhouette above me. Her hair tickled my neck as her vanilla scent filled my nose. I could still taste the kiss that lingered on my lips. "I can't feel anything," I said, my voice tight past the knot in my throat.

She let out a musical laugh and leaned against my shoulder again. "Good," she said with a satisfied chuckle. After a few minutes of comfortable silence, she set a hand above one of the bruises again, covering it with her fingers. "I do think having Magnum with you is a good idea," she said, her voice somber. "I don't want you to get hurt, and it might give you a break."

I pulled her closer, touched by her concern. "I'll give it a try."

She nodded and ran her fingers lightly down my ribs. I closed my eyes and memorized the feeling of her hands on my skin.

<hr>

I PULLED UP TO the Ashby house and parked the four-wheeler in the back near the barn. Jake walked to his bowl and took a few laps of water before he collapsed in an exhausted heap near the door. He wagged his tail when I walked by. I paused and patted his head.

"I don't really like dogs," I reminded him. "But I think you're growing on me." He swiped my hand with a sloppy, wet tongue. I made a face and wiped my palm on my jeans. "Thanks for that."

I opened the back door and left my sneakers in the mudroom beside the myriad dress boots, sneakers, slip-on shoes, and farm boots from which wafted an odor that made me hurry past without identifying the substance caked to the soles. I grabbed one of Aunt Lauren's dinner rolls from the breadbox on the counter and opened the fridge.

"You're home late."

I straightened at the sound of Mom's voice. A twinge of guilt held me. I had forgotten she was there instead of in California where she had been a week ago. "Hi, Mom." I gave her a quick hug and indicated the roll with a tip of my head. "Want one?"

She sat down at the table. "No, thanks. We had roast and potatoes earlier."

"Farmers love their meat and potatoes," I said as casually as I could.

Mom's presence in the Ashby house threw me off. I had gotten
used to the tiny niche I had found for myself, mildly ignored unless
I was floundering through work on the farm or giving the cows
names they retaliated against at milking time. Mom flew in when I
was shot trying to distract gang members from taking out my loved
ones and most of the small town of Sparrow at the town's annual
fair.

Her presence, while filling a gaping hole in my heart, had me
walking on eggshells for fear that I would remind her of why she
had sent me away in the first place.

"Did you have a good time at the junkyard?"

She managed to say it without the laughter that usually
followed the question at the Ashby house, but I could see the
curious light in her eyes.

"I wasn't there the entire time," I admitted. I grabbed the butter
from the fridge, along with a jar of Aunt Lauren's raspberry jelly,
before sitting at the table.

Her eyebrows rose. "What else is there to do out here?" she
asked. Then her face lit up. "Is it that girl?"

I was tempted to say no, but I had never lied to my mother. I
tore the roll open, then realized I had forgotten a butter knife. "Yes,
Madelyn," I said without meeting Mom's eyes.

She let out a surprised laugh and clapped her hands.

I stared at her, wondering if she was crazy.

"I knew it," she gushed. "I told Lauren there was something
different about you, aside from the whole Black Rider thing." She
said it lightly as though it didn't bother her, but we both knew
she wasn't thrilled with the idea of me riding a motorcycle as the
city's vigilante. I couldn't help it that she had managed to arrive
in Sparrow at my most painful moment as the Black Rider. I was
grateful she chose not to confront the issue. "I told her Madelyn

must be special to you, but she said you were too busy with school, the junkyard, and the motorcycle stuff to look at girls."

"There's always time for girls," I said, surprising both of us with my candor.

A true smile spread across her face. "Tell me about her," she asked eagerly.

I leaned back in my chair and slid open the silverware door. I managed to locate a butter knife without getting up. I waved it in the air triumphantly. Mom rolled her eyes as I spread butter inside the bread. "She's beautiful," I said.

I glanced up and met Mom's blue eyes. They were so like my sister Zoey's that for a moment I stared at her, my heart in my throat and memories pounding through my mind with the force of a freight train. I set the knife down and stared at the roll for a second.

"Are you okay?" Mom asked gently. Her tone reflected my heartache as if she guessed my thoughts.

I took a deep breath and nodded, forcing my mind back to Madelyn. "I didn't think she was beautiful at first," I admitted. I saw Mom's eyebrows lift again from the corner of my eye and smiled down at the roll. "I just didn't take a good look at her. She was reading on the bus and kept looking at me whenever I glanced her way." I smiled at the memory. "Then she gave me a handkerchief in class after I got in a fight."

"A fight!" Mom exclaimed.

I spread a generous helping of jelly across the roll and avoided meeting her gaze. "It wasn't a big deal. I stopped the Bullets from destroying the set for a play. The lights were out and they could barely see me."

"How many were there?" she asked.

I thought for a second. "Thirteen." The number surprised me. I hadn't thought of the Bullets in terms of individuals before. From the outside, it definitely appeared foolish to take them on by myself. I guess from the inside it had as well—I just didn't care at the time.

Mom shook her head and opened her mouth to protest, but I hurried on, "That's beside the point. When I was done with the handkerchief, I drove to her house to give it back to her. That's when I really saw her."

Mom's expression softened and she waited.

"She's incredible, Mom." I searched for words to describe her. "She's, well, she makes me feel like I can do anything, but also, I don't know, vulnerable, like I'm just a kid." I stopped, knowing how badly I was botching what I wanted to say. I shook my head. "She just makes me feel . . ." I blew out a breath. "Zoey would like her."

I stared at Mom, suddenly aware of what I had just said. So many emotions flooded her eyes; I didn't know what to say to make it better.

"Mom, I'm sorry," I said softly. "I shouldn't have—"

She shook her head, cutting me off. "If Zoey would like her, then I'll like her too." Tears filled her eyes, but she refused to let them flow over.

I set my roll down and leaned over the table, giving her an awkward hug. "Thanks, Mom," I said, my own voice choked with the emotions I tried to hide. "I'm glad you're here."

She hugged me tightly, then sat back in her chair. "I'm glad to be here too."

I watched her carefully. "Are you sure?"

She thought about it for a second before nodding. "I really am. I think we could start a good life out here."

I was surprised at the intensity of the emotions that filled me at the thought of leaving California for good. There were bad memories, painful memories associated with our home, but leaving it behind permanently meant letting go of the good memories as well. I took a deep breath and let it out, then nodded. "I think so too."

Mom rose from the table and patted me on the shoulder when she went by. "Get some sleep, kiddo. You've got school in the morning."

"I will," I promised.

She turned off the light in the hall. I stared at the roll, my appetite gone. I ran a hand through my brown hair. It was getting longer than I usually wore it. With all the cowlicks I had inherited from my dad, I had to keep it fairly short to be manageable.

I blew out a long breath at the thought of Dad and rose from the table. I tossed the roll out the back door to Jake, then made my way to the small living room. I collapsed on the cot next to the fireplace and kicked off my shoes, then shut my eyes. Firelight flickered on my eyelids, lacing its way through my dreams.

Chapter Four

A KNOT OF DREAD tightened in my throat when I climbed onto the bus the next morning. Mondays were difficult, but I had the impression that this one was going to top it all.

Sure enough, as soon as Cassidy's friend Sandy skipped onto the bus, I realized where the dread had been coming from. Sandy held her phone out to Cassidy and they both burst into laughter from the middle seats.

I slumped in the back seat next to Maddy. "You didn't happen to check the *Bulldog Bulletin*, did you?" I asked casually.

Madelyn threw me a compassionate smile. "You mean the *Bulletin* with the front page picture of the Black Rider sharing his bike with what looked like a pot-belly trucker and a rider closely resembling Magnum? I may have laughed for an hour."

I tipped my head against the back of the seat and moaned.

"It's not that bad," she tried to reassure me despite the smile she couldn't keep from turning up the corners of her lips.

It didn't help that all I wanted to do was kiss her. That would definitely make me feel better, if public displays of affection weren't grounds for expulsion from the bus. Walking the fifteen miles to school definitely wouldn't help my mood.

I settled for slipping my fingers through hers. "Skip school with me," I said.

Her mouth fell open and a warm laugh escaped. "Kelson Brady is asking me to sluff with him?" She gave me a piercing look. "If I didn't know you better, I'd think you were trying to get me alone."

"I think they call it parking, but I don't have a car," I answered with my most charming smile.

She tipped her head to the side as if considering. "I don't suppose it'd be as fun on the motorcycle."

I shrugged. "You could be known as the girl caught making out with the Black Rider."

"Oh," she said with a giggle. "You really do have a bad-boy flair, don't you?"

I stared at her. "Did you just giggle?"

"No," she blurted out, her cheeks turning red.

I nodded with a laugh. "You did. You just giggled!"

She shook her head quickly. "I laughed."

I sat back. "Madelyn West giggled over the thought of making out with the Black Rider."

Several heads turned our way. Madelyn's eyes widened. I realized she feared that I might have blown my cover. I stood up in the back of the bus. "I'll make out with the Black Rider," I said. "That guy's sexy." Laughter erupted at my words. Cassidy and Sandy laughed the loudest. I sat back down and met Madelyn's gaze. "Better?"

She rolled her eyes and laughed. "You're hopeless."

I grinned. "Hopeless with the thought of running away with you."

She flashed a teasing smile. "You're just trying to escape that picture of you with Magnum and the other guy on your motorcycle.

It's too bad, Kelson. You have to face both the fame and the hardship of your decisions."

I let out a sigh of defeat and leaned back. "He was a truck driver running stolen merchandise."

She nodded and brushed her fingers over mine. "I know; the article told how you guys pulled the truck over and then rescued the driver before it fell to the bottom of an abyss."

"It says that?" I smiled despite the thought of the picture no doubt running like a virus through school before the day even started. "I guess that's not too bad."

"That's not what happened?"

I laughed. "That's mostly what happened. Let's just say I owe Martin a thank you for always putting a positive spin on things."

The bus pulled up to school and we climbed off. Sure enough, everyone was talking about the picture. I left Madelyn at calculus and slowly made my way toward English class through the rush of students. I was almost to the door when a shoulder caught mine and threw me into the lockers.

I forced down any show of the pain that laced through my ribs and turned around.

"Watch where you're going, Keldon," Magnum said with a sneer.

I kept my face carefully expressionless as I tried to figure out what he was up to.

Magnum tipped his head minutely to indicate the members of the Bullet gang that surrounded him. It dawned on me that he was putting on a show for them, trying to keep up the front. I dropped my eyes and stuttered, "Oh, um, s—sorry, Magnum. I didn't see you there." Magnum's eyes widened slightly and I realized I had never apologized to the gang leader before. I was obstinate even when I wasn't the Black Rider. I lifted my chin. "Guess it's hard to see garbage with all these students crowding the hall."

His eyes narrowed. I was good at taking it too far. My mouth often worked faster than my good sense. I gritted my teeth as his fist slammed into my stomach. I fell to my knees on the ground, wanting more than anything to take him down but knowing both of our covers depended on me taking on the role of the coward.

"Watch the garbage talk," he growled in my ear.

Another member of his gang kicked me in the side. I sucked in a sharp breath to keep from yelling at the pain that stabbed through my healing ribs.

Magnum grabbed the green-haired girl by the arm. "He's had enough," he warned.

"But you barely touched him," she protested.

He met her eyes with a gaze even I wouldn't mess with. "He's had enough," he reiterated. She quelled under the look. The bell rang and he jerked his head toward the others. "Let's go."

They followed him down the hall without a word. I watched them go, fighting to catch my breath and vowing to remind Magnum who had saved his life when the gangs attacked. He met my eyes just before he turned the corner. "Sorry," he mouthed; then they were gone.

I sat up slowly, holding my ribs that now throbbed with every breath. I leaned my head against the locker. I definitely needed a new hobby.

I WAS DRAGGING THE backseat of a car with the four-wheeler when a familiar motorcycle sped into the junkyard. I gritted my teeth and kept my face expressionless as I climbed off the four-wheeler and levered the seat against the pile of other faded, burned, shredded, or otherwise discarded car and truck seats. Each

movement sent pain through my ribs and increased my anger. I tried
to lift the seat to move it further onto the pile, but the movement
hurt too badly.

I grabbed it with both hands, gritted my teeth against the pain,
and threw the chair on top of the pile before I leaned against the
four-wheeler and fought to catch my breath.

Magnum's footsteps were hesitant. "Gotcha pretty bad, huh?"

I refused to look at him. I turned to climb back on the four-
wheeler for the next chair, but he grabbed the key from the ignition.
I glared at him.

"Look, I'm sorry," Magnum said. He studied the ground near
his feet, then looked up at the sky. "I don't say that much, but I
mean it."

"Do you enjoy picking on those who are weaker than you?" I
demanded.

He glanced at me. "We both know you're not weaker than me."

I grimaced. "That's beside the point. Do you like picking on
kids and making them scared of you?"

Magnum shoved a hand in his pocket. He looked at the four-
wheeler key in his other hand, then closed his fingers around it,
gripping it tight. "I like feeling in control."

I thought about it for a minute as my anger slowly left. Magnum
wasn't one to open up. I knew I needed to take his words at face
value. "So being stronger than others makes you feel in control?"

He didn't meet my eyes. His fist turned white as he gripped the
key even harder. "In control of some things," he said quietly.

What little I had seen of his home life left little doubt as to what
he meant. I climbed off the four-wheeler and fought back a wince.
"Could you do me a favor?" I asked.

He looked up at me in surprise. "What?"

"Could you leave me alone until these ribs heal?"

He let out a laugh. "I'll find someone else to pick on." He slid the key back in the four-wheeler's ignition.

I hesitated, then shook my head. "On second thought, keep picking on me."

He studied me for a minute. Understanding dawned in his eyes and the color ran from his face. "Are you saying you became my target on purpose so we wouldn't beat up the other students?"

I shrugged. "Not the brightest plan."

He leaned against the four-wheeler and crossed his arms. "Not a coward's plan, either." He paused, then glared at me. "So the punch on my tuxedo?"

I grinned. "Not an accident."

He shook his head. "You need to come up with better plans."

I rubbed my stomach. "Tell me about it."

He nodded at the motorcycle and we both walked toward it. "The little theater?"

"Yep, that was me."

"The mascot?" he pressed.

I nodded.

He blew out a breath and rubbed the knuckles of one hand. "You really had a vendetta."

I stared at him. "Vendetta?"

Embarrassment crossed his face. "We're reading *Hamlet* in English."

"You're actually paying attention?"

He chuckled. "I know. Tell me about it. For some reason, I'm actually interested in school."

"If you get good grades, you could get a scholarship out of here."

"That's what they keep telling me," he admitted.

I kept my tone carefully even. "Who tells you?"

Magnum was quiet for a minute, then said, "The school counselors. My grades are close to passing. If I work hard, I can graduate this year with a GPA good enough to go to the university."

I couldn't help feeling surprised. Magnum had never appeared to me to be the ambitious type, but apparently my assumptions of him had been as wrong as those he'd had of me.

"Good," was all I said.

He turned to look at me fully. "Good? That's it?" His gaze darkened. "You're not gonna laugh or tell me it's ridiculous?"

I shook my head. "I'm happy for you," I said honestly. "You should do whatever you want." A thought occurred to me. "What about football?"

His eyes narrowed. "What about it?"

I kicked a bolt sitting in the dirt. It bounced against the motorcycle's tire. "I heard you were good at football once. Why not get out of here on a football scholarship?"

"I'd have to play," he said with a tone that indicated the stupidity of my statement.

I didn't let it bother me. "So play." His head jerked up and I felt his stare, but I kept my eyes on the bolt, nudging it with the toe of my shoe. "You could pick it up again. I'll bet the coach would be happy to have you."

He was about to reply when a truck turned onto the junkyard road.

Jagger threw open the door to the shack. "This'd be more traffic 'n we 'ad in months," he said as Mick barked with all the threat his tiny body could contain.

I squinted against the sun setting behind the truck. It was hard to make out who was driving, but there was something tied in the back.

The truck stopped a few feet from the shack. A hat bobbed, then

Sheriff Bowley climbed out. "Hello, boys," he said with a smile. He tipped his head. "Jagger."

"Howdy, Sheriff," Jagger replied. "I s'pose you been busy."

"Always," the sheriff answered amiably. He waved a hand toward the back of the truck. "I brought your bike back with the modifications Magnum *requested*." He said the last word as though the request had been more of a demand.

Magnum snorted. "About time."

I followed them to the back of the truck. It was the second time I had seen my motorcycle brought back in better condition than I had left it. I reached up a hand and touched the flat black side.

"Get 'er down b'fore Kelson 'ere starts cryin'," Jagger said. I threw him a look and he grinned, showing several missing teeth.

I was about to climb onto the truck bed, but Magnum grabbed my shoulder. "Let someone do it who can handle a bit of rough riding."

"I can ride my own bike," I protested, but Magnum climbed on the truck anyway.

The sheriff looked at me. "Did you get hurt pulling that truck over, or is it from the bullets?"

I shook my head. "Got in a bit of a fight at school."

Magnum snorted as he shifted the motorcycle into neutral. "I don't think you can call it that."

The sheriff looked between us. "Let me get this straight. You're riding together and still fighting at school?"

Magnum shrugged. "Got to keep up appearances."

"That ain't right," Jagger commented.

Magnum backed easily down the ramp, then parked the bike at the bottom. "There you go, princess," he said with a grin.

I rolled my eyes. "Thanks, Dark Wing."

He glowered. "That's not what I decided on."

I nodded. "I think Night Goose works better."

At Magnum's look of death, the sheriff lifted his hands. "Whoa. I'm not sure if you two working together is such a good idea."

"I secon' that," Jagger muttered as I went to the shack.

Silence filled the air. I pulled my black riding outfit on over my jeans and shirt, making sure to fasten the bulletproof vest Jagger had given me before zipping up the jacket. I then threw on my backpack and walked back out. "It's nothing a ride can't fix," I said, carrying my helmet and gloves.

I swung a leg over the motorcycle and sat on the newly upholstered seat. "You overhauled it," I said with an appreciative smile.

"Try to keep it in one piece," the sheriff replied gruffly.

"Hopefully merchandise runs near Sparrow will slow now that they've seen what we did with the last one," Magnum said.

A laugh burst out of the sheriff before he could stop it. "You boys be careful."

I turned the key and pressed the starter. The motorcycle rumbled to life with a much louder growl than it had before.

Magnum started his and revved the engine. "Let's ride," he said, pulling on his helmet.

"Wait," Jagger commanded.

He hurried back to the shack with more haste than I had ever seen the old man use. The three of us waited in the rumbling silence until he came back out carrying a black bundle. I grinned when he handed it to Magnum.

Magnum accepted the bundle warily and straightened it out. His eyes lit up when he recognized the vest. "Awesome," he said.

Jagger nodded. "If'n you ride wi' Kelson, you always wear it."

"I will," the Bullet leader promised. He pulled the ballistic vest on with an awe that made me wonder when the last time was he had received a gift of any kind. He zipped it up, then shrugged into his jacket. "Thanks, man."

Jagger waved him away. "Go 'ave fun and stop trouble if'n ya find it."

"We will," Magnum said.

I led the way out of the junkyard with the knowledge that Magnum was smiling inside his tinted helmet whether I could see it or not.

Chapter Five

WHEN WE PULLED UP to the junkyard an hour later, all thoughts of the fight and my ribs were far from my mind. Magnum shoved his visor up and grinned. "Now I know why you like this bike."

I climbed off and patted the seat fondly. "Not a bad ride."

"And did you see the looks we got? People are freaking out that there are two Black Riders now."

I nodded. "I have a feeling crime's going to drop drastically around here."

He set his helmet on the passenger footrest and took off his gloves. "What now?"

I shrugged. It wasn't late enough to go to the Ashbys' and eat, but I was tired of sorting through junk. "I could teach you how to fight."

Magnum bristled. "I know how to fight."

I nodded. "You brawl like a boxer. I could teach you how to fight with finesse."

He lifted an eyebrow. "Why would I want to do that?"

I held in a sigh. "Take a swing at me."

He shook his head. "No way. Have you seen the shape you're

in?"

I nodded. "Come on. Trust me."

He held up his fists. "If you're sure about this."

"I am," I said.

He blew out a breath and shook his head. "Don't say I didn't warn you."

He punched at my head. I stepped to the side and caught his arm, then ducked and used his momentum to send him over my back and to the ground. Dust rose around him, then settled slowly as he stared up at me in surprise.

"That's finesse?" he asked.

I nodded.

He clambered back to his feet and attempted to dust off his black clothes. "I suppose I could use some of that." He paused. "But I have a better idea."

"What's that?" I asked slowly.

He grinned. "Come on."

I followed him to the back of the junkyard where I had piled the tires in rows by size and tread. He pushed the biggest pile over.

"Hey, I stacked that," I protested.

"And I'm sure you'll do it again. Look." He climbed inside a stack of tires. "Now you duck behind another stack and I'll pop out. With our matching clothes, it'll look like the Black Rider is super fast. If we can get our timing down, no one will know what hit them."

I laughed, but did it anyway. When I was hiding, Magnum hesitated. "How will I know you're gone?" he asked.

"I'll yell. Be ready. It'll distract them anyway."

We practiced for several minutes, then switched positions.

"Go!" Magnum yelled.

I jumped out from the tires and did a roundhouse kick. "Take that, evil bad guys!"

He laughed so hard, he collapsed behind the tires. "I'm glad you didn't say that when you fought us in the store. I would have laughed to death."

"Not intimidating enough?"

His face was red from laughing. "The mighty Black Rider slays evil with his witty name-calling."

I chuckled. "It could be worse."

"Oh, really?" he said when he could breathe again. "How's that?"

"Their name could be Dark Wing."

He made a swipe for my legs, but I jumped out of reach. I tripped on a car hood and it skidded across the dirt with a screech.

"What's that?" Magnum asked.

We both stared at what appeared to be a full-sized metal door embedded in the ground.

"Ya found it!" Jagger exclaimed.

We both jumped at the old man's appearance. He rubbed the few pieces of hair on his head excitedly. "I couldn' 'member where I left et!"

"You lost a door?" I asked wryly.

He shook his head. "Not jus' a door, ye sarcastic cuss—my bomb shelter. Open et up!"

Magnum looked at me dubiously. I shrugged and reached for the C-shaped piece of metal that made up the handle. It took both of us and Jagger's crowbar to lift the metal door. A smell drifted from the exposed hole that almost floored us.

"What is that?" Magnum demanded, plugging his nose.

"I 'spect ets my canned pork," Jagger replied, unconcerned.

Magnum and I exchanged a glance. "You canned a pig?" I asked.

He nodded. "What else ya gonna do with et?" He stuck his bum leg out and knelt down gingerly. "I know ets around 'ere somewhere." He fumbled around the lip of the door for a minute, then exclaimed, "Aha!" He pulled something and a lightbulb flickered on.

Magnum and I stared at a set of dusty steps that led into the earth.

"Go'n then," Jagger said.

"This feels like *Silence of the Lambs*," Magnum breathed in my ear.

I hesitated at the top.

"Oh, come on," Jagger growled. He pushed past me and limped down the stairs. His crowbar banged loudly on the wooden steps.

Magnum and I exchanged a look before we followed Jagger into the musty hole.

The light led to another light, then another. We reached the bottom of the steps and stopped in a space about eight feet square. A dirty bed with twisted blankets sat in one corner and a table lined with what appeared to be Jagger's now-green canned pork took up the opposite side. I squinted into the gloom, surprised to see that Jagger had vanished.

"This is crazy," Magnum said quietly behind me. "What is this place?"

A light flickered in front of me, showing a rectangle against the dark wooden wall. "Ya comin'?" Jagger called back.

I walked through the door, then stopped in surprise. Magnum ran into me, swore, then froze when he saw the contents of the room.

Guns of every possible make and model sat on shelves along the walls and on a table. They appeared older, but were in good condition behind glass that kept the dust, moisture, and cobwebs from getting to them.

"This is awesome!" Magnum exclaimed. He reached out to touch the glass. "Seriously, Jagger, this is amazing! Winchesters, Remingtons, M16s, M21s, a Flamethrower!" He looked at the old man who was surveying his collection with pride. "What is this, a Vietnam weapons cache?"

Jagger nodded. "Pretty much. I've kept it 'round since my time in 'Nam." He winked. "I know a guy. Never know when ya might be needin' somethin'"

"Like a Minigun?" Magnum asked, his eyes wide as he studied the Gatling gun in the corner.

Jagger nodded. "Exactly."

Magnum looked back at me. "This is so cool, don't you think?"

I shoved my hands in my pockets and peered at the weapons. "Yeah, but what are you going to use them for?"

"Defendin'," Jagger said as if I had asked a stupid question.

Magnum's eyes narrowed thoughtfully. "You're a city kid. Have you ever shot a gun?"

I admitted defeat and shook my head.

Both Jagger and Magnum stared at me. "Well, now's the time to do it!" Magnum exclaimed.

Jagger slid one of the glass doors open and Magnum grabbed several different guns. He hurried back up the steps like a kid with an armful of candy. Jagger picked up boxes of bullets, then limped up after him.

I looked around the room one last time and my eyes landed on a box of grenades. There had been several times since my arrival in Sparrow when I felt I had landed in a twilight zone, but this one beat them all. I shook my head and hurried up the stairs.

Magnum already had car headlights set up and was taking aim at them with a pistol.

"Use bo' hands. Et's more accurate tha' way," Jagger instructed. Magnum complied, cupping a hand on the bottom of the pistol. He then lifted the gun again and closed one eye. "Watch 'er wi' the kick," Jagger said. "Ya drop et, ya buy et."

Magnum squeezed the trigger. A bang sounded and the glass on the headlight shattered. Magnum looked at Jagger with wide eyes. "That was awesome!"

Jagger nodded, looking as pleased as if he had fired the gun himself. "Kelson's turn."

Magnum grinned and grabbed a different gun off the table they had improvised from an old Chevy hood. "This'll be better for him."

Jagger looked at the gun, then shook his head. "I don' think that'd—"

Magnum glared at him. "Let Kelson try."

Jagger watched moodily as Magnum loaded the clip, then shoved it into the handle of the gun. He slid a lever on the top and pushed the gun into my hands.

"You have to hold it tight. It has a safety in the grip to keep it from firing accidentally," Magnum instructed.

"Where did you learn about guns?" I questioned him in an effort to cover up my nervousness at shooting the weapon.

He shrugged. "My dad got injured in 'Nam. Now we live on his checks while he reads everything he can get his hands on about the war. He's convinced there was another reason our soldiers were involved, but he hasn't found it yet. I used to read his books on guns when I was younger."

I nodded and turned my attention back to the weapon. It felt cold it my hands. I took a breath and aimed with the butt held close to my shoulder. It felt strange.

"I think my grip's wrong," I said, turning to show Magnum.

He and Jagger dropped to the ground when the gun turned in their direction. I had never seen the old man move so quickly.

"Watch where yer aimin' that gun, Kelson!" Jagger barked.

"Sorry," I apologized, turning it quickly back toward the targets.

"Just pull the trigger," Magnum said, rising back to his feet.

I took a breath and pulled. As soon as the trigger was back, the gun recoiled in my hands, spitting bullets in an arch. I ducked in surprise at the sound of bullets ricocheting off the car parts around us.

A sound erupted behind me. I turned to find Magnum laughing from his crouched position on the ground.

Jagger rose and tore the gun from my hands. "Givin' a greenie an Uzi," he grumbled, shaking his head.

He took the cartridge out and set the gun on the car hood without looking at Magnum, who was still cracking up on the dirt.

"You should have seen the look on your face!" he exclaimed. "That gun almost hit you with the recoil!"

I gritted my teeth and was ready to show him true boxing when Jagger set another gun in my hands. It was the one Magnum had fired earlier.

"This's a Colt M1911. Et should be more yer style," he said.

I shook my head, but he handed me a clip anyway. I shoved it in the base of the gun like Magnum had done, then looked at the target warily. Magnum was still chuckling from where he leaned against a pile of tires. I tried to block out the sound.

Jagger stepped closer to me and said in an undertone, "Et won't kick like the Uzi. Jus' squeeze slow like and keep yer eyes on the target."

I looked down the sights and let out a slow breath, pulling the trigger as I did so. A shot rang out and the bullet tore through the center of the headlight.

Magnum's laughter stopped. He rose and regarded the shattered headlight silently for a moment, then said, "That was luck."

I lifted the gun again and sent another bullet through the same hole.

Magnum glanced at Jagger, but didn't say anything.

I squeezed the trigger three more times. The bullets hit the headlight within an inch of the first hole. When the gun was empty, I allowed a small smile to cross my face.

"I think the joke was on me," Magnum said, glaring in my direction. "You've shot before."

I shook my head. "This is honestly my first time." I shrugged. "Guess I like the Colt."

Jagger laughed and slapped my shoulder. He set the guns back on the hood and checked the magazines. "Et's a good thing ya found my stash."

I stared at him. "You mean you lost it?"

He chuckled. "Why else ya think I'm havin' ya organizin' this place? Et's not gonna get any more beautiful."

Magnum burst out laughing. At my look, he grinned, "And here you thought you were doing something worthwhile."

I blew out a breath of frustration and stalked across the junkyard. Magnum and Jagger burst out laughing again. When I reached the shack, I sat on the step and glared at the ground. Mick surprised me by settling next to my leg and resting his head on his paws. I set a hand on his head. He licked my fingers, then returned to his vigil over the junkyard despite that fact that no one wanted to steal junk. Apparently there were two of us doing something worthless.

WHEN MADELYN JOINED ME on the bus the next morning, I

couldn't keep from smiling.

"What's going on?" she asked.

I took her hand. "Maddy, go on a date with me."

She laughed. "I've been on a date with you, remember?"

I shook my head. "Not to a dance—a real date with dinner and a movie or miniature golf. Maybe some flowers." I tried to make it sound as inviting as I could.

She pursed her lips. "I don't know. Mom hasn't been feeling good, and Dad said—"

"Your dad said you could have more freedom in the evenings because he wanted to spend time with your mom." I gave her my most winning smile. "You need to give them that opportunity."

She stared out the window for a moment and I watched her emotions in her reflection. Guilt and hope warred with each other. I knew better than to press her and tried to wait patiently, but the laughter and noise in the bus increased the closer we got to school. We were running out of time before her calculus class stole her away.

I took the ever-present book from her hand and began to flip through the pages. I made several non-committal sounds—grunts, noises of contemplation, and a few ahas, even though I didn't read a word. I grew aware of Madelyn's eyes on me and tried not to smile.

"What do you think?"

I studied the book for a few more seconds, then glanced at her, "I've always found," I looked at the front of the book, then fought back a laugh, "*Little Women* to be an excellent study of human life in social situations."

She attempted to keep a straight face. "Oh, really? Who is your favorite character?"

I thought for a minute. "That Maddy girl is always giving her boyfriend a hard time. He wants to spend time with her; she prefers her books." I tapped the novel on my knee. "It's difficult to see how she's stolen his heart and every moment of his thoughts, but doesn't care to be seen in public with him. Maybe she's embarrassed of his awesome hair or his charming personality—"

Madelyn grabbed the book from me. "Fine, I'll go out with you. Just stop inflating your own ego."

I grinned and kissed her on the cheek, then glanced at the front of the bus to see Mr. Benson glaring at us in the mirror. I ducked my head and laughed. "He's on to us."

Madelyn looked up, then waved. Mr. Benson shook his head and turned his attention back to the road.

"It's settled; I'll pick you up at six."

"I'll be there," she said with a warm smile. She propped her knees on the chair in front of us, then opened her book with one hand. She ran her fingers slowly up and down my arm while she read. I tipped my head back and closed my eyes, enjoying the tingles that ran along my skin at her touch.

I SWUNG BY THE sheriff's office after school. He looked up from the desk in surprise. "Hello, Kelson. What can I do for you?"

I glanced around to make sure we were alone before I slid into one of the chairs across from his desk. "How's everything going?"

A slight smile lifted his mustache. "Well, since the Bullets are under control for the moment, there's not much happening that you could help with."

I propped one knee on the other. "You're enjoying a bit of relaxation, aren't you?"

He tipped back in his chair as well and nodded. "I could get used to it. How long do you think it will last?"

The comment bothered me. "What do you mean?"

The sheriff sat up and put his elbows on the desk. "One member of the Bullets is occupied. How long do you think the others will sit idle waiting for him?"

I sat up and rubbed the back of my neck. "Not long, I guess."

He nodded. "Just keep that in mind. If Magnum can continue keeping them under control, great. If not, be prepared for someone else to take charge of the Bullets."

I leaned my elbows on my knees, but the position was uncomfortable with my bruised ribs, so I sat up again and found the sheriff watching me closely. "You could take a break, you know," he said.

The understanding in his tone made me angry for reasons I couldn't explain. I met his gaze. "I'm fine. What can we do to help?"

He studied me for a minute before letting out a quiet breath. "The gas stations along the interstate keep getting hit by the same three guys. They're gone by the time we show up, and they take the video surveillance tapes with them. You could drive by if you get time and check it out."

I stood and held out a hand. Sheriff Bowley shook it with a slight smile. "Take care of yourself, Black Rider."

"You too, Sheriff."

Chapter Six

"TAKE MY CAR," MOM insisted.

I eyed the beat-up green Volkswagen doubtfully. "I'm not sure it's much of a date car," I replied.

Mom gestured to the four-wheeler. "Were you planning on taking that?"

I looked from the four-wheeler to Mom's car, then to Uncle Rick's beat-up ton truck. He had offered it with a smirk before leaving in the nice Ram with my cousins Jaren and Cole to take care of a broken fence.

I gave in. "All right."

She smiled and handed me the keys, complete with a fuzzy pink rabbit's foot and a sparkly star that said "Shine". I unhooked the key and handed the rest back to Mom. She rolled her eyes. "Not manly enough for you?"

"Not by a long shot," I replied dryly.

She laughed and gave me a hug. "Have fun and don't do anything I wouldn't do."

I chuckled as I opened the car door. It gave a squeak of protest. "So I can eliminate sky diving and haunted houses. Anything else?"

"Spiders," she said. "Anything to do with spiders."

"Oh, right."

Mom pulled something from her pocket and set it in my hand. I smiled at the twenty-dollar bill. "I can pay for the date myself."

She shook her head. "Lauren told me Jagger doesn't pay you. I insist."

On impulse, I gave her a hug. She laughed and patted my back. "You'd better get going. Don't want to be late for your date!"

"Thanks, Mom." I said. She crossed to the porch to wave me off. Aunt Lauren walked out and stood beside her. Now that I knew she was expecting, her small belly was obvious beneath her plaid shirt. She set a hand on it and leaned contentedly against one of the supports. Mom said something to her and they both laughed.

I grinned as I started the car. It was great to see Mom laugh again.

———— ∽∾ ————

WHEN I PULLED UP to the house, my stomach twisted uneasily. It wasn't that I was nervous to pick up Madelyn—I was nervous to face her father. When Madelyn insisted they go to the hospital with the Ashbys after the fair, he found out I was the Black Rider. Since then, he had regarded me with respect, but also with the kind of wariness expected from a father who knew his daughter was dating a reckless boy.

It didn't matter that I saved the entire town. What mattered was if he could trust me the few times he knew we were together. I acted attentive and caring in their presence and tried to tone down my death-wish mentality when Madelyn and I were alone so I didn't give him further reason to worry.

Buck barked from his kennel as I crossed the sidewalk; it was only the second time I had ever really walked on it. I straightened my only button-up shirt and knocked on the door. I tried to smooth a particularly stubborn cowlick in my hair, then realized I was fidgeting and shoved my hands into my pockets.

The door opened slowly a minute later. "Yes?" Mr. West demanded. He saw who it was and waited for a moment before he opened the door entirely. "Come in," he said grudgingly as he made his way back to the couch.

"Hi, Kelson!" Mrs. West said from her place in the wheelchair on the far side of the couch.

Madelyn had inherited Mrs. West's long brown hair and fair skin. Mrs. West looked a bit paler than usual and her smile looked weary. Much to Mr. West's chagrin, I crossed the living room and took her hand, kneeling so we could speak to each other easier.

"It's wonderful to see you again, Mrs. West. You are looking lovely, as usual."

"Oh, stop," she said with a shadow of Madelyn's brilliant smile. "Save it for your date."

"A date?" Mr. West grumbled.

"Yes, dear," his wife replied patiently. "Madelyn told us about it when she got home and you said it was all right."

"That was before I knew who she was going with," he replied. He changed the channel on the television, but didn't turn the volume up past a slight hum.

"Don't listen to him, dear," Mrs. West said quietly, though we both knew her husband could hear. "He'd be grouchy no matter who she went with."

"I'd pick any of the other boys who come to the door," he said.

At my curious look, Mrs. West laughed, then tipped her head back wearily against the electronic wheelchair. "You're the only one. Don't let him give you a hard time."

"Are you okay?" I asked gently.

She nodded and gave me another warm smile. "Have fun and take care of yourself. You're a good kid, Kelson."

I gave a slight frown for show. "That's what everyone keeps trying to tell me. I think they're hoping that if they say it enough, it'll come true."

Mr. West gave a snort, his attention still on his show.

"Is Kelson here?"

My breath caught at Madelyn's voice. Her eyes lit up when they met mine, and my heart skipped a beat. I rose to my feet. Everyone watched her hurry down the stairs. She had a sneaker in one hand and a pair of earrings in the other. Her footsteps made a thump-pat sound on the steps.

"Sorry, Kelson," she said, pausing at the bottom of the stairs to lean on the banister and pull on the other sneaker. "I tried to hurry, but the curling iron wouldn't work and my hair is always so flat. I wanted to do something special, but it just didn't work out and I—" She paused and gave an embarrassed smile. "I'm babbling, sorry."

"It's a good thing," Mr. West said. "Boys don't like girls who babble."

"Oh, honey," Mrs. West chided.

I crossed to Madelyn's side and caught her arm before she could trip and hurt herself. She gave me a grateful smile and pulled her shoe on all the way, then stomped on it to make sure it was secure. "You look absolutely gorgeous, Maddy," I told her.

She wore a red shirt that fit her curves and her hair was down instead of swept back in her usual ponytail. She had traded her glasses for contacts even though I knew they bugged her, and the slightest hint of makeup highlighted her hazel eyes and reddened her lips. I couldn't believe I had the chance to spend the evening with such a beautiful girl.

"Maddy?" Mr. West repeated.

I grimaced at the annoyance in his tone, then turned to him with a smile. "It's a nickname my cousin started. Madelyn doesn't mind."

"I love it," she replied with a spark of defiance.

Mr. West watched us both for a minute, then turned back to the television as if we were a minor disturbance in his cinematic evening.

"Have a wonderful time," Mrs. West called.

"Thank you, Mom. We will," Madelyn replied. She hurried across the room and gave her mom a quick kiss on the cheek, then met me at the door. I opened it for her and was grateful when I was able to shut it and leave Mr. West's palpable glare behind us.

"He really doesn't like me," I said.

She shook her head. "The Black Rider stealing away his little girl? No father would like you," she replied with a laugh.

I opened her door. It gave a loud screech and she stood back to look at the car. "Where did this come from?"

"It's my mom's," I explained, trying to ignore the rust that ate at the paint under my hand. "She thought it would be classier than a farm truck."

Madelyn gave me a doubtful look.

I laughed. "That's the look I gave her, but it's better than the four-wheeler, and Uncle Rick took the blue Ram. We'd be left with the old white ton that's still loaded and tarped so the hay doesn't get ruined by rain."

She smiled up at me, her eyes so entrancing I could barely keep my mind on the date at hand. When she looked at me like that, everything vanished but the warmth that flooded through me at her expression. My heart slowed, my breathing stopped, and I felt bare and exposed. She made me more vulnerable than I had allowed myself to be in a year. "What?" I asked past the knot that tightened in my throat.

"You're starting to sound like a farmer," she teased, her eyelashes fluttering.

I pushed a strand of hair back from her face and couldn't help letting my fingers linger on her cheek. "If it makes you smile like that, I'll be a farmer for the rest of my life."

Her smile deepened. "I don't know if Sparrow could handle it."

I laughed and held her door open further. She gave me a quick kiss on the cheek and then slipped inside. I looked up to find Mr. West watching us from the window with a very disapproving expression on his face. I ducked my head and hurried around to the other side of the car, worried he would appear at any moment and shoot me for getting fresh with his daughter, even though she had been the one to kiss me.

I made a mental note to kiss Madelyn good night *before* I brought her home.

I sat in the driver's seat and started the engine. The fan belt whined for a few seconds before it settled into an uneven mutter. I threw Madelyn an apologetic smile before pulling onto the road. "I know this car is going to guarantee another date."

She smiled and slipped her hand through my arm, leaning over to rest her head on my shoulder. "I'm enjoying it."

She turned on the radio and I listened to her sing softly to several country songs.

"You have a great voice," I said.

She gave me a wry smile. "Did you expect something horrible?"

I nodded. "I pictured a mixture of alley cats and Aunt Lauren's rooster."

Madelyn laughed at the image. Aunt Lauren's rooster had a crow that sounded more like a strangled sheep than cock-a-doodle-doo. Aunt Lauren called it "eccentric." She was fond of all the animals on her farm, especially if they took such an effort to stand out.

"Sorry to disappoint you," she said.

I gave a dramatic sigh. "I suppose I'll get used to it. I should have guessed you would be the complete package—bookish but mysterious, not a mean bone in your body." I looked down at her. "Beautiful without realizing it, and now you sing like you belong on a stage." I gave her a searching look. "Why are you with me, Madelyn West?"

She gave me her special smile as I pulled into the parking lot of the town's pizza house. I would have preferred to take her for anything but pizza, except that there were only two other dining options in Sparrow. The first was Chaser's burger joint, which was always flooded with students and therefore not the best place for a conversation. The other was a Chinese restaurant Aunt Lauren told me I should visit if I wanted to experience dysentery. Since that wasn't my idea of a good date, I chose pizza.

"Two mediums, please."

"To stay or to go?" asked a teeny bopper with short brown hair and green glasses.

"To go," I said without giving Madelyn a choice.

"I thought this was a real date," she said.

I nodded. "It is. I just want to give you a better view to eat by."

The girl at the cash register batted her eyelashes at me. I smiled and ordered one Hawaiian and the other pepperoni and olive.

"Don't forget cheesy bread," Madelyn said. At my surprised look, she also batted her eyelashes. "It's my favorite."

I grinned and motioned for the cashier to ring it up. I paid and we settled down on red bar stools to wait.

"Come here often?" Madelyn asked.

I laughed. "Actually, no. I've never been here before, but I was reassured this is the best date food one can get in Sparrow."

She leaned back on her stool too far. I grabbed her arm before she could lose her balance. She gave me a searching look as she straightened back up.

"What?" I asked, suddenly self-conscious.

"I've never had anyone watch me close enough to catch me before I fell," she replied with an unsure smile.

Her tone made my heart stutter, as if she was on the verge of kissing me but didn't want to be too forward. I took a chance and lowered my head. She covered my lips with hers in a soft kiss that told of her gratitude better than any words.

When she sat back, it took me a minute to remember where we were. I pushed the hair back from my forehead. "You have a great way of saying thank you."

She blushed and was about to reply when the cashier called out, "Kelson, order's ready."

I picked Madelyn up before she could move, then spun around and set her on the ground. The action surprised us both. I had never acted that way with a girl—or with anyone, for that matter. The light sensation that filled me when I was around her made me invincible. I felt like I was in one of the movies Zoey used to watch where the guy falls over his own feet and would cross lava to bring whatever his girl requested. Madelyn hadn't asked for anything, but somehow she had possession of my heart.

Her hand slipped in mine, jarring me back to reality and pizza that needed to be carried. I breathed not quite evenly as she walked at my side to the car. The sound the door made didn't even bother me. I stood beside it and watched Madelyn lower herself into the seat with all the grace of her white geese gliding across the mirror-faced pond.

"Are we going somewhere?" she asked with a cute little smile that looked as though it held in a laugh.

I realized I had been standing with the door open gawking at her for far longer than was appropriate. I shut the door with a stupid grin and hurried around to the other side. If this date was going to go well, I had to get it together.

"Normally, I would take a date to a lookout over the ocean or high in the mountains so we could eat beneath the trees, but both are severely lacking in Sparrow," I explained as I pulled up to the city's park, a little tree-lined flat of grass with a man-made stream on one side.

Madelyn's tone was carefully expressionless. "Did you date many girls in California?"

I nodded, but I couldn't keep in a laugh. "No. I never went on a single date. We usually just hung out in a big group."

Her smile touched her eyes. "But you're so good at this."

I grinned. "Zoey made me watch lots of romantic comedies. They were her favorite." I paused, wondering why that had come rushing out.

Madelyn smoothed my emotions by covering my hand with hers and giving me a kiss on the cheek. "I'm happy we're on a date."

I smiled at her. "Me too."

I opened her door and led the way to a shady patch of grass near the stream. The rocks had been stacked so the water trickled pleasantly with much the same sound as Madelyn's laughter.

The sound reminded me of the camping spot where Dad used to take Zoey and me. That was way before Mom and Dad's financial struggles, back before he walked out of our lives without looking back. He always staked the tents by the stream, saying the sound was better than a mother's lullaby. Mom disagreed with that, but her smile chased away any argument. I wanted to see her smile again, like she used to before I lost Zoey in the fire. I owed that much to her.

"What are you thinking about?"

Startled, I looked at Madelyn. "I'm sorry. I must be the worst date ever."

She held up her pizza with a teasing smile. "You brought food. What more could a girl ask for?"

"More than someone staring off into space, I'm sure," I said, feeling a little lost.

She touched my arm. "You looked sad, Kel. What was it?"

I glanced at the stream, then let out a breath. "Regrets, I guess. I feel like if I had known then what I do now, I could have prevented a lot of the bad stuff from happening."

Her eyes lowered thoughtfully and she nodded. She looked at the water and slipped her hand into mine. "I've always wondered if I could have prevented Mom's accident."

I stared down at her, my heart constricting. "It wasn't your fault, Maddy."

She gave a little shrug, her eyes not meeting mine. "I begged Dad for that horse. It was all I wanted, and the Stevensons offered her to us because she was gentle and they knew how much I wanted to ride." Her hand tightened convulsively and even as a small smile touched her mouth, tears filled her eyes. "He said no and I went to bed heartbroken. Mom came in and promised she would talk him into it."

Her voice caught and she took a shuddering breath. "She smoothed my hair and kissed me on the cheek like she used to every night before bed, tucking the covers in snug even though I wasn't a child anymore. 'I'll tell him I want it,' she whispered, and we both smiled at each other because we knew Dad would never deny Mom anything she wanted. He loved her that much."

I wrapped an arm around Maddy's shoulder and she leaned against me, turning her head toward my chest, her pizza forgotten on the napkin that balanced on her knee. "Mom rode her everywhere. I think she loved the horse even more than I did. Nessi was spirited, but Mom loved that about her, and I didn't mind because she always calmed down when Mom rode her."

She lifted our entwined hands, studying our fingers as she spoke. "Then Mom took her out and didn't come back. We waited until evening and then Dad called everyone he knew, which was half the town. They combed the fields where Mom liked to ride." She sniffed and I could feel the dampness of my shirt where it absorbed her tears. "Mark Stevenson was the one who found her. They had jumped a ditch, but Nessi landed wrong on the other side and broke her leg. She rolled over Mom in the fall, crushing her. I heard the shot when they put Nessi down, and I knew something was terribly wrong."

"It wasn't your fault," I whispered, smoothing her hair. "You couldn't have known."

"If I didn't want the horse . . ." Her voice choked off with guilt.

"If I hadn't thrown that stupid party in the warehouse," I answered, holding her tight.

Her arms wrapped around me and I closed my eyes, feeling a strange release as though everything suddenly made sense, everything I had been fighting about the night Zoey died. "Say it's not your fault," I told Madelyn.

She sat back and looked at me. "What?" she asked with tears in her eyes.

"Say it," I repeated. "Say your mother's accident was not your fault."

She shook her head. I took her hands in mine. "I have carried the guilt of Zoey's death on my shoulders because I planned the party and I invited our friends." I blinked, refusing to let tears fall. "I didn't know how out of hand everything would get, and I didn't know Zoey and Jeff would die in the fire."

"It wasn't your fault," Madelyn said.

I nodded, feeling as though I could breathe easier. "I know that. You *helped* me know that. I didn't know there would be a fire. I didn't know Zoey and Jeff would go upstairs and I wouldn't be able to reach them in time." I swallowed and concluded softly, "I didn't know she would die."

She nodded and I caught her chin in my hand, gently forcing her to look at me. "And you didn't know your mother would jump that ditch and Nessi's leg would break. You didn't know, and so it wasn't your fault."

Tears spilled down her cheeks, but she didn't look away. Her eyes held mine as if she needed to hear what I was saying. The disbelief in her gaze warred with the want to believe. I pressed on, "You were a little girl who wanted a horse. That's all," I said.

She watched me for a second longer and then she nodded. At first it was a slow nod as though she was thinking everything through. Then she nodded quickly, her tears falling in a soft patter. "It was an accident," she said softly.

"Of course it was," I replied, pulling her close. "A horrible, painful accident that you couldn't have prevented. Your mother would never want you to carry that guilt with you because you don't deserve it."

She cried harder, the sobs of someone who carried such a heavy burden but feared no one else would understand. Deep down, she felt that they blamed her, but they didn't. For the first time, she allowed herself to accept that she was that little girl who wanted a horse, not the one responsible for her mother's quadriplegia. The sobs broke and turned into sounds of relief, of loss and gain, of finding one's self again.

I held her and blinked past the tears that had broken free at her heartache. I wouldn't cry for myself, but I couldn't stop myself at her pain. "You're amazing," I said softly, running a hand along her hair. "You carry so much by yourself, and you are the most wonderful person I've ever met." Her crying slowed and she listened as I continued, "You are so beautiful, inside and out. I can't even begin to describe how grateful I am to have found you." My voice dropped to a whisper. "You give me something to live for."

She tipped her head up and pressed her lips against mine. Our tears mingled with a taste of self-forgiveness. Afterwards, I tipped my forehead against hers, staring into her eyes and wondering again at the fact that she trusted me and wanted to be with me.

"You are amazing, Madelyn West," I said, lost in her gaze.

Her eyes searched mine. "How is it that you're everything I need fifty times over? I don't deserve you."

"You've trapped me in your spell," I answered with a grin, feeling such relief after our conversation that I couldn't stop smiling.

She took my hand and smiled a sweet smile at me before she dipped my fingers in ranch dressing. Before I could process what had happened, she took off running. I ran after her, laughing so hard I could barely keep up. I finally caught her by a stand of little trees and wiped ranch on her nose. She gave me an Eskimo kiss, smearing the sauce on my nose as well. We were both laughing so hard by the time we reached the pizza boxes again that we could barely walk.

We fought over who got the last piece of cheesy bread, and when I gave in, Madelyn tore it in half, so we shared it. I threw away the boxes and escorted her back to the car. I felt proud to have such a beautiful woman at my side with her hand resting on my elbow.

"Thank you for the lovely date, Kelson Brady," she said after I shut her door and hurried to the driver's side.

I shook my head. "We're not done yet. Not by a long shot."

Her eyebrows rose. "What are we going to do next?"

I grinned, but didn't explain. She waited patiently until I pulled into the parking lot of the town's only true entertainment facility, a place called At Shairo's that housed pool, laser tag, and miniature golf all under one metal roof that looked very much like Uncle Rick's Quonset hut.

"Whaddya wanna do?" asked a boy with short black hair and freckles.

"Your pick, my lady," I told Madelyn.

I thought she would go for miniature golf, but she surprised me. "Laser tag."

At my look, she smiled, showing all her pretty white teeth. "I've always wanted to try it."

I nodded. "Then a duel it is." I gave the attendant a ten-dollar bill and we followed him into a little room that was more of a closet lined with tattered vests, banged-up guns, golf clubs with broken shafts, sun-faded colored balls in a row of buckets, and broken pool sticks.

Madelyn slipped on the vest he handed her, then laughed at the name on the gun. "The Lady Killer," she read. "I think it's calling you a girl!"

I pretended to be offended, but when I checked the name on my gun, I couldn't hold in the laughter. "War of the Roses—really? Who names these guns?"

The black-haired kid shrugged, obviously not as enchanted by our situation as we were. He ran through a monotone list of rules as though there were no spaces between the words or sentences, then he gestured at the opposite side of the closet and disappeared back through the door where we had entered.

Madelyn gave me a confused look. "Are we supposed to go through there?"

I lifted my gun. "From what I could catch of his rundown, we'll either find the ultimate laser lair or a nest of poisonous neon spiders. Either way, I'm ready."

She laughed and pulled the door open. Both of us stared at the black room lit by florescent painted walls.

"This. Is. Awesome," Madelyn breathed. She looked back at me. "Save yourself," she said before ducking in.

I was laughing so hard, I got shot by three different people the second I set foot in the room.

I had never had so much fun playing laser tag. Madelyn turned into a whole different creature when she was wearing a vest and had a gun in her hands. She dove, rolled, dodged, and spun around corners to take down our opponents from the red team. Before long, everyone on that side was gunning for her.

I backed into a corner in an attempt to catch my breath and found myself shoulder-to-shoulder with Martin, the writer of the school's *Bulldog Bulletin*. I didn't have anything against him, but his uncanny ability of uncovering every photograph of the Black Rider to post on his bulletin left me wary. It didn't help that his brother was also my personal repairman when it came to patching up my myriad scuffs and scrapes from my life as a vigilante.

"Hey, Kelson," he said, pushing his glasses back up on his nose. His blond hair stuck out in all directions despite the amount of gel he used on it.

"Hi, Martin. How's it going?"

He shrugged. "Your girlfriend's making us all look bad. She's killer with that gun!"

I grinned despite my reservations. "Who knew?"

He tipped his head. "We'd better get back out there. She can't hold it on her own."

"I'm not so sure about that," I replied, but I followed him anyway.

Three members of the red team had been lying in wait. Martin and I dove to each side. I shot as I slid, feeling as though I were in an action sequence straight out of the movies. The vests of two of the members buzzed, signaling that they had been hit and needed to back away in order to reset. The third dropped to his knees and attempted to shoot Martin. I scrambled to my right and shot from the hip; the boy's vest buzzed.

"Geesh, it's just a game," he said. He shook his head as he retreated from our little corner.

Martin and I laughed. I leaned against the black carpet-covered wall, wishing Madelyn had seen it.

"You saved my butt," Martin said, crawling over on his knees. He paused and his expression changed. "Where'd you get those?"

I looked down and realized that the last move had forced my shirt to slide up, revealing the bullet bruises across my lower ribs. We sat underneath a yellow light that made the bruises look angry and purple. I shoved the shirt back down and stood. "Cow kicked me."

His eyebrows rose suspiciously. "More than once? What, you didn't think to move?"

"She had me pinned between the milking bar and the barn door," I said quickly. The story came to mind because the exact same thing had happened to Cassidy's younger brother Cole a week before. After making sure he was all right, we had laughed all through breakfast. I only hoped it was realistic enough to fool Martin.

He studied me for a minute. "Okay, Kelson, but I'm watching you." He disappeared around the corner, where an unmanly scream heralded the red trio's victory.

I hit my head against the carpeted wall and let out a frustrated breath.

Chapter Seven

"YOU TOOK HER TO play laser tag?" Magnum asked.

I grinned at the surprise in his voice. "You should have seen her. She beat us by more than all of our scores added together. It was amazing!" We were sitting in the junkyard in the dark, throwing rocks at a tin can lit by one of Jagger's porch lamps. I hoped the sheriff would call with something for us to do soon because any peace I had found organizing junk had been taken away with the realization that I had really only been doing it to help Jagger find his lost door.

"Maybe she should be a Black Rider," Magnum mused.

I shot him a look. "You're not a Black Rider. You're a sidekick."

He glowered at me. "I sure look like the Black Rider. And I'm not a sidekick, I'm a partner," he concluded with a self-satisfied nod. He threw a rock and it echoed inside the can.

I rolled my eyes. "And what's your name again? Night Pony?"

A curse escaped his lips. "What about Midnight Bullet?"

"By the time I say that, the crime will have already happened."

He pitched a rock at me. I moved my foot just far enough to

avoid it.

"Being a Black Rider is boring," he said. "You think I could get them to take the time off my community service?"

Because Magnum had officially been only a hostage, an unarmed bystander during the shooting at the fair, the sheriff had let him off with only community service hours, but he hated every minute of it. I rolled my eyes and decided not to take up the argument again. "Let's go patrol the roads. Maybe we'll be lucky and find the guys who keep hitting the gas stations."

"Maybe we can break in and steal the principal's car."

I shook my head. "Where did that come from?"

"It's what I used to do when I was bored. He started leaving the keys by the door so we wouldn't go rummaging through his house." He shrugged. "We didn't beat it up much."

I gave him a sideways glance. "You really have some issues."

"Seriously, city boy?" he shot back. "You're the one who came up with the vigilante idea in the first place."

"To stop you!"

He grinned. "How'd that work out for you? Now you get to put up with me all the time."

"Lucky me," I muttered.

"Better believe it," he shot back, rising to his feet.

I climbed on my motorcycle and smiled. It didn't matter what was going on in my life—the instant I sat on my bike, all my frustrations vanished. I didn't care if we found the robbers or not. I was just happy to be on the motorcycle again.

I glanced at Magnum. "I've been meaning to ask how you like that bike."

He slid his visor down and said from beneath the helmet, "It's no CBR, but it'll do."

We both revved our engines and took off into the night. The

hum of the tires on the road reverberated through my body, carrying away everything but thoughts of Madelyn. She had become my sacred place, my peace. As we took the turns, two midnight forms preceded only by headlights that lit bare circles on the worn pavement, I thought of her kiss, of holding her while she cried, of the taste of our tears. She broke me down like no other person had, yet she made me stronger and forced me to believe in myself by seeing the good I had thought long gone. I smiled at the stars and pressed the motorcycle to go faster.

TO MY SURPRISE, WE happened upon what looked exactly like the gas station robbers the sheriff told me about, except there were four of them instead of three. A beat-up old Charger was parked to the side of the last gas station before the interstate split. No other vehicle was in sight except for a rusted blue Chevy I assumed belonged to the gas station attendant.

I turned off my headlight and circled around back. I had forgotten to check if Magnum's motorcycle had been rigged with the same ability. I let out a breath of relief when he turned off his light as well. Apparently the sheriff thought it might come in handy.

We pulled up behind the store and left our bikes in the shadows.

"This is it," I said quietly. "Just stay calm and do what I do."

He nodded, his eyes wide. I slid my dark-tinted visor shut and he did the same, effectively blocking out any view I had of his face. I took a breath to calm my pounding heart, then walked around the side of the station.

Two of the robbers were in front of the counter, another stood behind it with a gun to the cashier's head, and the fourth wandered the aisles perusing candy and chips as though unconcerned by the terror they were putting the attendant through.

"We should call for backup," Magnum whispered loudly.

"Do you have a cell phone?" I asked, realizing mine was still at the Ashbys' plugged in on the lamp table by my cot.

He pulled a phone from his jacket, then shook his head. "Battery's dead."

The sheriff would be mad if we didn't call, but at least the dead battery was a better excuse than forgetting the phone. I shrugged. "The attendant's probably already alerted the police. If we don't act now, they'll leave with the money and maybe hurt the guy in the process."

He let out a loud breath, but then gave a nod of his helmet to indicate he was on board.

I started toward the door, then paused in the shadows of the gas pumps. "We should try what we practiced at the junkyard."

"What did we practice?" Magnum asked, his voice a bit tighter than usual.

"You know, the 'I distract them, you jump out. Crap, there's two Black Riders' thing."

He tipped his head toward the back door. "I go in that way?"

I nodded. "Check to see if it's locked."

The knob turned under his hand. I couldn't read his expression through the tinted visor, but his voice was apprehensive when he said, "It's open."

"Just be careful and don't take risks you don't have to," I said before leaving him there.

"How do I know if I don't have to?" he asked in a loud whisper.

I didn't answer because I hadn't figured out that part either. I took a calming breath and pushed the front door open. "Hey, fellas, looks like I almost missed the party."

The man with the gun tipped his head at me. "I 'eard 'bout you," he drawled.

"Funny, I haven't heard anything about you," I replied.

The robber's eyes narrowed. "From what I've 'eard, you ain't a pusho'er when it comes ta fightin'."

I shrugged noncommittally.

"The silent type, eh?" he pressed. "We have ways of getting' ya to talk."

I gave a low chuckle. "Didn't know I'd stepped into a B-rated movie about backwoods Mafias."

His jaw clenched. One of the men closest to me took a step forward. He wore a straw cowboy hat that had been torn along the brim. "Let me rough 'im up a bit, Charlie."

The leader swore. "Now ya done it! Gone and blown all our covers, Frankie. Yur not supposed ta say names. He's friends wi' the cops!"

Cowboy hat stopped and glanced back at him. "All the more reason for me to shut 'im up."

During the exchange, the gas station attendant was inching to the right out of Charlie's grasp. I took a step forward to keep the leader's attention on me. "I'm game if Frankie is."

He gestured with the gun. "You lose, I shoot you."

My heart clenched at the thought of another bullet bruise; of course, he might just aim for my head. I was pretty sure helmets weren't tested for their bullet-stopping abilities. The store clerk watched this exchange with wide eyes, his hand cautiously reaching to the right where the phone sat. My breathing slowed with the realization that he hadn't called the police yet. The cops didn't know the gas station was being hit.

Did the leader know that?

"You'd best be steppin' back a bit," he said as if in answer to my unspoken question. "Don't wanna be grabbin' that phone 'n endin' our little rally short now."

The store clerk backed up against the far wall, his hands up and fingers trembling visibly. His blond hair stood up in moussed spikes. I wondered if he was any relation to Martin. It seemed the entire town of Sparrow was.

"Bring it on," Cowboy Hat said. He moved a big wad of chewing tobacco from one side of his lip to the other, his grin revealing big bucked teeth outlined in brown juice.

I stepped forward, and his companion, a bald man with a black handkerchief around his mouth, stepped forward as well.

"What's it like fightin' in a helmet?" Cowboy Hat asked, trying to distract me. "Get in the way much?"

I shrugged. "What do you think?"

He threw a punch and I ducked so his fist slammed against the side of my helmet. He let out a howl of pain while his three companions burst into laughter.

"It ain't funny!" he shouted, which made them laugh even harder. He turned tear-filled eyes to me. "I think ya broke my hand."

I shook my head. "You did that all on your own."

The tall, skinny man who had been wandering the aisles was slowly making his way toward me. I turned slightly to the right to keep an eye on him. I wondered where Magnum was and if the Bullet leader could take him down; it was a little too late to find out his skill level.

"You'll pay for that," Cowboy Hat said. His bald companion swung a right hook.

I blocked the hook with my left arm and punched Baldie in the throat, then blocked a haymaker from Cowboy Hat and slammed the heel of my palm into his nose and chin. His head whipped back and he stumbled against the counter. Baldie attempted a kidney punch. I swept a low block and slammed my helmet into his nose.

A quick glance showed Magnum sneaking through the aisles

from the back. He was almost to Toothpick, who had his full attention on our fight. The tall, skinny man hefted a glass bottle of ketchup. I blocked a punch and heard the leader shout, "Look out, there's two of them!"

The bottle of ketchup hit the floor. I looked back to see Magnum punch Toothpick in the face again, followed by a blow to the stomach. Toothpick turned, up to the challenge. I realized by his stance that he was a brawler. He covered his head well and threw three punches for every one of Magnum's. Magnum's stomach and ribs got pummeled while Toothpick barely looked winded. Their fight took them through the aisle closest to me.

I blocked a poor attempt at a kick from Cowboy Hat, then turned and drove a jab into Toothpick's ribs. He swore and turned, giving Magnum an opening. Baldie caught me in the ribs with a jab of his own. The force sent a rush of pain through every bullet bruise. I bit back a curse and slammed a two-handed punch into his chest hard enough to propel him back against the counter.

Cowboy Hat's nose was bleeding and his lip was split, but he looked too angry to realize he was beaten. He came at me with both fists swinging. I grabbed a package of peanuts from the end of the aisle and threw it. It hit him in the face.

He caught the package before it fell to the ground and stared at it. "Did you just throw peanuts at me?" he demanded.

"Yes," I replied, then landed a haymaker on his jaw with a loud crack and he fell to the floor.

Baldie tried to take a page out of my book and threw a package of chips at me. It hit my visor and I fought back a laugh. I dropped to the floor and spun as I kicked, sweeping his legs out from under him.

A quick glance showed Magnum backed against the door, his hands raised in an attempt to protect his body from the shower of blows Toothpick was raining down. I took a step and caught Toothpick with a glancing blow to the head as he turned. He put up his hands in a defensive guard, but I slammed two punches to his stomach, then one to his face when he dropped his arms to protect himself.

I drove another fist into his stomach. When he bent over, I caught him in the jaw with my knee, then drove an elbow into his back. He sprawled to the ground. Magnum stepped over him and slammed a fist into Baldie's jaw, knocking him out cold.

"Not bad for a sidekick," I said.

Magnum's hands clenched into fists. "I'm not a sidekick. This is a sidekick." He kicked Toothpick in the ribs.

"Enough," the leader growled.

I turned to see him aim the gun at me.

His finger tightened on the trigger.

"You sure you want to do that?" I asked carefully. "Adding murder to theft is a big jump."

"I'm sure," he replied with a tight smile.

I held my breath, hoping he aimed for my heart where the vest would protect it.

Something flew through the air and hit the leader on the side of the head. I took advantage of the distraction, using my hands to propel me over the counter and on top of the man before he could react. We fell to the ground wrestling for the gun. He elbowed me in the throat, but I tipped my head so the helmet caught most of the blow. I jerked a knee between his legs, then rolled over and grabbed the gun firmly before twisting free and ripping it from his grasp.

"You got it?" Magnum called from the other side of the counter.

"Got it," I replied, pushing myself up.

The leader glared at me, but the sight of the gun in my hand took the fight from his eyes.

"Call the police," I told the attendant. He watched me with wide eyes, his face pale. When he made no move to comply, I glanced at Magnum. "Call Sheriff Bowley. Tell him we have his robbers."

Three sheriff cars pulled up to the gas station a few minutes later. I met the sheriff out front as soon as the robbers were under control.

"Got to give you credit for the quick response," I told him.

He tipped his hat and eyed the men who were being handcuffed and led to the waiting cars. "And you get credit for a smooth job. I look forward to watching the surveillance videos."

"Let me know if you see any areas that need improvement," I said.

He stared at me for a second, and then a chuckle escaped from him. "I'll do that."

We watched quietly as the leader was loaded into the car. "He jumped us!" the man protested. "We were set up! We were just here for gas."

"Tell it to your attorney," the officer said before shutting the door and blocking out further protests.

"The trio's still out there," the sheriff said.

I let out a slow breath. "You mean they weren't the ones?"

He shook his head. "I was hoping, but they carry knives instead of guns, and their leader's a big dude with tribal tattoos down one arm. You'll know him when you see him."

I nodded. "I'll keep an eye out."

The sheriff turned away, then paused. "Call us first next time. It might make the job a bit easier."

"I keep forgetting my cell phone, and Magnum's battery died." I said apologetically.

The sheriff smoothed his short beard with one hand. "Isn't that what a sidekick is for?"

Magnum let out a growl from where he waited by the motorcycles.

"What's his deal?" Sheriff Bowley asked, his gaze thoughtful.

I shrugged. "He's still struggling with a name he likes."

"I'm sure when Martin figures out there's two of you, he'll come up with one himself," the sheriff replied amiably.

I spoke before I finished thinking my words through. "I'd prefer it if Martin didn't know."

"Why is that?" he asked, his expression curious.

I shrugged, searching for a reason. "It might give us an edge if the people we're up against think there's only one Rider."

Sheriff Bowley nodded with a slight crease to his forehead. "That makes sense. I'll tell the boys not to mention it."

"I'd appreciate that." I held out a hand.

The sheriff shook it. "Call us next time."

"I will," I said, though we both knew I probably wouldn't.

Chapter Eight

"YOU WENT ALL KUNG fu back there," Magnum said while we wiped down the motorcycles in the junkyard.

"Not my best work," I replied.

Magnum glanced up at my tone, then scowled. "Beating up the Bullets wasn't your best work, either."

I shrugged. "The odds were a little better."

He turned back to his bike, but I could see the humor that tried to battle his glare. He finally said, "If you mean thirteen on one, given the way you fight, I might have to grant it to you. You're kind of an all-or-nothing fighter."

I looked at him curiously. "Meaning?"

He let out an exasperated breath. "Like you couldn't care less about your safety. I saw you take a punch in the ribs protecting me. I could have handled it."

"I know you could have," I said levelly.

"I could have," he shot back.

I held up a hand. "I know," I repeated. "Sometimes I'm not careful."

He slowly wiped the spotless seat again. "Sparrow isn't the

end of the world. If they don't get caught here, they'll be caught somewhere else."

I wiped off the gauges even though there wasn't any dust on them. "I know. It just gives me something to keep my mind off things."

He looked over at me. "What things?"

I shook my head and threw the rag at him. "That bag of M&Ms you chucked at the gunman changed everything back there."

Magnum grinned. "I know. It was pretty awesome." He chuckled. "You gave me the idea when you threw the peanuts at the other one."

"I had to come up with something," I admitted. "That blow to the ribs slowed me down."

He laughed and put both rags and Jagger's cleaner back on the porch. I stashed my bike in the lean-to next to the shack and Magnum parked his alongside it. I swung the door shut and looked at the four-wheeler. It was a paltry trade.

"See you around," I said, sitting on the machine.

Magnum crossed to the rusty red Ford parked on the edge of Jagger's lot. "Take care of yourself," he called before starting up the engine.

I drove the four-wheeler slowly up the lane, then turned onto the main road. It took a few minutes before I realized the horizon was lighter than it should have been. I followed the road with my eyes and my heart slowed. Flames danced against the night sky where the Ashbys' house was.

Magnum's truck skidded to a halt beside the four-wheeler. "Get in!" he shouted.

I turned off the four-wheeler and climbed in, unable to speak or even breathe with the sight of the flames lapping at the midnight sky.

A brief glimmer of relief surfaced when I saw that it wasn't the Ashby house but the barn that was on fire; shadows appeared within the doors.

"Someone's in there," I said to Magnum.

"Kelson, wait!" Magnum yelled, but I was already running across the lawn.

I ran through the doors, then froze at the sight of red, orange, and yellow tendrils lapping at the floor and walls of the massive barn. The cows were gone, and the straw on the floor of their stalls burned in fierce orange.

I made out the form of Uncle Rick near the middle of the barn. Somehow, a beam had fallen and trapped Jaren underneath it in the blazing inferno. Uncle Rick was trying to lift the timber off him, but it weighed too much.

"Kelson, help!" he shouted.

I couldn't blink, I couldn't move. The sound of the fire devouring the wood around me had my feet pinned to the floor as effectively as if the beam was on me instead of Jaren.

Magnum's shoulder brushed mine as he ran past me. He grabbed the beam and tried to lift it with Uncle Rick, but they couldn't make it budge.

"Kelson!" Magnum shouted.

Two scenes danced in front of my vision. In one, a warehouse reached around me with faded white paint that peeled under the fingers of fire. A car that had once filled the walls with music sat as an empty shell that burned from the inside. Beer bottles were scattered along the floor and the trash barrel was overturned.

In the other, my uncle and friend tried to free my cousin before he burned to death in a barn painted red and tan by loving hands. I had learned to milk cows under its roof, and saw Uncle Rick smile with pride in my accomplishments for the first time. Cassidy had patched the roof numerous times, though a small leak still persisted stubbornly in one corner. Now, the roof burned red with raging flames.

I couldn't face it. I couldn't stand in fire again and watch a loved one burn. It followed me. It was a part of me. I felt like I burned from the inside out.

The visions blurred together and I saw the warehouse stairs where the barn stairs stood. Two forms ran up them, one with long blonde hair and eyes that I knew would be as blue as a summer day—my sister Zoey. The other had dark hair and a grin that charmed all the girls, my best friend Jeff. Their forms faded as the stairs burned and fell away just as they had that night.

Smoke clouded the air. "Kelson," Uncle Rick shouted.

"Kelson, save him," Zoey's voice echoed.

I blinked at the sound of her voice. I took a step forward, suddenly free of the fears that held me. I ran through the fire to Uncle Rick's side and picked up the beam with all the strength I possessed. The other two barely had a chance to lift before the beam was high enough for Jaren to wiggle free. The four of us stumbled out of the barn. A beam creaked, and then the entire roof fell in.

I had to get away from the fire. Aunt Lauren threw her arms around Uncle Rick and Jaren with tears streaming down her face. I walked past without really seeing them and went straight inside to my cot. I collapsed in a heap on the bed and felt the tears flow down my cheeks.

The kitchen door opened and footsteps came inside.

"What was that?" Magnum demanded from the kitchen.

The door opened again and more footsteps sounded. "The fire department is on its way," Aunt Lauren said. "But there won't be anything to save."

"What happened to Kelson?" Magnum demanded.

All sounds in the kitchen stopped. I wasn't crying, but I couldn't stop the tears that continued to overflow. I glared at the darkness in the living room, unbroken for one blissful moment by the flames that lay dormant in the fireplace.

"Oh, Rick," Aunt Lauren whispered.

"Somebody fill me in," Magnum said, his voice softer in answer to Aunt Lauren's tone.

Aunt Lauren took a calming breath. "Kelson lost his sister in a warehouse fire a short while ago. His mom sent him here to help him get over it."

I gritted my teeth against the pain that flared through my heart. There was no getting over it. I was broken, haunted, no longer functioning at the level of a normal human being. I had almost let my cousin die because I couldn't figure out the difference between reality and a nightmare.

"What do we tell Sarah?" Aunt Lauren asked.

The sound of the fire engine's siren answered as it raced down the road. They went outside to meet the crew and help out in any way they could, leaving me to numb silence.

"Are you all right, Kelson?" Magnum asked from the kitchen.

I didn't answer. He waited a few minutes, then crossed into the living room.

"I didn't know," he said quietly. "I hadn't heard what happened to your sister. I'm sorry."

He waited, but when I still didn't respond, he set a hand on my shoulder. "Let me know if you need a drinking buddy."

I nodded. He squeezed my shoulder and left through the kitchen door. His absence made the room feel small and strange, as if I sat in a black box without any of my senses. I felt numb and vacant, like a stranger in my own body.

Mom's voice pierced the void. I didn't know how many hours

had passed. It was still dark outside, but the fire engine had left. Mom had gotten a job at one of the town's two grocery stores. She didn't deserve to come home from a long day of work to find out what had happened.

Hushed voices spoke outside, then Mom's footsteps raced through the kitchen and up the hallway to the living room.

"Oh, Kelson," she exclaimed. She threw her arms around me and held me tight as if afraid until that moment that I had been burned in the fire.

"I'm all right," I forced myself to say.

"You're shaking like a leaf!" she exclaimed. She smoothed my hair over and over again, holding me against her like she would never let me go. "You're all right," she said, probably as much for herself as for me. "You're all right."

More tears broke free. I didn't know a person could cry so many tears and still have some left over. I didn't bother to dry them because others took up residence the second they were gone. I had never been a crier, and now it seemed my body was determined to make up for the times I had forced back the tears.

Mom just held me as if she knew it was exactly what I needed. She cried into my hair. I felt the rivulets soak down to my scalp and my soul. "It's okay," I found myself whispering. "Everything's all right, Mom. We're all right."

She eventually sat back and wiped her face, watching me through the darkness of the unlit living room as if wishing she could read my thoughts.

"Are you okay?" she asked.

I nodded even though it wasn't true. I could be strong for Mom. She didn't need to suffer with me.

I stood up.

"Where are you going?" she asked, her voice filled with

concern.

"I need to get some fresh air. I think I'll go for a ride." I touched her shoulder. "Will you be okay?"

She took a deep breath and let it out in a rush. "I will." Her eyebrows pulled together. "Don't be too long."

"I won't."

I wiped my cheeks as I made my way to the kitchen. Uncle Rick and Aunt Lauren were talking and holding hands across the oblong kitchen table. When I appeared, they stopped whatever they were saying. Aunt Lauren rested a hand on her stomach and Uncle Rick squeezed her other hand reassuringly. I rushed through the mudroom and out the back door, forgetting to catch the screen before it slammed shut behind me.

I ran back up the road to where I had left the four-wheeler. My ribs ached with every pounding step, and I was glad for the distraction to my thoughts. I tripped on a clump of weeds and rolled, but righted myself and kept running. My heart pounded as if the flames were chasing me, lapping at my ankles and forcing me to run faster. I collapsed against the four-wheeler, but refused to let myself pause because pausing meant thinking, and I couldn't let myself do that.

I climbed on the four-wheeler and drove to Madelyn's house. It was the only place I wanted to be. She was the only one who could calm my thoughts. I parked in her driveway instead of stopping at the corner of their lot and jogged across the lawn.

It was so early in the morning that the sun hadn't even touched the horizon with gray, but the lights were on and commotion showed through the living room window. On impulse, I knocked on the front door instead of climbing the tree to her room.

The door opened and my heart slowed at Madelyn's pale face. "Kelson, what are you doing here?" she asked.

Caught off guard, I took a step back. "I just needed to talk to you. I—"

She shook her head before I finished speaking. "Mom's sick. We're taking her to the hospital."

"Madelyn, let's go," her father called from the garage.

"I've got to go," she said, her expression desperate.

I caught her hand. "Maddy." At the look on her face, I gave her what I hoped was a reassuring smile. "Everything will be okay."

She nodded, gave me a quick kiss on the cheek, then ran through the kitchen to the garage. I was left in the open doorway and listened to the sound of their van as they pulled around the four-wheeler and out of the driveway.

She was gone. My rock, my peace, my heart. I shouldn't have felt betrayed by her absence; her mother needed her there and she was where she needed to be, but I couldn't face the emotions that threatened to tear me apart from the inside out. I couldn't face the side of me that surfaced beneath the fire, the coward who froze instead of saving lives, the person who brought danger to those around him.

A voice deep inside said that wasn't true, but the whirlwind of my thoughts was full of such chaos that I couldn't listen. I didn't recognize myself anymore. I was a shell of despair, a hopeless wreck who let his sister die and almost lost his cousin in yet another inferno.

I crouched on the porch and held my head in my hands. A cry of defeat broke from my lips. I no longer knew myself. I despised myself.

I slammed a fist on the wooden porch. Chips broke where the brown paint was crumbling. It felt like my sanity, slipping through my fingers as so much dust.

I jumped to my feet and ran to the four-wheeler. The hum of the tires against the road was loud in my ears as I pushed the machine faster than I ever had before. I sped past the Ashbys' house and continued up the road to the junkyard. I didn't slow when I hit the dirt road. The four-wheeler slid on the dirt as it skidded around the corner. I jerked the handlebars hard and stood, forcing it to stay upright. I drove around the shack and braked to a halt. A cloud of dust surrounded me when I climbed off.

I barely saw the two forms sitting in the shadows on the porch.

"Where ya goin'?" Jagger asked.

"I'm not sure," I replied. I pulled the door to the lean-to open and backed my motorcycle out.

"You're not going alone," Magnum said. He moved his motorcycle out as well and pulled on his helmet.

Jagger put a hand on my motorcycle. "Yur all right," he said, his gaze boring into mine.

I shook my head. "I don't know what I am anymore." My steady tone surprised me. Inside, I felt like everything was shaking, threatening to explode.

"Ta fire warn't yur fault," Jagger said. He stood in front of the motorcycle with a hand on the shield to keep me from pulling forward.

I closed my eyes, unable to meet the directness of his gaze. "If I don't ride, I'm going to do something stupid. I need to get away."

I heard Jagger step back. "'Member, you've always got a place to come."

I opened my eyes and looked at the gauges on the motorcycle. "I know," I said quietly.

He limped back to the porch.

I started the engine and heard Magnum do the same. I pulled on my helmet and revved the throttle. The growl of the motor combated some of the heaviness that ate at my mind. I pulled around the shack and took off up the road. My tires skidded when I hit the pavement, but I rolled the throttle and sped up the road.

I didn't let myself think. My motorcycle raced through town with the efficient ruthlessness of a well-working machine. I didn't slow down. I swerved around the two farm trucks that were on the road, then drove through the red of the single light in town and crossed into the dark wash of predawn. The growl of the engine filled my heart and soul, crowding out all other thoughts but the call of unknown roads and the darkness beyond.

I lost track of the distance I traveled. I forgot why I was running and what waited for me when I got back. The only world I knew danced within my headlights, a pale expanse brushed at the edges with shadow, a beam that threatened to be consumed by the black agony that surrounded it.

The road narrowed and took a turn into a mountain pass I had never traveled. I didn't slow the bike. Instead, I pushed it faster, rounding bends with my knee scraping the ground, barely righting it before another turn. At the last bend, the valley spread out before me. Scattered dots of light showed from the few farmhouses awake before the sun. The homes were nestled in darkness, cozy in their blissful ignorance.

I drove toward the edge. Darkness bounced beyond my visor with open arms to embrace me. I took an accepting breath.

At the last second, I grabbed the hand brake and stomped on the foot brake. The tires locked and the motorcycle slid. I jerked forward when it stopped at the farthest edge of the road, and stared at the depth beyond my front tire. I turned off the engine. My heart pounded in my throat with an erratic rhythm. It was a few seconds before I could reassure myself that I was still alive, not broken and twisted in the valley far below where even the rising sunlight didn't reach.

A curse sounded to my right. The rough scrape of a motorcycle kickstand sliding against the pavement echoed harshly against the rock wall behind us. A loud bang sounded when Magnum ripped off his helmet and threw it to the ground. His footsteps were loud in the sudden silence.

"I thought you weren't going to stop," he said, his voice thick.

I shook my head. "I didn't think I was either."

Magnum hit the back of my helmet so hard my ears rang. I stared at him in surprise. He glared back at me, his fists clenched and expression more angry than I had ever seen him.

"Don't you ever do anything so stupid again," he said, his shoulders tight and chest rising and falling as if he was fighting to catch his breath. He grabbed the front of my shirt. "Don't you ever think to throw your life away so cheap." He forced my visor up so we were staring eye to eye. "I refuse to let a friend die because he feels guilt from some freak accident."

I stared at him, my heart pounding and my thoughts puny compared to the outrage on his face. It was then that I remembered he had watched another friend die, his best friend Kyle who perished racing a train on a motorcycle.

"Life is always worth living, always," Magnum said, his eyes boring into mine. "Say it."

I swallowed against the knot in my throat.

"Say it!" Magnum yelled.

"Life is worth living," I whispered.

"Louder," Magnum demanded.

"Life is worth living," I yelled.

He let me go and I slumped on the motorcycle. I felt drained as if I had been sick for weeks.

"Don't ever do that to me again," he said in a voice so low I barely heard it.

We stared out at the dark gray expanse in silence. Eventually, Magnum took a deep breath. "I need to get some sleep." He glanced at me. "Crash at my house—it's closer. You can call your mom and tell her where you are."

The thought of what I would meet at the Ashby house filled me with dread. I nodded. Magnum climbed back onto his motorcycle and led us at a much slower pace toward his house. By the time we pulled into the cracked driveway, the horizon was light gray and roosters were already calling the farmers to rise.

"MOM?"

"Kelson, are you okay?" The worry in Mom's voice tore at my heart.

"I'm fine. I'm at Magnum's."

"I was so worried," she said. "You promised you wouldn't be long."

"I just . . . I had some things to work out, so we took the bikes on a ride."

I sat on one of Magnum's rickety porch steps watching the sunrise bathe the houses in a wash of pink and orange. Birds chirped in the trees and a dog barked in the distance. The sunrise felt like something new, a gift when I had all but given up.

"I'm glad you're okay," Mom said. The depth to her voice said she guessed more than I let on.

"Magnum's a good friend," I replied. The words couldn't cover what I owed to him.

"I'm grateful you have him."

"Me too."

An uncomfortable silence fell. Mom and I had never been good at discussing emotional stuff. That had always been Zoey's realm.

She had been the peacemaker and therapist of the family. I closed my eyes and rubbed a hand across them, trying to think of what Zoey would say. She would just tell the truth.

"Mom?"

"Yeah?"

I let out a slow breath. "I'm sorry I worried you. I shouldn't have left like that; I just didn't know how to deal with everything."

"You carry so much by yourself." She sniffed. I realized she was crying but trying not to sound like it. "I just want you to come to me if you need someone to talk to."

"I will, Mom. I promise." She needed closure as much as I did. I swallowed the knot in my throat. "I love you, Mom."

I could hear the smile in her voice when she replied. "I love you, Kelson. Take as much time as you need there. Just promise me a hug when you get back."

"It's yours," I promised.

Chapter Nine

THE HARD SPRINGS OF an unfamiliar couch told me I wasn't on my cot. I opened my eyes a crack and met the serious gaze of a dirty-faced five-year-old.

"Leave Kelson alone, Tommy," Magnum said. "Go brush your teeth; breakfast is almost ready."

The little boy obliged, but it was obvious he would have preferred to continue staring at me.

Memories of the day before crowded my mind. I sat up and rubbed my face.

"Sleep all right?"

I cracked a smile at Magnum's doubtful tone. "This couch isn't bad."

He snorted. "That's because you were only on it for two hours." He jerked his head toward the kitchen. "C'mon. Eggs are ready."

"You cook?" I asked in amazement as I followed him through the door.

He glared at me. "No one else to do it."

I put up my hands. "I can barely make toast. I'm impressed."

He shook his head and gestured toward a chair. I took a seat at a round plastic table with a hole in the middle where the umbrella used to go. Someone had drawn skulls and snakes in permanent marker on the white plastic. A few clumps of dried ketchup sat near one edge.

"Get in here," Magnum yelled over his shoulder as he dished slightly overdone eggs onto five paper plates. He handed one to me, then sat down with another plate and a bottle of ketchup. He proceeded to squirt more ketchup onto the plate than there were eggs.

The little boy from earlier came into the kitchen wearing a pair of gray shorts and a shirt with a yellow stain across the front.

"You can't wear that. Go change into something clean," Magnum commanded.

"It is clean," the boy argued.

Magnum pointed to the stain. "You'll get sent home from school again. Hurry up and change or you'll be late."

Tommy sniffed and walked slowly from the room.

Magnum's brother Derek came in next. I recognized him from the time Jaren pointed him out at the middle school. Derek had been following his brother's footsteps bullying students; since Magnum and I spoke about it, I hadn't heard any more complaints from Jaren.

Derek squinted at me. "Where'd you come from?"

"We were out riding late; forget about it." Magnum answered shortly.

Derek grabbed a plate of eggs and scarfed them down in four big forkfuls. He ducked his head under the faucet and drank a few gulps of water, then wiped his mouth with the back of his hand and grabbed his backpack.

A horn honked outside. "Jess, bus is here," Magnum yelled.

"Coming," came a shout from the back of the house.

Magnum held out the plate of eggs. It was grabbed by a tall, skinny girl with scraggly red hair as she rushed past. She barely glanced at me before she slammed the door.

"Wait up," Derek yelled. He grabbed a handful of eggs from Magnum's plate and shoved them in his mouth.

"Hey!" Magnum protested, but Derek was already out the door. Magnum muttered a creative string of curses before he yelled, "Tommy, move it!"

The five-year-old ran past wearing a green Hulk T-shirt and his gray shorts. Magnum forced him to take a plate of eggs as he bolted out the door. A few seconds later, the huff of a bus taking off sounded. Magnum fell back in his seat. "I swear that gets harder every day." He then glanced at me as if just remembering I was there.

I hefted the eggs. "These aren't bad."

"Shut up," Magnum growled.

I grinned and ate the last few bites, then stood up.

"How you feeling?" Magnum asked, his tone cautious.

I shrugged, not willing to put too much thought into the question. "I could use more sleep."

He laughed, but the sound was cut short by a shout from the other side of the house.

"Charles, get in 'ere," a male voice demanded.

Magnum's head jerked toward the command. For one second, he froze, his entire body completely still. He blew out a slow breath through his nose, then glanced at me. "I'll be right back."

He scraped what was left of the eggs into a blue plastic bowl from the counter, then left the kitchen.

Mumbling ensued from the back room; Magnum's voice responded. The voice sounded louder, followed by the sharp crack of a slap. I tensed. I wanted to intervene, but I knew better than to get involved in family matters.

Magnum came back down the hall a few seconds later. A red handprint colored the side of his face. He grabbed a set of keys off the counter without looking at me and shoved the front door open. I followed him without a word. We climbed into his rusty red truck and soon the only sound was the hum of the tires over the road.

Magnum broke the silence just before we reached town. "It's not perfect, but it's my family."

"You invited me into your house. You don't have to defend your family to me," I told him.

"It must look like a mess from the outside." He paused, then gave a small, wry smile. "It looks like one from the inside."

I shook my head. "At least it's a family. You heard my story. There's just me and Mom left now." My voice lowered. "Pretty pathetic, considering what we used to be."

Magnum glanced at me. "So you put your energy into fighting crime and stopping gangs?"

I shrugged, lost in the darkness of my thoughts.

Magnum broke the silence again as he pulled into the school parking lot. "It's Thursday. You up for a race?"

His words turned my thoughts in a completely different direction. Excitement brushed through me. "Always. Should I race as the Black Rider, or as Kelson?"

Magnum glanced at me and chuckled. "Last time you raced as Kelson, I was the one who paid for it. Nobody would mind another race against the Black Rider."

I nodded, knowing we both needed a new picture in the *Bulldog Bulletin* to take over the three-seater on my motorcycle with the truck driver. My thoughts turned to Martin. "I need your help with something."

"I'm in," Magnum replied.

I looked at him in surprise. "You don't even know what it is."

He shrugged. "When you say it like that, I know you're up to something and I'd rather be part of it than read about it later."

I nodded. "Fair enough." I moved to open the door, but Magnum held up a hand.

"Wait until I leave. We shouldn't be seen entering together."

"Want another brawl?" I asked.

"I'm game if you are," he said with a grin.

I lifted an eyebrow. "One of these days, I might not be able to just curl up and take it."

He paused. "I've been on the real receiving end of your fists before. It's not a great feeling."

It was my turn to grin. "Watch the cheap shots."

He shook his head with a wicked smile. "I can't promise anything."

I shook my head as he climbed out, waited until the rest of the Bullets met him at the side of the building, then slipped out to join the throng making their way to school.

I STOPPED BY MADELYN'S calculus class, but she wasn't in her usual seat. Second-period music history crept by slowly. Madelyn's empty seat next to mine was a constant reminder of last night and everything that had happened. I wanted to be with her again, to make sure she was all right. I needed to feel things move on so I wasn't haunted by the reminders that were obvious in her absence.

Martin stopped me in the hall before I reached macroeconomics. "Have a good time at laser tag?" he asked.

I nodded. "It was fun," I answered carefully.

His eyes narrowed behind his thick-rimmed glasses. "Was that before or after you stopped a robbery at the gas station near Enton?"

I widened my eyes in what I hoped was an innocent expression.

"What are you talking about?"

He lowered his voice and stepped forward, staring up at me with all the fierceness his five-foot frame could muster. "The Black Rider stopped four men from robbing the gas station. According to the sheriff, it was quite a fight. Unfortunately, something happened to the security tape and it didn't record properly, so I'll have to take his word for it."

"They would have let you watch the tape?" I asked doubtfully.

He shrugged with an air of confidence. "The gas station owner and my dad are good friends. It's not hard to call in a favor when you have the right contacts."

"That's handy," I replied dryly.

He watched me with all the careful scrutiny of a little boy with a bug under a microscope. "Your knuckles are bruised."

"The Ashbys' barn caught fire last night. Jaren was trapped under a beam and I scraped them trying to help him get free." I lifted an eyebrow. "You must have heard about the fire from your contacts."

He cocked his head to the right, reminding me of Jagger's Chihuahua when he tried to figure out a strange noise. "I'm watching you, Kelson."

"Have fun with that," I said with false confidence. "I work in a junkyard and on Uncle Rick's farm. You'll be able to write about junked cars and alfalfa."

"And maybe a black motorcycle, an Er-6n with an updated exhaust system and a newly installed fender eliminator kit?" He watched me shrewdly. "It looks a lot better."

I gave him a small smile. "Did you see the last time I was on a motorcycle? Magnum's still out for blood."

He opened his mouth to reply, but the bell rang.

"I've gotta go to class. It was nice talking to you," I said. I stepped into macroeconomics and left him staring through the door.

MAGNUM MANAGED TO MAKE lunch exciting. I had just paid for my tray when the Bullets happened to mosey by. Thompson, a tall, skinny boy with a shaved head, hit the tray from my hands. It landed on the floor, sending chicken nuggets, green beans, and applesauce everywhere. An expectant hush fell over the cafeteria.

"Look what you did, loser," Uzi, a thick-set boy with rings through his eyebrows, said. He waggled his eyebrows mockingly.

"Do you get good reception with those things?" I asked.

His expression turned confused, but the green-haired girl shoved him to the side. "You've got a mouth on you."

"You do too," I noted.

She glared at me. "Your respect for the Bullets is severely lacking."

"It might be the lack of bullets," I pointed out. I glanced at Magnum and saw that he was fighting not to laugh. If he wasn't careful, he would blow our cover. I met his gaze. "How's life treating you, Capgun?"

His smile vanished and was replaced with a glare. "It's Magnum."

"Are you sure that's a real name?" I asked. "I like Capgun better."

Whispers spread through the lunchroom, but it was stilled at one look from Magnum. He took a step toward me. "You spilled your food."

I shrugged. "I'm a bit clumsy."

"I wouldn't want the lunch ladies to have to clean up after you," he said with a pointed look at the floor.

I bent down and began picking up chicken nuggets.

"He's getting away easy," a boy with a red Mohawk said.

Magnum crouched next to me. "Uh-uh, Keldon," he said loudly, stressing the wrong name. "Clean it up with your mouth."

I fought to keep the anger from my face. I met Magnum's eyes with enough of a glare to warn him that he was about to cross a line. His gaze tightened slightly with humor.

He stood. "I guess Keldon's afraid of germs," he said. Students around the lunchroom broke into uneasy laughter.

"Make him eat it anyway," one of the Bullets urged. The others echoed the heartfelt sentiment.

"What's going on here?" Principal Dawson asked. I gave a sigh of relief.

The Bullets immediately backed away.

"Nothing," Magnum said. "Just helping Keldon clean up his spilled lunch."

The principal looked at the mess on the floor. "Better get a rag from Ms. Smith," he advised.

I nodded and turned away, grateful for both my sake and Magnum's.

Chapter Ten

I MET MAGNUM AT his truck after school.

"I need you to take me to the hospital."

Surprise lit his face. "Did you get in another fight?"

I rolled my eyes. "Madelyn is there with her mother. I need to go visit her."

"I don't know how I became your chauffeur," Magnum grumbled, but he motioned for me to climb into the truck.

"Lucky, I guess," I answered when we were both inside. "And for the record, Magnum is a far better name than Capgun."

He fought back a smile and started the truck.

I made him stop at a grocery store for flowers, and then he dropped me off in front of the white stucco building. "I'll wait here." At my surprised look, he shrugged. "Someone needs to get you to the factory."

I had forgotten about the races. I shook my head. "It might be better if I don't race today. Martin's been asking questions. I think he's figured out that I'm the Black Rider."

"Does he know there are two of us?"

"I don't think so. He said the surveillance tape at the gas station had a problem and didn't record."

He chuckled. "Then I think you definitely have to ride today."

I fought back a smile. "It could be risky."

He shrugged. "Isn't that what being the Black Rider is all about? Taking risks, saving lives, all that boring stuff?"

I grinned and opened the door. "It's definitely worth a try. Martin's too curious for his own good."

"Makes for a good reporter."

I laughed. "You didn't think so a month ago."

His eyes narrowed. "That's because everything he wrote was against the Bullets."

"You gave him a lot to write about."

Magnum grinned. "Yeah, we did."

I grabbed the flowers. "I'll be right back."

The nurse at the desk directed me toward Mrs. West's room. I peeked through the partially open door to see Mr. West sitting in a chair with his head against the wall, and Madelyn hunched over with her elbows on her knees. She looked up suddenly as if expecting something. When her eyes met mine, such joy filled her features that I felt my heart would burst. She jumped out of her chair and threw her arms around me.

"I'm so glad you're here," she said. "I'm sorry about last night."

"You have nothing to apologize for," I told her, smoothing her hair. "Your mother should be your biggest concern." I looked at Mrs. West's pale form on the bed. She looked so tiny surrounded by IVs and beeping machines. I wondered how she managed to sleep through all the noise. "How is she doing?"

Mr. West rose and shook his head. "Not well." He held out a hand and I shook it. "Thank you for coming. They'll be transporting Mindy to the city in an hour."

I looked at Madelyn in surprise. "I didn't realize it was so serious."

Her brows pulled together in worry. "It started as just a cold, but it settled into her lungs. She has pneumonia and they don't have the equipment to care for all her needs here."

I nodded and gave her my most reassuring smile. "I'm sure she'll be all right."

"She's a fighter," Mr. West replied, but there was a heaviness to his tone that he couldn't suppress.

"Is there anything I can do to help?" I asked.

I held out the flowers to Madelyn and she took them with a grateful smile. "If we don't get home tonight, could you feed Buck?"

"I'd be happy to." The thought of spending a night without seeing her was painful, but I knew the emotion was selfish compared to a daughter's concern for her mother's health. I wanted to kiss her and tell her how much I would miss her, but her father didn't know how often we saw each other. I settled for kissing her forehead. "Call me if you need anything."

"I will," she said softly. I held her in my arms for a moment, and then she stepped back with a sigh. "Thank you for coming."

"Let me know if you need anything at all," I repeated.

I made my way back to the truck with slow steps. It wasn't until I was almost there that I noticed the blue crossover motorcycle in the back. It was the same motorcycle I had wrecked during my first race at the factory. Magnum had fixed it up so it was in much better shape.

"We're getting there late, so no one will notice if you're the one driving," Magnum explained.

A thought occurred to me. "What happened to your black truck?"

He clenched his jaw as he turned the engine over. "You mean the one you dented with my motorcycle?"

At my amused nod, he looked like he wanted to punch me. I wondered if I could goad him into fighting me away from anyone's view. It would be nice to get a little payback for the fight at lunch.

His gaze simmered as if he guessed my thoughts. "Dad took it back and left me with this junker. Said I didn't deserve a vehicle I couldn't take care of."

I laughed out loud. "What did you tell him happened to it?"

Magnum's eyes narrowed. "The truth. I said some new kid wannabe hit it with a motorcycle."

"Did you tell him it was your motorcycle?"

He nodded and grinned in spite of himself. "That's when he took the truck away."

I dropped him off at his house to pick up one of the motorcycles we left there the night before, then made my way to the factory. The crowd was cheering on the beginner racers, newbie bikers who didn't really race so much as survive the trip around the track while the audience waited for the real race to begin. Small handfuls of cash, candy bars, playing cards, and anything else students valued were exchanged for bets on the fastest bikers.

The air smelled like burning rubber and the bags of popcorn an enterprising student sold from the back of her truck. Everyone jostled each other in an effort to get a good view. Cell phones recorded the first bikers in the hopes that something exciting would happen. The races were well underway when I found Martin in the crowd.

He pushed his glasses up when he saw me. "You're not racing?"

"Of course he's not," Cassidy said, surprising me with her sudden appearance from the crowd. My cousin gave me a knowing wink.

"Don't you remember how he nearly killed himself last time?" Sandy asked, leaning against her friend. I felt a surge of gratitude for the wispy girl who was inseparable from Cassidy.

Martin shrugged, unconvinced. "The students will be disappointed if the Black Rider doesn't show up."

Sandy stared at him. "Are you implying that Kelson's the Black Rider?" She laughed so hard she snorted. "He couldn't jump from a roof on a motorcycle if his life depended on it!" She gave me an appraising look. "He's not tall enough, not muscly enough—no offense—and he's kind of a pushover."

Cassidy smothered a laugh while I tried to take it good-naturedly. "I'm not a pushover."

Sandy grinned to show her black-and-yellow braces. "The Bullets walk all over you. The Black Rider laid them out, like, a dozen times. There's no way he would stand for Magnum's bullying."

I rolled my eyes while Martin pointed out that it hadn't been nearly a dozen times that the Black Rider had bested the Bullets. Then the roar of a familiar motorcycle filled the air. I grinned at Martin's still-suspicious gaze. "If I'm the Black Rider, how is he over there?"

More people had been following the conversation than I realized. At my comment, nearly half the crowd turned to see Magnum dressed as the Black Rider as he parked near the first warehouse. He revved the engine and a cheer went up from the crowd. Cassidy turned back to me with her mouth open. She was the only one there who knew my secret, so her surprise was the greatest of all. I threw her a smile before I turned back to Martin.

"Sorry," I apologized to the high school journalist. "Guess you'll have to find a lead elsewhere."

He let out a disappointed huff and stalked through the crowd in an effort to get a picture of the Black Rider for the Bulletin.

Cassidy leaned close to me. "If you're here, who's that?"

I winked at her. "Guess I still have some secrets."

"Kelson," she said in frustration. I left her steaming next to Sandy.

I grabbed a set of gray-and-blue riding clothes from Magnum's truck, then drove his motorcycle to the back of one of the warehouses. He showed up a few minutes later and changed quickly.

"It's gotta be hard on your self-esteem to meet cheers like that," he said as he pulled on his blue helmet.

I zipped up the black jacket he gave me and slid up the dark visor on the black helmet. "It makes our little quarrel in the lunchroom a bit easier to face."

He laughed as he climbed onto his crossover motorcycle. "It was just a chicken nugget."

"From the floor," I said in disgust.

"Next time, you're eating it," he threatened.

"You'll have to catch me first," I replied. I gunned the engine and drove out to face the crowd.

"Dibs on the Black Rider!" someone called out. Soon, everyone was exchanging gum, candy bars, allowances, and anything else they could place on the race. The black-and-blue crossover pulled up a few seconds later. A girl with a white cowboy hat crossed to the starting line.

"About time you got here," the boy with the red Mohawk said. It was the first time I had ever heard any of the Bullet members say something so pointedly rude to their leader's face.

Magnum silenced him with a glare.

"Thought you'd show up and take charge?" asked Beretta, a girl with spikey hair now held in check by her neon pink helmet.

"Shut up and ride," Magnum barked.

He revved his engine and took off as soon as the white cowboy hat hit the ground.

I followed close behind, my mind more on the attitudes of the Bullet members than on the race. The first turn through the warehouse doors brought me back.

I swept low, my left knee brushing the ground as I rode with my front tire inches from Magnum's back one. We pulled upright, then ducked through a low-framed door and raced across the cracked cement floor. Magnum drove like a demon followed on his heels. I trailed him closely, but the Bullet members and other riders fell back.

We turned right and crossed the expanse to the second warehouse, then took the ramp up to the stretch of metal set between the two rooftops. Magnum barely slowed when he reached the stairs. His back tire clipped the corner of the sharp turn at the bottom and nearly sent him off his motorcycle. He kept his seat and surged forward. I followed close behind.

Another left turn put us at the last stretch. Students shouted and jostled each other when they saw Magnum in the lead. The other riders began to catch up, pushing their skills to the very edge. I held close to the last corner, cutting in to Magnum's left side. We crossed the starting point shoulder to shoulder.

A glance showed fierce determination on Magnum's face. He glared at the ground as if daring it to slow him down. He threw a look over his shoulder, then took the left turn. The riders behind us pressed forward at the challenge.

I realized that winning meant more to Magnum than it did to the Black Rider. He had something to prove; the Black Rider didn't. We crossed the metal span side by side; I had to back off at the stairs because there wasn't room for two riders abreast. When we hit the ground, the riders behind us pressed at our backs.

I took the next turn wide, nearly clipping two of them with my back tire. They fell behind at the stretch, then the boy with the red Mohawk downshifted and tried to cut the next corner. I took the turn with my knee scraping the ground, blocking him from effectively gunning past. Magnum cleared the finish line, and I followed in the next second. Three disgruntled members of the Bullet gang came next.

Magnum didn't stop at the finish line. He rode straight to his truck and drove the motorcycle up the ramp and into the bed. A crowd of students pressed around me, patting my back and reaching forward to touch my helmet. It had become something of a lucky totem to the students. They dared each other to touch it, then laughed in triumph when they were successful.

"Awesome ride," said a boy with a black eye. "You almost had him."

I nodded. "Thanks."

I kept my eyes on Magnum as he tied the motorcycle down. Students surrounded his truck, congratulating him on the ride. He spoke to a few of them, but his answers were short and his frustration clear. The two girls from the Bullets hurried over and tried to talk to him, but he didn't bother to hide his annoyance with them and they eventually gave up.

"Thanks again for what you did at the fair," a girl with long brown braids and a red bandana around her head said. "You saved my cow."

I really looked at her. There were tears in her eyes. I never could understand the relationship some of these farmers had with their livestock, but it was obvious how much it meant to her. "I was happy to help," I said honestly.

"It was incredible!" gushed a young boy who must have been

brought to the races by an older sibling. "You took a picture with my friend Mark. He got a bullet taken out of his arm. He said you were shot too!"

I nodded and saw Martin out of the corner of my eye. Any impulse I had to show off my battle wounds vanished completely at the knowledge that he had already seen the bruises. "It was a bit uncomfortable," I said.

The audience around me laughed.

A kid with bright red hair and a tie-dye shirt held up a handful of dollars and several candy bars. "This is your share."

"But I didn't win," I said in surprise.

He shrugged. "They said you'd make top three. No one can beat Magnum every time." He paused with a smile. "Actually, until you got here, no one could be Magnum at all."

I accepted the loot and shoved it in my jacket pocket. "Thanks."

I looked over to see Magnum arguing with the red Mohawk Bullet. He waved an arm to indicate the crowd, then shouted something. The Bullet member turned away and stalked through the crowd. Magnum watched him go, his expression livid. He punched his truck hard enough to leave a dent in the hood, then climbed inside and stared unseeing out the windshield. I decided that I was my cue to go.

"See ya around," I told the crowd. They backed up and left an empty patch for me to leave. It was obvious what they wanted. I fought back a smile and popped the clutch to jump the front tire in the air, then rode out of the factory grounds on a wheelie. The cheers of the crowd echoed in my helmet long after they had vanished far behind.

Chapter Eleven

"A BIT OF A showoff, aren't you?" Magnum said as we pulled a car hood close to the door in the middle of the junkyard.

It was Magnum's idea to turn the junkyard into a hideout for our escapades. Since I was so used to spending my afternoons organizing car parts, it didn't bother me to work them into a stack that effectively hid the entrance to the fallout shelter.

"It comes with the territory," I said, pushing a car door up to hold the hood in place.

"What, being cocky?"

I looked up at the challenge in his tone. "Receiving gratitude. They were thankful for what happened at the fair. It'd be rude not to let them express how they felt when I saved their lives."

"Glory hound," Magnum muttered.

I gritted my teeth and fought back the impulse to hit him.

"If I didn't know you better, I would say you did it for the attention," he goaded.

I clenched my hands around a steering column and shoved it in place. "You know that's not true."

"Maybe your fear of fire is just to get attention," he continued.

I slammed him in the chest with a two-handed punch before he could react. He fell backward into the dirt, then came up swinging. I blocked a right hook and popped him in the jaw with a quick right of my own. He let out a roar that would have done a lion proud and tried to run me down. I stepped to the side and spun on one knee, bringing my other leg around to sweep his legs out from under him. He hit the ground hard, then rolled and kicked, catching me in the leg.

I grabbed his foot and turned it, forcing him to flip over on his stomach again. I slammed a knee into his low back and kept ahold of his ankle, twisting it to the point of excruciating pain.

"Argh! Let go!" Magnum shouted.

I let go and stepped back in case he decided to retaliate. He stayed on his stomach in the dirt, his chest heaving and sweat trickling down his face. After a minute, he ran a hand through his red hair. "I didn't mean it," he said into the ground. When I didn't answer, he rolled over and looked up at me. "I'm sorry. I didn't mean it."

I walked to a far pile of crooked bike tire frames to let the adrenaline fade, then grabbed one and brought it back. I tossed it on our hideout before sliding down to sit near Magnum. "I know what the other Bullets said got under your skin. I shouldn't have let you get me fired up."

He sat up and grabbed a bike chain. "I shouldn't have said what I did."

I shrugged and kept my eyes on a patch of dirt caking the knee of my pants. "Maybe I do take it too far. It's just nice to hear people who are proud of me for a change."

"You deserve it," Magnum answered. He squinted at me. "You got shot for them and for me. You did the bravest thing this town has ever seen. You deserve the gratitude."

Uncomfortable, I changed the subject. "The Bullets are rebelling."

Magnum let out a sigh and nodded. "They feel like I've abandoned them. They don't understand what I do at night."

"You mean instead of roughing up new students or petty theft at convenience stores?" I asked with a joking tone.

His countenance darkened. "You make it sound like we were no better than those gas station robbers."

"From my point of view when I first came to Sparrow, you weren't," I said honestly.

He fell silent for a few minutes, turning the bike chain over and over in his hands. Finally, he spoke with his gaze on the chain. "It was different because the town knew us. They knew we wouldn't hurt them."

I thought about it and nodded. No matter what it had looked like to me, there was a big difference between a town gang of friends who were lost and causing trouble and a group of four guys with a gun holding up a gas station. Magnum had never shot anyone.

"I know you lost the race today on purpose."

I glanced at him, keeping my face carefully expressionless. "I don't know what you're talking about."

He blew out a breath and chucked the bike chain onto a random pile. "Cut the crap, Kelson. It was obvious."

"Hopefully not to everyone else," I muttered.

He shook his head. "Why not keep the Black Rider's perfect streak? I don't get it."

I glanced at him. "I heard the way the Bullets were talking to you. You need their respect more than I do."

He squinted at the ground, his expression distant. "I'm not sure if I want it anymore."

I studied him, but kept silent. He was obviously going through some things with his gang, but I wouldn't press him. If he needed someone to talk to, he knew he could talk to me.

He stood up and held out a hand. I grabbed it and he pulled me to my feet. "Let's go for a ride."

I was more than happy to jump on my motorcycle and lead the way out of the junkyard. Night fell around us, chasing away the thoughts of daylight and leaving the clarity of headlights and shadow. Stars chased each other through the black tapestry above, white streaks that served as a stubborn reminder that our lives were merely tiny specks within a grand display of fire and fireworks. We could only try to burn bright and hope to leave a mark worth following. The thought was both hopeful and sobering. I wanted to leave a mark worthy of both me and my sister.

WE WERE ABOUT TO head back to the junkyard after an uneventful night ride when a cluster of teenagers in an empty grocery store parking lot caught my attention. The store had been closed for at least two hours, and no car was in sight. I motioned for Magnum to circle to the back of the lot.

I drove slowly across the pavement, curious what held their attention. At the sound of my engine, all of the boys looked up. The wide-eyed looks they shot each other when they realized who I was made me smile beneath my visor. A few of the older boys glared, not happy to have their fun broken up. They held a black-haired kid between them. My smile faded at the sight of a small switchblade in one boy's hand.

"Let him go," the boy they were holding yelled.

I realized then that the form at their feet was a medium-sized brown dog. His paws had been tied with bailing twine and someone had looped a belt around his muzzle to keep him from biting.

I turned off the engine and climbed from the bike. "What's going on here?" I asked.

"They took my dog," the dark-haired boy said. A light of hope showed in his eyes. It was obvious how much he cared about the animal.

I turned to the leader with the switchblade. "What were you planning to do with it?"

He shrugged. "We were just having a little fun. No big deal."

I nodded toward the dog. "He thinks it's a big deal." The animal's brown eyes were wide and he whimpered. The belt was tight around his muzzle, pulling at his skin.

"We were just going to rough them up a bit and let them go. Honest. Tell him, Rod," a younger boy said from behind the leader.

Rod turned and glared at the boy. "Shut your mouth."

"Let the boy and the dog go," I said in a steel voice that carried across the parking lot.

One of the kids moved to comply, but at Rod's look he backed away and studied the cement under his feet. "What if we don't want to?" Rod asked. "You're outnumbered."

"You're kids," I said with a touch of humor he didn't like.

"And there's two of us."

All the teenagers spun around at the sound of Magnum's voice. He had parked his motorcycle around the grocery store and walked to us without drawing attention. Now he stood a few feet away with his arms crossed, looking very intimidating in all black.

"There's two of you?" Rod said, followed by several curse words from others in the group.

I shrugged. "We wouldn't mind a brawl with kids. Might help loosen us up. What do you say?"

Rod shook his head. "Naw, man. I think we're good." He backed away and motioned for his comrades to let go of the boy.

As soon as he was free, he dropped to his knees next to the dog and tried to untie the twine from its paws.

Rod's teenage gang turned to leave. "Rod, wait," I said, using the tone Uncle Rick did when he demanded obedience.

Rod turned reluctantly as the rest of the boys took off across the parking lot. I closed the space between us until his face was inches from my visor. He stared at his own reflection, his face pale.

"If I ever catch you picking on kids or animals again, you will answer directly to me. Do you understand?"

He nodded a bit reluctantly.

I grabbed the collar of his shirt and lifted him up. "Do you understand?" I shouted.

"Yes," he squeaked.

I set him back down, but didn't let go of his shirt. "You are an example to those kids back there. Make sure it's one worth following. You got me?"

He nodded and dropped his eyes. "Y—yes. I'm sorry."

I let him go and he took off running across the parking lot after the others. I turned back to the boy with the dog. Now that the teenage gang was gone, tears were streaming down his face. He pulled at the twine, but couldn't untie it. Magnum watched with his arms still crossed, his shoulders hunched like he didn't know what to do.

I knelt next to the boy and pulled off my gloves. Taking the dog's paws from him gently, I undid the twine as quickly as I could. The dog didn't make a sound as if he knew I was trying to help. I then slid the belt muzzle carefully from the dog's face, aware he could try to bite me as soon as it was free.

Instead, the dog jumped up and licked the boy all over, wagging its long tail and whining with relief. The boy laughed through his tears, hugging the dog to his chest and smiling when it licked his cheeks with an eager tongue.

The dog then ran back to me and tried to do the same. I stood up quickly, but not before it managed to lick my visor and smear drool across my vision. It then licked my bare hand with the energy of Cole on caffeine.

"That's enough," I told the dog as I pulled on the gloves to hide them from his enthusiasm.

"Thank you," the boy said.

"You don't need to thank us," I told him. "Just get both of you home safe and avoid empty parking lots at night, especially if those guys are wandering around."

He nodded quickly. "I will."

Magnum slapped his knee. "Come here, pooch."

The dog stopped its happy tail wagging and bared its teeth at Magnum. He took a few steps back.

"Rosco, no," the boy said. He patted the dog's head. "Sorry about that. I think he's just worried about me."

Magnum didn't say anything.

"We've got to go," I told the boy. "See you around."

"Bye! Thanks again!" he said. He hugged the dog to him once more, then hurried in the opposite direction the boys had gone. The dog trotted at his heels, happy to be free once more.

Magnum and I watched until they disappeared at the end of the block. "I hate dogs," Magnum said in a low voice.

"Me too," I replied. He threw me a look, but I just smiled inside my visor and climbed on my motorcycle. "At least it was a night worth riding," I called to him as he walked back to his bike.

He made a rude gesture in the air and didn't turn around.

***

MOM MET ME IN the driveway when I pulled up on the four-wheeler later that night. "I'm glad you're finally home," she said, giving me a tight hug.

I gave her a sincere smile. "I'm glad too. I'm so sorry I scared you. Sometimes I don't think."

She shook her head. "Kelson, you think of everyone but yourself. If you need a little you time now and then, I understand. Especially after something like that."

We both looked at the dark mounds that made up the remains of the barn. A shudder ran up my spine at the thought of the fire. I turned my back to it and put an arm around Mom. "Let's go inside."

If she was surprised at my actions, she didn't say anything. When we entered the mudroom, she gave a warm smile. "Lauren says their insurance is going to cover it because the fire was started by a faulty electrical outlet."

"So we don't have to help rebuild it?"

Mom stared at me for a minute, then started laughing. "Thank goodness! It would just fall down."

"I don't think Uncle Rick would trust me with a hammer anyway," I replied with a laugh of my own.

I kicked off my shoes and crossed to the kitchen, then paused at the sight of Uncle Rick and Aunt Lauren at the table in much the same position as when I left.

Aunt Lauren gave me a careful smile as though she was worried about what to say. Uncle Rick nodded at her. She rose with a hand on her stomach and gestured toward her sister. "Let's see what the boys are up to," she said. Mom gave me a worried look, but followed her sister through the doorway.

"Sit down, Kelson," Uncle Rick intoned.

A pit formed in my stomach, but I sat where he indicated. He studied his hands on the tabletop. When he opened his mouth to speak, I blurted out, "I'm so sorry about Jaren. I shouldn't have frozen like that. I almost got him killed. I'll go if you want me to." I blinked back the sharp burning of tears.

Uncle Rick's voice filled the room, a voice used to calling cattle, commanding horses, training dogs, and heralding ranchers, and now used to calm the troubled soul of his aching, lost nephew. "The fire wasn't your fault," he said in a tone that left no room for doubt. "You hold no amount of blame for the danger Jaren was in."

I listened to him with my gaze firmly locked on the scratched tablecloth. In one place, a flower had been torn in two by somebody's fork, probably Cole's.

"If anything, I am at fault for asking so much of you." His voice softened. "I can't imagine what courage it took for you to enter the fire after everything you went through with your sister."

I swallowed against the tightness of my throat. It felt like somebody held it in a fist. I couldn't have spoken even if I had known what words to say.

"Kelson, I didn't know what to expect when you came here." He paused and a hint of humor touched his voice. "I'll have to admit when you first showed up, I thought you were a useless city boy who didn't know a swather from a backhoe."

A begrudging smile crossed my face. "The last part was true."

He chuckled. "I know, but you didn't let that stop you. You threw everything into pulling your own weight around here. You even learned how to milk."

I shrugged with my gaze still on the table. "Barbecue hates me."

He let out a snort that was part humor, part derision. "It's the name, most likely." I laughed despite my mood and he continued, "I expected the city bit; what I didn't expect was a boy I was proud to call my nephew."

I glanced up at him warily, uncertain what I would see.

He gave me a warm smile, one of the few that ever crossed the stern farmer's face. "The example you give my boys is one even I can't hold a candle to." He took a deep breath and let it out slowly, then said, "If they turn out just like you, I couldn't be more proud."

I stared at him, amazed to hear so many compliments strung together and relating to me. He looked away as if embarrassed to be caught saying so many words. He jerked his head toward the oven. "Lauren saved you a plate of ribs and potatoes. You'll regret it if you let them get cold."

He rose and left out the back door as if anxious to put some distance between the mushiness that filled the kitchen. I slid the plate out of the oven and set to eating Aunt Lauren's cooking with an appetite made doubly ravenous by Magnum's overcooked eggs and my chicken nuggets abandoned on the cafeteria floor.

I WAS LOST IN my thoughts when Madelyn climbed onto the bus. A smile spread across my face at the sight of her, even with the worry that pinched her brow. I stood up and let her take the window seat she preferred, then sat down beside her.

"I thought you would be gone a few days," I said, just happy to have her next to me once more.

"My mom's going to be in the hospital for a while, so Aunt Masey brought me home. Dad worried about me missing school," she explained.

I lifted my arm and she leaned against my side with a weary sigh. "I've missed you," I said.

She gave me a small smile. "It's only been a day since I saw you."

"Two nights," I replied. "Two nights without my Maddy. Those may have been the longest nights of my life."

Warmth flooded her smile and filled my heart. "I've missed you too," she said.

When we entered the school, tables lined the hallway. "What's this?" I asked.

"College day," Madelyn responded with a quiet sigh.

We wandered down the row looking at the different colleges. I picked up a few packets even though I hadn't even begun to consider a field.

"With your grades, you should apply for a scholarship," I told Madelyn.

She shook her head. "I'm staying in Sparrow."

I wanted to protest, but the weight of her mother's sickness rested heavily on her shoulders. I picked up a few extra applications in case she changed her mind, then escorted her to calculus.

"Everything will be all right, Maddy," I said softly as I set her backpack at her feet.

She gave me a worried smile. "Thanks, Kelson. I appreciate it."

I left her looking forlorn and lost. My heart ached at the sight. I wanted more than anything to sweep her away from it all, to see her smile without worry once more.

I wandered back up the hall and found Magnum staring hard at an application for a state college known for their football team.

I pretended to look at their brochure for band even though I didn't play an instrument. "You could probably get in on a scholarship if you played for the Bulldogs the rest of this year," I said in an undertone.

Magnum stared at me, shock clear on his face. "What makes you think I want to play again?" he demanded in a harsh whisper.

I gestured at the application. "Not too subtle."

He cursed and set it back down. I picked it up and put it in my stack.

"What are you doing?" he demanded.

"Shh!" I cautioned.

He glanced around to make sure nobody was paying attention to us, then asked in a quieter tone, "What are you doing?"

I shrugged. "I have a friend who wants to apply."

He looked at me for a minute, then shook his head and walked away.

Later that day during sixth-period physical education, I was surprised to see Magnum talking to Coach Farston. A few of the Bullets hung around him as well. I fought back a smile and finished jogging my laps around the track.

Chapter Twelve

WHEN I CLIMBED OFF the bus, Jaren and Cole were waiting. They usually raced home the second their feet touched the dirt road, so their presence surprised me. Cassidy was already walking up the road talking animatedly to Sandy on her cell phone.

"C'mon, Kel. Let's race," Cole said, hopping from one foot to the other.

I shook my head. "I'm not much of a racer."

Jaren gave me a weighted look. "If I heard right, the Black Rider was racing at the factory yesterday."

I glanced at the bus, but it was already heading toward Madelyn's, leaving us in a cloud of dust and exhaust. I waved the fumes away and took a better look at Jaren. It was obvious by his expression that something was bothering him.

I needed to head to the junkyard, but my dedication to the tasks Jagger sent out wavered greatly under their obvious uselessness.

"What's going on?" I asked my cousin.

Jaren's usual easy-going smile had disappeared. He ran a hand through his sun-blond hair and glanced at Cole. His brother had the sense to appear uninterested in our conversation. He dug for what I assumed to be bugs around the base of the mailbox.

Jaren let out a sigh that made him sound well older than his twelve years. "I want to apologize for what happened in the barn."

I stared at him. It was the last thing I expected. My heart clenched away from the memories of that night and I shook my head. "If anything, I should be the one apologizing. You were nearly killed because of me."

Jaren kicked a rock. He looked at Cole again, but the ten-year-old had climbed the fence and was following a trail through the alfalfa. Uncle Rick wouldn't be happy about his son stomping down the hay, but I cared more about what Jaren had to say than repeating the same lecture Cole had heard a thousand times.

Jaren let out another breath. "I wasn't supposed to be in the barn." Before I could question whether I wanted to know the reason a farmer's son snuck into a barn, he continued as though it was hard for him to say. "I was building a computer."

He gave a small smile at my surprised look and confessed, "I've been collecting computer parts from school. Mr. Murphy let me take apart two computers he was going to throw away. I've been trying to build a better one by piecing them together."

I tried to suppress a smile. "And Uncle Rick has no idea you like computers?"

He shook his head quickly. "He despises them. I told him once that I wanted one and he said I'd be better off with a bummer lamb to sell at the fair."

I thought about Uncle Rick's declaration that the Internet was a fad. To know that the farmer's son had a passion for computers would have been hilarious if it wasn't for Jaren's woeful expression.

"You've been hiding them from him?"

He nodded. "The far corner of the barn has a closet Dad uses to store extra shovels and pitchforks. I rigged it with a light and have been using it as my workroom."

A hint of trepidation touched my thoughts. "Are your computers the reason the barn burned down?" If an investigation showed as much, I doubted the insurance would replace the building.

He shook his head. "No. The fire started long before I realized it was even going. I smelled smoke and came out to find the building falling down." He gave me an embarrassed look. "I guess that's where you came in."

I rubbed the back of my neck. "Not that I helped much." It was strange to talk about my weakness to him. His expression showed none of the scorn or derision I felt I deserved. Instead, a hint of awe touched his gaze.

"You lifted that beam pretty much by yourself," he said in amazement.

I shook my head. "Your dad was there, and Magnum."

"They tried, but they couldn't do it." He spoke faster in his excitement. "You were in front of the barn doors and they kept yelling to you because they couldn't free me even though they tried several times. The beam was burning and I was worried everyone was going to die." He blinked quickly to keep back the tears as he continued, "Then you ran over with a look on your face even a bull wouldn't mess with. You picked up the beam and had it high enough for me to get out before Dad and Magnum could move to help."

To hear it in Jaren's words made the whole event surreal. It hadn't felt that way to me. I had almost let my cousin die, and he acted as though I was his hero. "I chickened out, Jaren," I forced myself to admit. "I got scared."

He nodded as though that was the most normal thing in the world. "Of course you were scared. I was terrified! We all could have burned to death. But we didn't."

His last three words echoed through my mind, reminding me

that I had survived a fire yet again and this time brought someone with me, the thing I had been unable to do when the warehouse burned.

He gave me a hopeful smile. "Are we all right?"

I let out a breath I hadn't realized I was holding and nodded, squeezing his shoulder. "Yeah, we're fine."

"Good," he concluded. He took a step toward the house, then glanced at me. "Wanna race?"

At that moment, the bell tolled from its stand behind the Ashbys' residence. I wondered if Uncle Rick had been watching us, waiting for the reconciliation.

"You're on," I said.

He took off running and I followed close behind. Cole darted across the field, then ducked under the fence to fall in at our heels. The three of us stumbled into the mudroom laughing and jostling each other. We stopped at the sight of Uncle Rick standing in the kitchen next to several burlap bags.

"Ladybugs!" Cole exclaimed.

Cassidy appeared behind us. "Oh, gross," she said. "Not again."

Uncle Rick nodded. "Kelson, I already told Jagger I needed your help. The aphids are bad this year and we need to clear the alfalfa out."

"With bags of ladybugs?" I asked doubtfully. I poked one of the sacks with a finger. It was full of something that moved subtly under my touch.

Mom came into the kitchen and gave me a hug. "How was your day?"

"It just got weirder," I said, nodding toward the bags.

She gave a sympathetic smile. "I know. When Lauren told me they bought bugs, I about died."

"We could have got spiders," Cole teased.

Mom gave a visible shudder. "Then we'd be moving back to California."

Uncle Rick laughed. "They're just ladybugs. They're harmless, really."

"Except to aphids," Cole expounded with a wicked grin. "Those little bugs won't know what hit 'em."

"Or what ate them," Jaren corrected.

Mom waved a hand, careful to stay far away from the bags. "Go have fun with your little bugs. Just make sure none of them follow you home."

Cole picked up a sack and carried it to the mudroom to get his work shoes. "We'll save you a few," he called over his shoulder.

"Please don't," Mom replied.

Uncle Rick picked up two bags and motioned for the rest of us to do the same. Cassidy made a face, but carried her bags carefully to the backyard. "I don't mind ladybugs by themselves. But so many of them together are scary."

I didn't understand what she meant until we carried the sacks to a field and opened the first one. Hundreds of the little spotted bugs crawled over my hands.

"Be free!" Cole yelled. He threw ladybugs in every direction. Some landed on Cassidy and she shrieked.

"Walk in a row," Uncle Rick chastised. "They aren't cheap little critters. I want to make sure they stay put." He pulled out a handful and began to drop them as casually as if he was letting sand slip through his fingers.

I sighed and grabbed a handful from my bag, then kept pace a few feet from him. After a few minutes, the feeling of millions of legs across my hands stopped bothering me. I let them fall in little clumps and watched them climb up the alfalfa, ready to begin their work of ridding the dark hay of aphids immediately.

"We work in the evening because ladybugs don't like to fly at night," Uncle Rick said. He appeared to be in a rare conversational mood. "This way, hopefully they'll stick around."

"Maybe they'll have all the aphids eaten before the sun goes down," I replied. I pulled another handful from the bag and spread it through the hay.

"That would be nice," Uncle Rick agreed.

"Ew, one's in my ear!" Cassidy shrieked. Cole laughed and Uncle Rick walked over to help her remove the invader.

By the time we called it quits, we had walked through eight different fields and left thousands of ladybugs in our wake. I pictured it as a surprise attack on the invading aphid army. It was satisfying to know Uncle Rick had told Jagger he needed my help. It wasn't much, but I had assisted in the improvement of his fields and saw the satisfied look in his eyes because I had completed the task exactly as he needed. Even if it was just spreading bugs through the alfalfa, I had done something to better Uncle Rick's farms.

We sat around the table and joked as we ate pork chops and the fresh asparagus Mom and Aunt Lauren had picked from the ditches close to the house.

"She was screaming like a girl," Cole told his mom about Cassidy's close encounter with the ladybug.

"I *am* a girl," Cassidy replied with a sniff. "And it was in my ear."

"I would have screamed too," Mom told her with a sympathetic smile.

My cell phone rang. I gave Uncle Rick a sheepish smile. He didn't approve of cell phones at the table.

"Go on; get it," he said with a touch of humor.

I set my fork down moved into the hall for privacy. Cole waited in the doorway, but when I looked at him, he disappeared back into the kitchen.

I lifted the phone to my ear. "Hello?"

Concern filled me at the sound of sobbing I heard. "Kelson?"

"Maddy?" Her voice tore a hole through my heart.

"Kelson, I need you here."

"I'll be right there."

I hung up the phone and stared at it for the space of a heartbeat. Whatever had happened, it wasn't going to be easy. I gritted my teeth and hurried through the kitchen. "I've got to go to Maddy's. I don't know when I'll be back," I said to no one in particular.

I heard Mom follow me to the mudroom. She stood in the doorway as I pulled on my shoes. "Is everything all right?"

I shook my head and met her gaze. "Maddy was crying. She doesn't cry easily. Something is definitely wrong. I need to go to her."

Mom nodded. "Be careful. Do you want to take my car?"

"Thanks, but the four-wheeler's fine. Her house is close."

She gave me a quick hug, catching me by surprise. "What was that for?" I asked when she stepped back.

She hesitated, then shrugged. "It just seems like you're always helping others. I wanted you to know that you have support here too."

I smiled, touched. "Thanks, Mom."

I left through the back door and jumped on the four-wheeler. Jake, the Ashbys' Border Collie, fell in beside me as he always did when I went to Madelyn's. I drove straight to the front lawn and barely took the time to turn off the four-wheeler before I made my way to the door.

Madelyn opened it before I could knock. She fell into my arms and sobbed against my neck. "My mom . . . she . . . she . . ."

I knew without her having to say the words. The heartache in her voice and the hollow, lost expression in her eyes echoed exactly how I had felt when I awoke to find that Zoey had never made it out of the fire. My heart clenched and I blinked quickly, struggling not to cry. I smoothed her hair. "I'm so sorry," I whispered, holding her tight.

The world fell away. It was just us. The girl I loved with all my heart had lost someone precious and dear to her, someone who could never be replaced. Her sorrow burned through me as her sobs racked both of us. My breath caught in my throat at the thought of an empty spot in the living room where her mother's wheelchair had always been as she smiled at us with such warmth and gave her blessing to our relationship despite her husband's misgivings.

Mrs. West was pure love despite all she had gone through. In the place of bitterness, she carried joy and gratitude for the life she still had. In the quiet moments of the few evenings I spent at their place, she made me feel welcome and let me into the tiny circle of their family.

I closed my eyes, remembering one such event.

Madelyn had invited me over to watch *The Last Samurai*, which was surprisingly her mother's favorite movie. "You like sword fights and Tom Cruise?" I teased her.

Mrs. West replied with a spunky, "Who doesn't?" Then her smile softened and she tipped her head toward Mr. West. "Actually, Joe used to look a lot like Tom in his younger days."

I studied Mr. West, but couldn't see the similarities. Madelyn's dad gave me a grumpy glare as though he guessed my thoughts. I turned my attention quickly back to Mrs. West as she said, "But that's not the reason I like it. Watch, and you'll see."

By the end of the movie, everyone had tears in their eyes. Mr. West held his wife's hand and leaned against her chair from his place on the couch. The worn cushions told that they sat the same way a lot more often now. She blinked to clear the tears from her eyes and Mr. West wiped her cheeks gently with a handkerchief. I smiled at the sight of the handkerchief, remembering one of my first encounters with Madelyn.

"There's something to that," Mrs. West said quietly. Mr. West nodded as though he knew exactly what she was talking about.

I didn't want to break the soft hush that fell over the room, but it felt very important that I knew what she was talking about.

"Something to what?" I asked quietly.

Both of them looked at me as though they had forgotten my presence. Madelyn's fingers traced my palm fondly. I hoped her father didn't mind.

Mrs. West's eyes sparkled. "He says all the flowers were perfect. Earlier he mentioned that you could spend a lifetime looking for the perfect flower and it would not be a wasted life, and at the end of the movie he realized that all of them were perfect in their own way." She looked at her husband. "It's like life, I think. Each life is perfect in its own way, whole in its own way."

A tear fell on my hand. I glanced over to see Madelyn watching her mother. The trail of a single tear showed on her cheek. I doubted she even knew it fell. The silence that filled the room was a warm one, a welcome one. Madelyn's fingers tangled in mine and we listened to the movie soundtrack weave its way subtly within the silence, creating a bubble of peace and contentment I wanted to live in forever.

Now she was gone. I took a shuddering breath and the tears broke free, soaking into Madelyn's hair. An angel was gone, and I could feel the void she had left in the house. I didn't want to go inside and see her gone. I wanted to pretend she was there even though I knew she wasn't.

The door pushed open and a lady with mascara streaks down her cheeks gave me a watery smile. "You must be Kelson. Please come in," she said.

I didn't want to. The house was dark and emptier than it had ever been when Mrs. West was alive. I didn't want to step into the bare reminder of her absence. I could feel Madelyn's reluctance as well and knew she felt the same way. We both needed whatever comfort we could find from the starlight shining down and bathing the dark grass. "Can we sit on the porch?" I asked. I sounded like a child and hated feeling lost again, looking for a way to avoid the hollow place in my heart that was filled with sorrow and loss.

"I would like that," Madelyn whispered.

The woman nodded. "It'd probably do us all good." She sniffed. "I'll bring some lemonade."

It was a strange comment. Madelyn sat down and when I settled next to her, she gave me a small half smile. "That's Aunt Masey, Mom's sister. She can't ever sit still."

"I'm glad she was here with you," I said.

She nodded and tears filled her eyes again. I couldn't think; I didn't know what to say. I rubbed Madelyn's back with numb fingers. Her mother was gone. I held her close, wishing I could take away her pain.

The moonlight fell on our shoulders, warming us with silver grace that failed to penetrate the pain of loss. Eventually Madelyn's sobs slowed and she merely leaned against me, tears still fresh on her cheeks and her face turned to the stars.

Masey's footsteps sounded and the door opened with a quiet creak. She flipped on the porch light and it bathed the area around us. The sound of glasses chinked together before she set a tray down and sat near us on the stairs. We watched in silence as she poured from a glass pitcher with pictures of strawberries on the outside.

"That's Mom's favorite pitcher," Madelyn said softly.

Masey nodded. "I know. That's why I used it. It would make her happy."

Madelyn nodded in agreement and accepted one of the glasses. She took a tiny sip, then held the glass in her hands, watching the drips of condensation run down the outside.

Masey handed me one, then poured a glass for herself as well. She sipped it, then made a sour face. "A bit more sugar next time. I'll have to remember that." Her voice cracked when she continued, "Silvia used to make the best lemonade."

Madelyn nodded again and I realized Silvia was her mother's name. I had never heard anyone say it before.

"I'm so sorry about your sister," I said, my voice scratchy from crying.

Masey sniffed and wiped her eyes as fresh tears spilled over. "We didn't expect it. They thought it was pneumonia and wanted to keep her for observation." Her words choked off and she sobbed, then continued, "But her heart stopped and they couldn't revive her."

Madelyn turned her head into my shoulder and cried. "I should have been there," she said.

I smoothed her hair gently. "You didn't know. You couldn't have known. It's not your fault."

Masey nodded. "We came home because Madelyn had school and Sylvia was stable. They had no idea . . ." Her words trailed off, leaving a painful void in their wake.

"It's not your fault," I told them both.

Madelyn shook her head against my shoulder. "I've always been there for her."

"And she knows you would have been there if you had known," I replied in a soft voice.

We drank the lemonade and cried, three people lost in a night that felt like it would never end. Madelyn eventually settled on my lap and fell into a restless sleep. I swallowed my reluctance to enter the living room with the signs of Mrs. West so recently gone; Masey held open the door while I carried Madelyn in and settled her onto the couch. She stirred and fresh tears showed when she looked up at me. I sat beside her and pulled her close. A shuddering sob shook her shoulders before she fell asleep again.

I tucked her hair behind her ear, then brushed the tears from her cheeks with the backs of my fingers. There was nothing I could do to ease her pain. I knew that from harsh experience. When a loved one is ripped from your life, there is no way to fill the void. It hurts like a raw, aching wound and there is nothing that can stop the pain because they are gone. The only thing that would end it is if they came back. The hardest part is realizing they never will.

I could feel the emptiness where Mrs. West's electronic wheelchair used to sit beside the couch. Once in a while a sob would tear from me, waking Madelyn. I stifled my pain, pushing it down so she could get whatever rest she could manage.

Masey settled a blanket over us and gave me a grateful smile. The sounds of her bustling around the kitchen were long to fade, echoing Madelyn's assessment that she never kept still. When she finally went to bed, I settled back and pulled Madelyn closer to my chest. She leaned her head on my shoulder, tears drifting down her face even in sleep. My heart ached that she would awaken and realized that the pain of her dreams was real and sharper in its permanence.

My phone buzzed in my pocket. I worked it out carefully so I didn't wake up Madelyn, and glanced at the text.

Hope everything's okay—Mom

I clenched my teeth to keep my emotions in when I wrote back,

Maddy's mom died. I'm staying with her tonight. Hope that's okay.

Mom quickly wrote back, *I'm so sorry. Is there anything I can do?*

I blinked and texted, *I don't even know what to do.*

You're doing it, Mom replied. *Take as long as you both need.*

Thanks.

I was about to put the phone away when it buzzed again. I looked down and read, *Are you okay?*

My breath shuddered in my chest. I typed *Yeah* and was about to send it, but the truth was more complicated than that. I stared at the word on the screen for several minutes before I erased it. With hesitant fingers, I wrote, *Not sure. Guess I'm more shook up than I thought. She was a great person.* The word "great" was far short of what she really was, but describing her would take far more than the tiny screen allowed.

Mom's reply took a few minutes, and when I got it I realized why. I could hear her heartache through the words. *I didn't cope well with Zoey's death. I had never lost anyone like that, and to know my daughter was gone took away my stability. I felt like the world crumbled under my feet.*

I blinked and rubbed my eyes. *I sent you away instead of us getting through it together. I needed you, but didn't realize it until you were gone, and you seemed to do better without me. I'm so sorry.*

The guilt in her words ate at my aching heart. I needed my mother and she sent me to Sparrow because the sight of me reminded her of Zoey's death. She blamed what happened on me, one of the reasons I had carried the guilt so close. Madelyn had helped me overcome it. Madelyn was my place of peace, and she was the one who was hurting.

I kept reading. *Be there for her like I should have been there for you. It will help you both through it. You are so much stronger than me. You help so many people because you can. You never let the world tell you that you are beaten, and that is why you are so much better than me.*

I wanted to protest, but another text appeared before I could write her back. *I am proud to have such a son. Thank you for the example you have been to me. You have carried me through even when you didn't know it, and you are strong enough for Maddy. She is so lucky to have you. I am so lucky to have you. I love you, Kelson. Hang in there.*

I stared at the last few words. Something lightened in my soul to hear the depth of my mom's feelings. Her belief in me helped me believe in myself. I could help Madelyn through this because I had survived losing Zoey, even though there were times when I lost myself. Madelyn had found me, and I would be her place of peace.

I pulled Madelyn closer and she slept wrapped in my arms, her breath a warm brush against my cheek and her hair tangling along my arm. "I'll take care of you," I whispered.

A few hours later, the front door opened. I sat up slowly at the sight of Mr. West entering the house. He met my eyes, his gaze bare and empty. He had ridden home in a van that usually carried his wife, but now was as vacant as the living room. The worn places where the tires of her wheelchair usually rested near the couch reflected in his expression.

I was about to rise when he surprised me by motioning for me to stay and not disturb his daughter's rest. He crossed to the armchair on the other side of the television and collapsed into it. He buried his face in his hands and sat there in silence. After a few minutes, he spoke in a muffled voice, "I used to think it would be easier if she died." He let out a loud breath and scrubbed his face with his hands, then buried his face in them again without looking at me. "It's not that I wouldn't miss her—it's just that we both felt so trapped sometimes. Now I hate myself for those thoughts."

He glanced at Madelyn to make sure she was still asleep, but was careful to keep his gaze from meeting mine. "She hated that she couldn't dance or run like she used to. She missed walking with Buck, and the trips we used to take on our bikes in the canyon." He ran a hand wearily across his nose and mouth, then looked at the ceiling. "I told her I would never ride a bike again because she couldn't." He sniffed. "I think she hated that most of all."

He looked at me, meeting my gaze with a directness he never had before. "I thought it would be easier for her if she died because then she would be free, but I never thought about the empty shell I would be when she left me behind." He sighed. "It's different when you lose your wife. She was a part of my soul, the best part of me. Her accident made me bitter toward God and anything to do with heaven, even though she kept reading the Bible and holding on to her faith like it was a lifeline for both of us."

Sorrow cracked his voice, but his eyes remained red and free of tears as though he had cried them out before he reached home. "I guess she knows now if she was right." He looked at the ceiling. "I just wish she could tell me where she was."

The defeat in his words ate at me, tearing at the scars Zoey's death had carved into my heart. It didn't matter than Mrs. West was his wife and Zoey was my sister. Loss was loss, and the emptiness of heartbreak hurt the same. I bowed my head. "When my sister died, it almost killed me. I didn't want to live and I didn't want to breathe because she was gone. I never realized how much of my life she filled until she was no longer in it."

Mr. West sat in silence with his shoulders hunched and his gaze turned in the direction of the space his wife's chair used to occupy, but it was obvious by his expression that he wasn't really looking at anything. The lines of his face were carved deep and he looked as though he had aged ten years overnight.

I swallowed and continued, unsure if my words even made an impact. "The only thing that got me up was a reminder that because I was the one who had survived, I had to live for both of us."

The silence was so thick I stopped talking. I smoothed the blanket around Madelyn's shoulders, my own thoughts spiraling around the path my journey had taken me.

"So you live for her by stopping those who hurt other people?"

I looked up at Mr. West in surprise. The thought brought a small smile to my face. "Something like that, though I've never thought about it in those terms." I looked down at Madelyn. "Sir, you've got a beautiful daughter who loves you very much. You both need each other now more than ever." My voice lowered. "Take it from my experience. The first thing a child needs after losing someone is the support of loved ones."

He glanced at me. "Why did your mother send you away?"

His question struck me with a pain I tried to hide. It grabbed at my breath and made my heart pound in my chest. I forced the feelings down as deeply as I could and gave him the truth. "Because she blamed me for Zoey's death."

"Was it your fault?"

The rational side of me put the frankness of Mr. West's questions toward a need to change his train of thought from the dark spiral losing his wife had taken him into, but after everything he knew of me, that question hurt worse than the first. The conversation Madelyn and I had in the park about her guilt for her mother's accident and my own regarding Zoey surfaced. I sighed and shook my head. "No. It wasn't."

He nodded as though the answer didn't matter, but it did to me. I brushed a strand of hair from Madelyn's face, grateful for the girl who gave me the truth about myself and helped me survive.

A few minutes later, Mr. West rose and crossed behind the couch on his way to the stairs. His hand rested on my shoulder for a brief moment. "Good night, Kelson."

I hid my surprise at the sign of acceptance. "Good night, Mr. West."

He paused by the base of the stairs and whispered, "Thank you." The words were so soft I wondered if I imagined them as he trudged slowly up the steps away from the quiet living room.

THE NEXT DAY BROUGHT fresh tears and sorrow as dreams and heartache from the night before surfaced into reality. I held Madelyn and comforted her the best I could. Mr. West wandered aimlessly through the house avoiding the living room while Masey cleaned everything she could think of.

Mom and Aunt Lauren arrived at the house shortly after sunrise. Mr. West opened the door in numb surprise. "We brought you some food," Aunt Lauren said without asking him how he was doing. I knew Mr. West wouldn't have appreciated it, and I was grateful for the sisters' foresight in leaving him with his thoughts.

Mom carried the basket into the kitchen, giving us a kind smile when she passed. Aunt Lauren spoke quietly to Masey about the food while Mom came back in with us. She pressed something into Madelyn's hands. The familiar smell of pumpkin and chocolate wafted through the air.

"Thank you, Mrs. Brady," Madelyn said as Mom took a seat in the armchair.

"It's pumpkin bread," Mom explained. She and I exchanged sad smiles. "It's helped our family through a few rough times."

"I appreciate it," Madelyn replied with an attempt at a smile.

Aunt Lauren appeared at the doorway. "We planned to bring dinner, but your aunt says she needs something to do to keep her mind off things. We got her to agree to let us bring breakfast tomorrow in case she's not feeling up to cooking."

"Thank you," Madelyn and I both replied.

"We're so sorry about your mother," my mom said, rising to give Madelyn a hug. She then hugged me, too. "If there's anything we can do to help, please let us know." She turned to go, then gave me a warm look. "Stay as long as you need, Kelson. Rick already talked to Jagger about you not coming in for work."

"Thanks, Mom," I told her, touched.

When they left, the house felt empty and quiet. Mr. West disappeared back upstairs, and the soft sounds of Masey working in the kitchen failed to chase away the melancholy of the living room. I wanted to get Madelyn out, but she said she was happiest where her mother had been.

"How did the pumpkin bread help you?" Madelyn asked numbly after a while. She took another bite, her second since Mom had given her the bread.

I pulled her close. "When my dad left us without a word, Mom started baking pumpkin bread every night when she got home from work so we could have it with our breakfast in the morning. She said it was to remind us that life always had a little something special to offer as long as we didn't give up."

Madelyn studied the dark orange-and-chocolate-chip-spotted bread in her hand. "Did she make it after Zoey died?"

I shook my head. Nothing more needed to be said.

I sat with Madelyn through the day. We ate the food Aunt Lauren and Mom had brought over, but I don't think any of us tasted it. That night, Madelyn told me I should go home.

"You need someone with you," I said, protesting.

She shook her head, her eyes sad. "I appreciate it, Kelson, but your family misses you and I know you have things to do. You'll sleep better in your own bed."

I thought of the cot in the Ashbys' living room compared to holding Madelyn on the couch. There was no debate about which I preferred. "I want to be here for you," I said gently.

She shook her head with a weary sigh. "I'm exhausted. I think I'll go to sleep now and I'll be fine until morning. Please take a break." She put a hand on my cheek, her fingers brushing the scruff on my jaw. She gave me a small, warm smile. "You need to rest too. You've been amazing."

I nodded numbly and told Masey good-bye before I walked out into the darkness. It felt right that the sun was down. To me, it felt like the sun had never risen again after Madelyn told me of her mother's death. I could barely think. I started the four-wheeler and drove down the road. I passed the Ashbys' property without thinking about it and continued to the junkyard. I stopped next to the lean-to and climbed off, feeling as though I had aged a decade since I had last been there.

Mick came out of the shack barking as though a million cats had invaded his property. Jagger followed closely behind. He flipped on the floodlights that hung above the porch, then squinted at the sudden brightness.

"Why ya here so late?"

I barely looked at him. "Maddy's mom died. I don't know what to do." I stared hard at the ground. "Nothing could help me when I lost Zoey."

Jagger was silent for a moment, then he said, "Take 'er for a ride."

I blew out a breath in frustration. "She's not going to care about some motorcycle ride after her mom just passed away."

Jagger used his crowbar cane to walk down the one step from his shack. He tottered my way and gave me the most serious look I had ever seen from him. "I seen the way ya look after a ride. Ets healin'. Ets what she's needin'."

The logic of his words rang true. I rode because it chased away all the troubles in my world. For those moments I was on the motorcycle, I could forget everything but the wind, the road beneath my tires, and the expanse of sky that promised no limits in front or behind me. I could be no one, just feel, and it was enough.

"Do we have another helmet?"

Jagger cracked a smile. "I got jus' the one." He moved back inside and came out a minute later with a helmet that was very familiar.

I accepted the flat black helmet, feeling as though I held something almost sacred. Grooves ran along two sides where it had protected me from bullets when I jumped through the window at the fair. I traced a finger along one, remembering the crash of glass, the sound of a dozen bullets, the feeling of ribs breaking under their impact. When I crashed, I landed on my back and head. I felt the scratches that cut through the paint along the back. The helmet had saved my life more than once.

"Ya prob'ly should 'ave her wear yours. I ain't sure this 'un'll save anyone again."

I gave a small smile. "Her life's worth saving a lot more than mine."

He grinned and patted my shoulder. "Now yer talkin'."

I strapped the new helmet to the back of the motorcycle seat and put the old one on. I slid the visor up. "Thanks, Jagger."

He saluted me and turned back to the shack. "What're friends for?" he called over his shoulder, followed by, "Mick, git in ta house."

I drove from the junkyard straight to Madelyn's. It was well after midnight, but I doubted she slept. The light in her window gave me the answer I needed. I parked the motorcycle by the edge of their property and crossed to the tree below her window. I climbed the branches as I had so many times before, the rough bark familiar under my fingertips.

Her yellow-and-white curtains hung in front of the window. I tapped on the glass, hoping she would answer. After a moment, I saw movement inside. Madelyn pushed the curtains aside and opened the window, looking even more exhausted than before. Her face was pale and her hair was mussed on one side where she'd been laying on it, but it was obvious I had found her in the middle of crying instead of sleeping. Her eyes widened when she saw me in the Black Rider outfit.

"Kel, what are you—"

I took her hand and pulled her into the night. I guided her gently down the branches even though she had climbed the tree more often than I. She slipped her hand in mine and I led her to the motorcycle. When I handed her the helmet, she gave me a questioning look. I told her quietly, "I can't make the pain go away, but I can help you forget about it for a while."

Tears filled her eyes again, but she put the helmet on before they could fall. I climbed onto the bike, then helped her get seated on back. Her arms wrapped tightly around my waist when I started the engine. I pulled slowly from their property and drove south down the road away from town and anything that was familiar.

Madelyn's grip loosened after a mile. She leaned against me with her head resting on my shoulder. Her body shook and I knew she was crying again. I put a gloved hand over hers. She slipped her fingers through mine and held on to the bare comfort my presence offered.

The sun rose while we rode. Clouds parted above the mountains just as the first rays peeked over the rocky expanse. The sight was breathtaking, bathing the road around us in shades of orange and gold I had never seen before. Madelyn's arms tightened around me as sunlight fell on our shoulders. Rose-hued mist drifted from the river that ran a few feet beyond the road, cattails waved in the golden light, and the shadow of birds rose above us, stretching their wings in embrace of a sunrise so beautiful I felt it was just for us.

I slowed so we could savor each subtle change in the sky. The clouds shifted, sending sunbeams down in golden shafts that looked solid enough to climb if we could only reach them. The road curved slowly to the east and we drove into the dawn, the morning light around us bathing in the glistening dew.

"She's all right," Madelyn said just loud enough that I could hear her above the sound of the engine.

I squeezed her hand and her fingers twisted through mine. By the time we arrived back at Madelyn's house, our tears had dried. She gave me a warm smile of thanks and kissed my cheek when I climbed with her back to her room and saw her safely tucked in bed.

Chapter Thirteen

BY THE TIME I traded the motorcycle for the four-wheeler, the sun was already hanging above the horizon. I fell into the cot and slept half an hour before Cole tipped my bed over to tell me it was time to milk the cows. I stumbled after the boys into the corral that had been turned into a makeshift milk yard until the barn was rebuilt.

Cole and Jaren were surprisingly quiet. Usually they roughhoused in the mornings, but today they milked without quarreling. The steady shush-shush of filling buckets was the only sound that broke the morning hush. I wondered why until Uncle Rick appeared.

"I heard about Mrs. West," he said. He gave my shoulder an apologetic squeeze. "How's Madelyn?"

"Not good," I replied. I leaned my forehead against Barbecue's side. The black cow swatted at my face with her tail.

"Long night?" he asked sympathetically.

I nodded. "I just tried to be there for her. I didn't know what else to do."

"Sometimes that's all you *can* do." The knowing look on his face made me uncomfortable. For the first time, I considered that might have been how they felt when I moved in.

The only thing I wanted to do was go to her and make sure she was all right. I finally gave in after breakfast.

"I'm going to the junkyard," I told Mom and the Ashbys. I could tell by the looks they exchanged that they knew I would be detouring to see Madelyn.

Aunt Lauren surprised me by following me out with a large basket. Mom joined us by the four-wheeler. "I know Masey didn't want more food, but if she goes home, we want to make sure they have plenty so they don't worry about having to cook," Aunt Lauren explained.

I met Mom's warm gaze. "There's more pumpkin bread in there," she said.

"Thank you," I told her, giving her a tight hug. "I told her what it means."

"I'm glad," she said, giving me a kiss on the forehead.

I strapped the basket to the front of the four-wheeler. The scents that wafted from it made my mouth water. "Thank you," I told them both. I hesitated, then met Mom's gaze again. "I don't know when I'll be home. I'll call you if it gets late."

A grateful smile spread across her face, reminding me that I needed to act like a son more often. "Take care of yourself," she said.

I drove off the property and smiled when Jake fell in beside me. The dog had been plenty put out when I returned last night. At least I could make him happy by letting him tag along.

I carried the basket to the front porch and knocked quietly.

The door opened a minute later. "What do you want?" Mr. West demanded.

Apparently our little talk hadn't made him like me any better. I swallowed and held up the basket. "Aunt Lauren and my mother send more food so you don't have to worry about cooking."

"I don't cook," Mr. West said as though the very thought offended him.

I tried to find the right words. "I—I didn't meant to imply that you cooked, Mr. West. I—I just wanted to, well, if Masey leaves and you don't have to—"

Madelyn's aunt saved me the trouble of figuring out just what I wanted to do by opening the door further and giving me a warm smile made all the more tender by her red nose and faint trails of mascara that had survived her scrubbing. "Hello, Kelson. Please come in."

"He doesn't need to come in," Mr. West pointed out. "He brought a basket and now you have it." He took it from my hand and gave it to her. "Done. Now he can leave."

"Give him a break, Joe," Masey chided gently.

Mr. West threw me one more dark look, then stalked back inside the house. I followed Masey in, wondering if it would have been smarter to obey Mr. West's wishes. If possible, he appeared to dislike me even more since he broke down. I waited at the edge of the living room in uncomfortable silence.

The fact that the television was off and no one occupied the living room pounded painfully against me. Mrs. West's absence made the room unbearable. I couldn't blame them for avoiding it.

Madelyn appeared at the top of the stairs. A shadow of a smile touched her lips as she made her way down. A memory tugged at the back of my mind. I saw Madelyn in the dark purple dress she had worn to the dance, her long brown hair collected in a diamond clip on her head that vied with the brightness of her eyes. Now, she looked worn and beat down, a whisper of the girl in my memory. The thought made my heart ache.

I crossed to her side just as she reached the bottom. She put her arms around my shoulders and held me quietly. No sobs racked her this time. I knew she had probably cried herself to the point of numbness. I could remember the feeling; it sent a shudder up my spine.

"It's going to be all right," I whispered.

She shook her head. "How?" she asked in a tone of defeat.

I didn't know what to say. I searched my mind for anything that had helped me, any little fragment of hope. I found one and gave her a small smile. "Remember the Towhee, the little bird that helped me survive my heartache when Zoey died?" She nodded with a flicker of a smile; I knew she thought about the time we were comparing each other to birds. She had been my Towhee. "It's time for me to be there for you."

"You're going to be my Towhee?" she asked softly. A slight smile touched her gaze.

I nodded and kissed her on the forehead. "I'll tap on your window until you are ready to see the sun. I won't give up on you."

Tears showed in her eyes. "Promise?" she asked.

"I promise."

She fell into my arms and held me tight.

"Maddy, I need your help with the obituary," Mr. West called from the other room.

"Maddy?" I asked in surprise.

She gave a true smile. "Mom loved it when you called me that, so Dad hasn't stopped using it." She blinked before her tears could fall. "It makes me happy."

I smiled back. As much as he hated me, Mr. West would do what he could to help Madelyn through this, even if it meant calling her by the nickname I used.

Mr. West made an annoyed grunting sound. Madelyn looked over her shoulder. "I should spend some time with him," she said softly. "He needs me."

I nodded in understanding. "Call me if you want to get away."

"I will."

I kissed her again, and watched her walk slowly to the kitchen. She paused at the doorway to give a little wave, then disappeared.

———∽∽———

I DROVE FROM MADELYN'S house straight to the junkyard. Magnum showed up about an hour later. Jagger told him what happened while I threw myself into stacking car parts for our hideout. I wanted to be with Madelyn and couldn't think of anything but the pain she was going through. I kept checking my cell phone, hoping she would call. The frustration I felt at being away from her ate at me. I put it into my work, chucking bumpers, pulling out steering columns, and using hoods to form a secure wall around the door.

I eventually gave up around noon and pulled the guns from the bomb shelter. Both of them watched with concern on their faces as I stacked cans along the fence.

I was surprised to find a sense of release as I shot at the cans. The methodical rhythm of loading, aiming, and the sharp ricochet of sound around the junkyard lulled me into a thoughtless cadence. I had killed more cans than I could count by the time Magnum set a hand on my arm. "That's probably about good," he said. "You've gone through more bullets than there are people in Sparrow."

I followed his gaze to the shells on the ground. I hadn't realized I had shot so many. The cans on the ground showed surprisingly accurate bullet holes.

I unloaded the clip back into the box and handed Jagger the Colt. "Sorry."

He shrugged. "No better use fo' a gun."

"Than to shoot it?" Magnum asked.

Jagger rolled his eyes. "Ta blow off steam, ya dolt."

"Let's go for a ride," Magnum suggested, ignoring Jagger.

We took the bikes, but I couldn't ignore the missing sensation of a pair of arms wrapped around my waist and a helmet leaning against my shoulder. My thoughts lingered on Madelyn as we toured the gas stations along the highway. It was probably better that we didn't find the robbers. I wasn't sure how I would handle them with all the pent-up frustration I was feeling.

I couldn't stand the silence. We stopped several times so I could call her, but she didn't answer. I knew better than to push my presence on her when she and her dad needed the time together. I arrived at the Ashbys' later that night and found Mom waiting up for me. She gave a sympathetic smile. "How was your day?"

I sat in a chair at the kitchen table and rested my head on my arms. "Infuriatingly uneventful."

"You wished something would happen so you could take your mind off what Madelyn's going through?" Mom asked.

I nodded without looking up.

She patted my back. "I worry about you every time you ride out. I know how much danger you put yourself in."

I knew if she truly realized the danger I faced, she would probably make us move back to California. I gave a noncommittal grunt.

She set something on the table in front of me. I glanced up to find one of Aunt Lauren's apple plates holding two slices of fresh bread spread with strawberry preserves. The smell made my stomach growl and I realized I hadn't eaten since breakfast.

"The funeral's tomorrow," Mom said gently.

I stared at her in surprise. "Tomorrow?"

She nodded. "Rick said Joe West wanted it over with as quickly as possible. They're only inviting immediate family and a few friends." She gave me a kind smile. "Of course you're also invited."

I nodded and pushed the bread away, my appetite gone. Mom slid it back. "You need to eat. Lauren said Jagger's cooking isn't the greatest."

I hadn't seen Jagger cook so I had nothing to base her assumption on, but some of the scents that wafted from the shack left little to the imagination. There was a reason I never asked for food when I worked at the junkyard.

I begrudgingly accepted the plate of bread. "Thanks, Mom. I probably should get some sleep."

She nodded with a look of concern. "You have circles under your eyes. You need more rest."

"I'll try," I replied.

She gave me a hug and I made my way to the living room. I fell onto the cot without changing into pajamas. It took too much effort and whatever sleep I would catch still wouldn't be enough to combat the weariness that seemed to come from my soul instead of my body. I kicked off my shoes and rolled over, but it was a long time before I could chase the heaviness from my mind.

I missed Madelyn. I missed her smile, I missed her vanilla scent, and I missed the feeling of her hand in mine. We had been apart for a day, but it felt like a century. I wanted to comfort her and be there for her. I had barely survived losing my sister. Even now, a glimpse of the right color of blue or a laugh at school that carried a few familiar notes were enough to send me into a sinkhole of loss. I didn't know if I had what it would take to carry Madelyn through her sorrow as well, but I needed to be strong for her.

THE FUNERAL WAS SHORT and to the point. Several ladies from

the local church said kind things about Mrs. West, and the pastor was to conclude the ceremony. Madelyn sat between Masey and Mr. West, but her hand slipped back to where I sat behind her with my mom. I held Madelyn's hand, tracing patterns on her palm in an effort to take away some of her pain. Mom rubbed my back and held a handkerchief to her eyes from time to time. Her presence comforted me more than I could express. I knew it was just as hard for her to go through another funeral so soon after Zoey's.

When the pastor rose, he carried his heavy books to the stand and opened them, quoting a few passages without looking at the text. In the end, he concluded with, "This life is but a gateway to the beyond. How we live during our time on this earth determines our place in the heavens. Silvia West underwent hardship and suffering following the accident that stole the use of her limbs, but she maintained a steadfast attitude despite her lack of attendance in church."

Madelyn's hand tightened in mine. The pastor concluded his sermon, but her fingers didn't loosen. The casket was closed and we were at the cemetery sooner than I thought possible. Madelyn sobbed as the casket was lowered into the ground. She leaned against me and turned her head against my shoulder when it was time to go. I knew what she needed; it was what I had needed when Zoey died.

I held her and let everyone pass us by. Mom whispered that she would get a ride home and slipped the keys to her car into my hand so we could stay as long as we wanted. The few family members and friends who came gave their condolences, and I accepted them for Madelyn with a grateful nod because she wasn't in a state to hear them. Eventually, even Mr. West drove away in the van they no longer had a use for.

Rain began to fall in a gentle patter. Madelyn and I were the only two people left in the cemetery except for the two workers who waited a respectful distance away to fill the grave when we were gone.

"He said she stopped going to church," she said, her voice broken.

"She had to," I replied. "She was injured."

She shook her head. "But what if that affects where she is now?" Her eyes filled with tears.

I took her face gently in my hands and waited until she met my gaze. "Madelyn, your mother is the best person I have ever known. She was an example to me of how to smile despite the most dire of circumstances. She was always kind, and never had a mean or negative thing to say about anyone or anything even when she was uncomfortable or in pain. Your mother's place is secure and she is safe and happy, watching over you and your dad. You know it in your heart. You said so when we watched the sunrise on the motorcycle. Trust your heart and know that she is whole and happy, and so proud of her daughter."

She nodded, the frustration gone from her gaze and replaced with tender sorrow. "I know you're right," she said. "But I don't know what to do now."

"You can talk to her," I said softly.

Madelyn looked up at me, her hazel eyes edged in red.

"It'll help," I urged. "I used to talk to Zoey every day." I swallowed back the lump that tightened in my throat at the thought of the distance between us now.

Madelyn took a step forward and surprised me by sitting at the edge of the grave. Flowers covered the top of the casket, lining the beautiful mahogany with white, red, and pink petals. Madelyn picked up one of the flowers and ran her fingers over the petals.

"I'm sorry, Mom," she said quietly. Her voice choked with

tears.

I wanted to tell her she had nothing to be sorry for, but knew better than to interrupt.

"I should have been there," Madelyn continued. "But we didn't know. I wouldn't have left the hospital if I had known."

Her words stabbed my heart. Her regret echoed the words I had said to Zoey. I saw myself standing by her grave in the cemetery that overlooked a quiet wash of green with the sound of the distant waves brushing past in quiet sighs. Zoey's tombstone had a picture of a cat and a dog in one corner to symbolize her love of animals. In the other, an angel spread its wings with the rays of sunrise behind it. I traced both pictures.

They were so inadequate in their ability to give anyone who visited Zoey's grave an idea of who she really was. I wanted to stand there and tell them everything she stood for, everything she meant to me, but there was no one to tell.

"I'm so sorry, Zoey," I choked out, tears streaming down my face. I wiped them away, ignoring the way the burns on my hands ached with the salt. "I should have saved you. It's my fault."

I shook my head and forced my thoughts back to the present, blinking back tears. I knew now, thanks to Madelyn, that Zoey's death didn't rest on my shoulders. The guilt of the boy who cried at her tombstone was no longer mine. Our conversation in the park had allowed me to heal and forgive myself for the stupid decisions that led to that fateful night. It was an accident, and the release of that thought left me lighter.

I would do all I could to help Madelyn feel the same way. She was such an amazing person. I didn't want to see her weighed down by guilt she didn't deserve.

Madelyn continued, oblivious to my thoughts. "I won't ever forget everything you did for me. I'll try to make you proud of me.

I'll take care of Dad and make sure he's happy. I won't leave him in Sparrow alone."

She set the rose gently on the casket and whispered a few final words. When she was finished, I helped her stand up. "Your mom would love the flowers," I said. I thought back to the conversation in their living room after we finished *The Last Samurai*.

I squeezed Madelyn's hand. "Do you remember what your mom said about flowers?"

She nodded and a slight smile showed on her face. "Life was like the flowers. Each one was perfect in its own way."

"And whole in its own way," I concluded.

"She lived a good life, didn't she?" Madelyn asked.

I nodded. "You helped make it great."

She rested her hand near my elbow and let me lead her to the car Mom had left for us. Before I could open her door, she gave me a tight hug. "Thank you," she said softly.

I drove us away into the fading light of the sunset. It looked like an exact reverse of the sunrise we had seen from the motorcycle. Golden light faded into pale yellow and rose until the deep purple mountains were all that remained. It felt like a farewell, like a heartfelt good-bye, and a reminder that we weren't alone. Madelyn's hand tightened in mine and her head rested on my shoulder.

Chapter Fourteen

I DROVE TO MADELYN'S house and walked her to the door. When she went inside, I paused in the doorway. Her words to her mother echoed in my head. "Do you want me to pick you up tonight?" I asked quietly.

She shook her head without meeting my gaze. "I need to stay home with Dad."

I held in a breath, then let it out slowly and nodded. "Call me if you need anything."

"I will," she promised. I turned to go, but she touched my arm. "Kelson?"

I turned back reluctantly, worried she would tell me she didn't want to see me for a while.

Instead, she gave me a small smile. "Thank you."

I nodded. "Let me know if there's anything I can do to help." I walked down the stairs, feeling as though I left my entire world behind me.

I MET MAGNUM AT the junkyard that night, but I told him I

didn't feel like riding.

"Come on, man," he urged. "It'll do you good."

I shook my head. "I'm just not feeling it."

A spark of anger showed in his eyes. "You get me to leave the Bullets without question and go tagging along after you, and now you're wussin' out on me?" He shoved the tinted helmet on his head. "Fine. I don't need you. I look like the Black Rider and I fight like the Black Rider. I can be the Rider without you."

"You don't fight like the Black Rider," I replied sharply. "If anything, I have to spend my time protecting your back."

He slammed the visor down, then said through it, "I'll save you the trouble." He revved the engine and sped off into the night.

I sat on my motorcycle, wondering at the direction my life had taken. There was only one person I wanted to see, and she didn't want me around. Madelyn had asked for time to be with her dad, and I knew that was important, but I needed to see her, if only for a moment. I couldn't think without making sure she was okay. Against my better judgment, I left the junkyard and turned south toward the West residence.

I didn't stop until I reached their property, but the sight of the van in the driveway reminded me who I could potentially run into. I was in the middle of debating whether I should turn back when the fact that Buck was barking dawned on me.

Madelyn's dog had grown so accustomed to my presence that he no longer barked when I showed up. Masey had been there long enough for him to grow used to her, and he knew far better than to bark at Mr. West. That meant he was barking at something or someone else. I climbed slowly off the bike and glanced around, but didn't see any vehicles.

I crossed to the road and looked along it. A small gray car was parked a ways down. It had been pulled off to the side so that it sat partially in the bushes. Something familiar about the vehicle nagged at my brain. I took a step closer, and then my heart clenched.

I tore off my helmet and threw it near my bike when I ran past. I reached the tree beneath Madelyn's window and was halfway up when I heard the screams. I reached the top limb and threw open the window. The curtains furled out and tangled with the night breeze. I pushed past them and froze halfway into the room.

Madelyn stood with a bat in her hands. The unconscious form of her uncle Mitch sprawled at her feet. Blood ran down the side of his face that had been battered to the point that I barely recognized him. Her chest heaved and her face was white. Red marks on her arms showed where he had grabbed her.

Mr. West burst through the door.

Madelyn didn't appear to notice either of us. She was about to bring the bat down against Mitch's head in a blow that would probably end his life, but I caught it out of her hands. She fought me for a moment and I was amazed at how strong she was. I held the bat in one hand and pinned her arms to her sides with an arm around her waist. She punched at my chest, her fists a lot weaker than her grip on the bat had been.

"Maddy, it's me! Maddy, it's Kelson! You're okay—it's all right now!"

She stared at me for a second, then collapsed against me with a sob.

"What . . . what just happened?" Mr. West managed to ask. He could only stare at the unconscious, bleeding form of his brother.

"He'll never touch me again," Madelyn said in a voice that was much more controlled than I would have guessed.

Masey came into the room, then let out a shriek. "What on earth!" she said in a high-pitched voice.

I walked Madelyn to her aunt's side. "Take her away from this room," I said in as calm a voice as I could manage.

Masey complied without asking further questions. I turned back to Mr. West. "He needs a doctor."

Mr. West acted as though he couldn't move. "Madelyn almost killed him."

I nodded. "We need to get him help, but they can't know it was Madelyn who did this. She's dealing with enough already."

"Then who?" he asked, his voice barely above a whisper.

"The Black Rider." My heart hardened as I said the words, but I knew it was the only way. "We'll tell them the Black Rider did it."

Mr. West's eyes turned to me for the first time. "Why would they believe that?"

I met his gaze squarely. "Because it wouldn't be the first time I beat up your brother for assaulting Maddy."

Understanding dawned in his eyes and he took a step back from the bloody mess that was Mitch's unconscious form. He then came to himself and reached for the bat.

I moved it out of his grasp. "Murder won't help your daughter," I said softly but in a voice that left no room for argument. "We'll tell the police what he attempted to do, but not with whom. Maddy doesn't need to deal with reporters and statements after all she's gone through. He will go to jail no matter what, and the Black Rider can tell the sheriff what happened to her so your brother is prosecuted."

Mr. West nodded. I could tell that after everything he had gone through, the events of the night were too much for him. I knelt and slung his brother not-so-gently over my shoulder, then carried him out of the bedroom. He was a tall man, but adrenaline fueled my steps. I made my way down the hall, happy to see Masey had the sense to keep Madelyn out of sight.

Mr. West helped me through the door, then we set his brother in the back of the van.

"Where do we take him?" Mr. West asked, breathing hard.

I had already made up my mind. "The Horseshoe Bar. It's where I beat him last time and chased him out of town. They won't question his presence there."

Mr. West nodded and climbed into the driver's seat of the van. I jogged back to the porch to tell Masey where we were going. She met me at the entryway. "I'm taking Madelyn to my house."

Madelyn stood pale and solitary in the middle of the living room floor. A bag sat at her feet, its contents hanging out haphazardly as if they had been thrown in at random. I crossed the floor to her and hugged her tight. The fierceness with which she held on to me told of her fear. Her arms shook and she let out a little sob.

"You did good," I told her. "I'm so proud of you." I blinked back tears of outrage that she had gone through such terror again. Masey's intentions of taking her away made perfect sense. It would be best for Madelyn to put some space between herself and the house until things settled down. "Go with your aunt. You'll be safe there. I'll call you."

She nodded and pressed her lips against mine. The kiss was fleeting, but tasted of her tears and heartache. "I love you," she whispered.

I almost let go of her hand to follow Mr. West, but her words stopped me in my tracks. I stared at her, my heart pounding in my ears and my chest so tight I thought it would burst. "I love you too," I replied.

She smiled through her tears and gave me one last kiss, then motioned for me to go. I walked out the door and made my way to the motorcycle without remembering the steps that took me there. I was certain I was unfit to drive, but knew I had no choice. I followed the van with so many emotions swirling through my mind even riding on the motorcycle couldn't take them away.

"YOU SAY HE WAS molesting a girl?" Deputy Nayton asked.

I nodded. "It wasn't his first time. I just couldn't control myself."

His eyebrows lowered. "Can't say I blame you. Where's the girl?" The deputy jotted notes on a pad of paper. He was one of the sheriff's closest men; he had two girls in high school and no sympathy toward anyone with intentions to hurt children. I had worked with him a couple of times after the fair shooting.

EMTs loaded Mitch West into an ambulance. The oxygen mask on his face was spotted with blood and both of his eyes were swollen shut. I wondered what he would look like if he survived the event.

"She didn't want her name revealed. She didn't get hurt, and I promised I would keep her identity a secret," I replied.

Officer Nayton wrote down a few more notes, then nodded at the sheriff. Sheriff Bowley motioned for me to follow him away from the lights and police cars. I was grateful he was the only one who knew who I was beneath the Black Rider outfit.

"This isn't good," the sheriff said in low undertones. "This isn't like you."

"It was me," I said steadily.

He gave me a doubtful look, but gave up the argument. "If his condition gets worse, I might have to hold you for attempted murder."

His words sent a spike of fear through me, but I nodded and didn't say anything.

"Lay low for a while," Sheriff Bowley continued. "I don't want to hear anything associated with your name for the next few weeks."

"Will do. Thanks, Sheriff." I climbed on the motorcycle and was about to drive away when he walked over to me.

"One more thing." He frowned and scratched his hair beneath his hat, then pushed the hat on more firmly. "There've been sightings of a few Brown Hawk gang members hanging around."

"What are they doing?" The fact that someone from the fair shootings was hanging around Sparrow concerned me.

"Not sure." The sheriff looked annoyed that they didn't have more information. "Several of them are still in custody for the shootings. These are either from other chapters or weren't involved in the shooting." His eyes tightened. "Just the same, be careful and warn your partner."

I nodded and didn't bother to mention that Magnum had decided to do things on his own for a while. I climbed on my motorcycle and drove to a stop sign, then sat and watched the police cars and ambulance head to the hospital. A few seconds after they passed, my cell phone rang. I slid it out of my pocket, worried it might be Madelyn. I was surprised to see Magnum's name on the screen.

"Hello?" I said reluctantly.

"Kelson, hey, I didn't know if I should call you but, um," Magnum paused, then rushed forward, "I was filling up my bike at the same place as last time, and you know those guys who keep robbing the gas stations? Well, I think they're inside."

Indecision gripped me. The sheriff had told me to lie low. I wasn't supposed to compromise myself further. "I'll call the police," I said.

"Seriously?" Magnum cursed under his breath. "These guys'll be gone before the cops get here. You know that." He took a breath, then said, "I'm going in."

"Magnum, don't—" I began, but he hung up.

I stared at my phone. I could try to call him back, but I knew there was no choice. I slid the phone in my pocket and revved the engine.

Chapter Fifteen

I PUSHED MY MOTORCYCLE to the red line, speeding down the interstate at one hundred and forty. I passed a few trucks as though they were standing still, then flew off the exit ramp and slid to a stop next to Magnum's bike. A quick glance showed him already inside. I crossed to the doors and studied the layout.

Magnum wasn't doing well. His helmet sat on the floor and he was sporting a black eye. Two of the robbers had him pinned against the counter with knives at his throat while the other was busy emptying the cash register to the frustration of the pale, raven-haired attendant. She stood against the wall and held her hands up, revealing swirling tattoos running down both arms. Her fingers were trembling and she kept looking at Magnum for help, but he was in no condition to be of assistance.

All the emotions from finding Madelyn's uncle in her room flooded my body—the adrenaline that filled me at recognizing his car on the side of the road, my desperate climb to her bedroom, then the fury at seeing her consumed by terror and outrage pounded through my chest. I took a steeling breath and pushed the door open. "About time we ran into you guys."

All three men looked up. The man behind the cash register had a black bandana around his forehead. His eyes narrowed. "I thought the Black Rider crumpled a little too easily."

He jerked his head and one of the men left Magnum and walked slowly to me. He handled himself with the cool grace of an experienced fighter. This wasn't going to be like our last fight at the same gas station.

"Be careful," Magnum called.

"Shut up," the man who held him at knife point hissed.

"Let's see if you're as good as he was supposed to be," the man near me said.

He passed his knife from one hand to the other. I kept my eyes on his face, reading his expressions and the subtle twitches that told of his intentions. His gaze sharpened and I realized he knew what I was doing. I dropped my focus to a point just below his throat so he wouldn't try to draw me out with fake signals.

His knife slowed. He threw a punch, then lashed out with the knife when I dodged to the side. I blocked his attack with my forearm and threw a punch in return. He lunged to the left and his grip tightened on his knife.

He made a swipe for my throat. I leaned back, then ducked low and drove a fist into his left knee. It snapped to the side with an audible crack. The man let out a yell. He slashed at my chest, stepping forward on his injured leg. When he stumbled, I slugged him in the stomach, then dodged back before he could drive his knife into my thigh.

"I'm gonna kill you," he hissed, his jaw clenched tight in pain.

I motioned him forward. His eyes narrowed, his gaze bright with outrage.

"Go help him," the man behind the counter commanded the others.

I caught the first man's arm before he could bring his knife down. I drove a punch into his ribs just below his arm and he dropped his knife. He tried to kick me in the groin, but I caught his leg and drove a chop into his groin in answer. I spun and elbowed the second man's arm away just before he stabbed me in the back. I slammed a fist into his side, then followed it with a low leg sweep that knocked him onto his back.

A quick glance showed Magnum at the counter with the leader's knife pressed against his throat. I picked up the knife the first man had dropped. I was tempted to throw it at the one behind the counter, but both men made it back to their feet. The one I had punched in the groin looked like he was about to throw up. I had to give him credit for resilience.

"You don't know when to give up," I said amiably.

The man with the knife advanced without a word. He made a quick swipe at my stomach, then sliced up toward my head in a blow intended to lay my throat open. I dodged the first, but the tip caught me when I blocked the second. It sliced deeply along the palm of my left hand, causing me to drop my knife. I backed up.

"So he can bleed," the man taunted, pursuing me.

His companion jabbed at my side. I turned and blocked the blow, then felt the fire of the knife as it tore through my jacket into my side. Rage burned through my limbs. I twisted and caught his knife hand, then hit him in the stomach followed by a haymaker to his face that made him spin in a complete circle before he fell to the ground.

I blocked a kick from the other man and answered it with a punch to the chest, a left jab to the stomach, then another chop to the groin that made him collapse, gasping, to the floor.

I picked up both knives and advanced on the man holding Magnum hostage.

"I'd suggest backing away from him," I said in a deadly calm voice.

Magnum stared at me with wide eyes while the man behind him laughed. "And give up my hostage? No way."

I shrugged and flipped one of the knives in my hand so I held it point first. "Either that or I send this blade through your eye."

His eyes widened, then narrowed. "You're bluffing."

A sign said "Donuts" above the counter of coffee and hot chocolate machines. I threw the knife, hoping to at least hit the sign. To my surprise, the blade hit the middle of the donut and sank into the wall.

The man dropped his knife and backed up. Magnum grabbed it and advanced on him, pressing him against the counter. "How do you like it?" he demanded. "Not very comfortable, is it?"

"We've got to go," I told him. I turned my attention to the pale attendant. "Call the sheriff of Sparrow. He's been looking for these guys."

She nodded and fumbled for the phone.

"Why do we need to leave?" Magnum asked. He pulled bungee cords from one of the stands and began to tie their hands behind their backs. "We should turn these guys in. It'd look great!"

"Madelyn's uncle came back into town."

Magnum's mouth fell open. "After the beating we gave him?"

I nodded, then lied, "I had a bat this time. The sheriff said I'd be lucky not to get attempted murder charges."

"But he's a rapist," Magnum argued.

"I promised the sheriff I'd lie low for a while." I gestured toward the men he left tied on the floor. "This isn't exactly lying low." I looked at the girl. "Can you handle them until the cops show up?" My voice sounded gruff beneath the helmet.

She nodded and grabbed one of the knives. I smiled at the grim look of determination on her face. "They aren't getting away this time," she threatened in a tone that left little doubt she would use the knife if needed.

As the adrenaline left, my side began to throb. I vaguely remembered the bite of a knife. I put a hand to my side under the jacket and it came away damp with blood. "Let's go," I said. I pushed the door open without waiting to see if Magnum followed. My hand left a bloody print on the door.

"Wait up," Magnum called. I made it to the motorcycle and glanced back to see him staring at the blood on the door. He hurried over. "You got cut?"

I pulled my glove off and showed him where the knife had sliced it. Magnum's eyes tightened. "That print was from your right hand."

I let out a slow breath between my teeth and lifted my jacket. Blood flowed down my side from a knife wound about six inches long.

Magnum swore. "We've got to get you to a hospital."

I shook my head. "Lying low, remember?"

"Then where?" Magnum demanded. "This is your life you're playing with."

I shoved the jacket back down and started the engine. "I'm going the Ashbys'."

"That's idiotic," Magnum shouted.

When he saw I wasn't going to be swayed, he climbed onto his motorcycle. I drove slowly from the parking lot and followed the interstate back toward Sparrow. Headlights blurred and the whirl of police car lights glared blindingly as they passed us on their way to the gas station. A loud humming sound pounded in my ears.

I blinked, then weaved as I forced the bike to stay up. Magnum gunned his motorcycle so he rode beside me. He threw his visor up.

"Pull over," he shouted.

I shook my head and hunched lower, forcing myself to concentrate on the lines of the road. The bike wavered again. I felt lightheaded. The headlights of the oncoming vehicles were all I could see in the darkness.

Magnum pulled in front of me. His red taillight was like a balm to my aching eyes. I concentrated on the light and followed him off the interstate. Each blink took longer. It felt as if a lifetime went by before I opened my eyes. The red light was the only thing that mattered to me.

My thoughts drifted to Madelyn. She would be upset with me for getting hurt. I had made a promise to her long ago that I would think about her before I did anything stupid. Turning away from the knife had definitely been stupid. I didn't want to disappoint her, and I really didn't want to be scolded for forgetting my promise, but I had. I owed it to Madelyn to work harder on that next time.

Something about thoughts of Madelyn weighed on my mind. Dark feelings pressed down as though something bad had happened, but my mind couldn't concentrate hard enough for me to remember what that was. I wanted to make sure Madelyn was all right.

I felt the road change from tight asphalt to the looser gravel near the Ashbys' property. The feeling brought me to a foggy version of the present. Magnum's taillight flashed when he slowed. I couldn't make my brain respond. I released the throttle and felt the bike tip. I hit the ground with a jarring thud and felt the motorcycle crash against my leg, pinning me down.

"Kelson!" Magnum shouted. He was immediately at my side. Shapes came out of the house, calling questions into the darkness. The back porch light flipped on, flooding the area around us.

"Kelson needs help," Magnum called. He yanked the motorcycle off my leg, then unstrapped my helmet and eased it carefully from my head. "Stay with me," he said, his expression worried.

Cassidy appeared, then Mom, followed closely by Uncle Rick and Jaren.

"Kelson!" Mom exclaimed. Her hand flew to her mouth.

"What happened?" Uncle Rick demanded.

"He stopped a robbery at a gas station, but one of the men got him with a knife," Magnum explained quickly. He lifted up my shirt. I didn't have the energy to protest. The flow of blood down my side felt warm and sticky.

"Oh, my goodness," Mom whispered.

"He needs a hospital," Aunt Lauren said, appearing at Mom's side.

Magnum shook his head. "Maddy's uncle tried to rape her and Kelson practically killed him. The sheriff told him to lie low so he doesn't get pressed with attempted murder charges. He can't be linked to the gas station."

I remembered what had happened to Madelyn. A sick feeling tightened in my stomach. Uncle Rick knelt and picked me up in his arms as if I weighed no more than a newborn calf. I tried to protest, but he didn't appear to hear me. Cassidy opened the door and he carried me straight to the living room. Someone picked up the phone and dialed. I blacked out to the muffled sound of voices.

Chapter Sixteen

"HE'S COMING AROUND," A familiar voice said.

I opened my eyes, then squinted at the bright light. Someone dimmed the lamp and I was able to see again. A small smile touched my lips. "I didn't know you made house calls," I said to Dr. Carrison. Pain flared along my side. I kept my gaze on him to avoid looking at it.

His eyebrows pulled together. "I normally don't," he replied with a touch of humor. "But I've learned to make exceptions in extreme cases."

My left hand was wrapped. I could feel stitches poking through the gauze. I attempted to sit up, but hands held me down. I looked up to see Magnum, Mom, and Uncle Rick standing over me. The hot ache that rushed across my stomach and ribs at the movement made me feel close to blacking out again. I settled back and took a shallow breath. "I guess this is an extreme case," I said quietly.

He nodded and finished cleaning my side with something cold, then pressed gauze to the wound. "Six stitches in your palm, and twenty-four across your side. Pretty nasty wound, but at least it was shallow enough to avoid clipping anything major." He gave me a serious look. "You got lucky."

I nodded. "Thanks for the help."

His eyes took on a troubled glint. "I'm supposed to report any signs of brawling or abuse." He looked up at the others. "But since we're not at the hospital, I'll keep this on the down-low. It could cost me my license if I'm found out, though."

"Thank you, Doc," Uncle Rick said. "We appreciate it. I didn't know who else to call."

"Bronson wasn't available?" Dr. Carrison asked.

Uncle Rick gave a snort of laughter. "I'm not positive the vet has your discretion."

I tried to see the humor in the situation, but failed entirely. "A vet?"

Mom rubbed my shoulder. "Take it easy," she said gently. "Dr. Carrison says you need bed rest."

I wanted to argue, but the look in her eyes stole any quarrel I could come up with. How many times would my mom have to worry about losing me? I didn't know what was wrong with me. I kept putting myself in situations where I didn't care if my life was in danger. If I admitted the truth to myself, it was obvious I was looking for them.

I shied away from that line of thought. "Thanks for patching me up again, Doc."

Dr. Carrison shook my hand and said in a chiding tone, "Take better care of yourself. If you're going to be any good around here as the Black Rider, it'd be best to survive the situations you pit yourself against."

"I'll keep that in mind," I replied wryly.

He smiled and crossed to the living room door, then paused and turned back. A thoughtful expression crossed his features. "You know, I worked on Mitch West."

The name brought a cold pit to my stomach. I kept my face carefully expressionless and waited to see what he would say.

"He survived—for now, at least," the doctor said. His tone stated he wasn't exactly sure how he felt about the fact. He shook his head and continued, "He was pretty messed up. I'm assuming it was a blunt object?"

I nodded. "A bat," I said carefully.

He rubbed his chin. "I assumed as much, but . . ."

"But what?" Magnum pressed, unable to maintain the patience the doctor's drawn-out story required.

A slight frown formed between Dr. Carrison's eyebrows when he looked at me. "I've treated a few of your victims, if you don't mind the term, and I've seen what the full force of the Black Rider's fist can do. Imagine combining that with the unforgiving clout of a bat." He gave me a very straightforward look. "Mitch West wouldn't have made it to the hospital. He would be in a body bag at the morgue."

He left through the front door. Tension hung in the air thick enough to choke a person. I swallowed and found my mouth very dry. Mom took a cup from the end table and held a straw to my lips so I could swallow. I finished two gulps, then rested my head back against the pillow. My body felt like it weighed a ton, and my head swam with every movement.

"What did he mean?" Uncle Rick asked. His voice was quiet, but he used the tone he handled like a weapon whenever he wanted the truth from Jaren or Cole—usually Cole.

I closed my eyes. His heavy footsteps shuffled slightly, but nobody left the room. I swallowed again and said in a voice that sounded as exhausted as I felt, "He's implying that I didn't beat Mitch."

"I got that," Uncle Rick pressed. "If you didn't do it, then who?"

"Madelyn," Cassidy said in a voice just above a whisper. All heads turned toward her and I opened my eyes to see the color run from her face. "He was trying to hurt her," my cousin continued. She kept her eyes on mine as if the truth was the most important thing in the world to her. "She was defending herself, right?"

Angry tears burned in my eyes. I closed them again and nodded. When I answered her, frustration and rage came out stark and plain in my voice; apparently pain and whatever the doctor had used to drug me took away my ability to hide my emotions. "I beat him once before, after she told me what he was doing to her. Magnum and I chased him from town and made him promise never to come back. But I forgot he would've heard about the funeral. He didn't attend the ceremony, but maybe he thought in all the chaos, he could get to Madelyn." I rubbed my closed eyes, heedless of the way the movement pulled against my stitches. "I shouldn't have left her alone," I choked out.

Hands touched my shoulders and arm. "It's not your fault," Mom said. "You couldn't have known."

"I was supposed to protect her," I replied. "I was supposed to keep her safe from him and I failed." I opened my eyes and she stepped back. Tears flowed down my cheeks, but whether from pain, emotional agony, or sheer exhaustion, I didn't know. "I love her and I couldn't keep her safe, even as the Black Rider."

The silence that answered my words was different this time. I stared at the ceiling, hoping to be swallowed up by the floor and never returned. I should have died so many times. I protected strangers from robbers and gangs, yet I couldn't save my loved ones.

A voice in the back of my mind argued that I had saved them at the fair, but I wasn't in the mood to listen to reason. The floor wasn't complying with my need to disappear. I wondered how many pain pills Dr. Carrison had left. The same voice maliciously said that maybe he had forgotten to leave any. It would serve me right.

"You love her?" Cassidy asked.

My gaze shifted to my cousin. She crossed the floor, leaned her elbows against the back of the couch, and looked down at me. Her eyes were alight and there was a tender smile on her face. "You care about her that much?"

When I nodded again, Mom's hand touched my cheek, wiping away the tears. "You can't protect those you care about from everything," she said. "You just have to do your best and hope you can live the full measure of your lives together. It's not easy." Her voice held aching experience.

I lifted a hand and covered her fingers with my own. "No, it's not."

She gave me a small, faltering smile. When I returned it, her expression touched her eyes. For a moment, I saw Zoey looking back at me the way she used to, pride and happiness making her blue eyes dance. "I'm okay." I repeated the words she had said to me long ago. I didn't know if I had heard the words the night she died, or if they had come later as I attempted to cope, but for the moment, they were right.

"You're sure?" Mom asked.

I nodded. "I'll be okay." I looked at the faces around me. Everyone looked extremely weary. I fought back a chuckle because I knew it would hurt. "You guys need some sleep."

Magnum let out a frustrated breath. "We've been waiting to see if you were going to die or not."

I smiled at him. "Thanks for the concern. I think I'll survive."

He surprised me by squeezing my shoulder hard. "Glad to hear it."

He headed for the back door and Cassidy ran to follow him. Uncle Rick stared hard after them for a moment, then turned back to me. "You need to take it easy for a while."

"I plan on it," I said honestly. "Think Barbecue will miss me?"

He snorted, holding back a laugh. "She won't know who to kick come milking time."

"She'll probably be happy," Cole said from the kitchen door.

"How long have you been standing there?" Aunt Lauren demanded with her hands on her hips.

He munched on a chocolate-chip cookie and smiled without answering.

"You're supposed to be in bed. It's way past your bedtime." She motioned toward Jaren. "You, too."

He nodded. "I'll be right there."

Cole grabbed two more cookies before Aunt Lauren could stop him, then ran down the hallway. Aunt Lauren trailed behind.

Jaren crossed to the couch and gave me one of his serious looks. "I almost saw you die tonight."

Guilt flooded through me and I nodded. "Sorry about that." From the corner of my eye, I could see Uncle Rick and Mom watching us quietly.

"Were you scared?" the twelve-year-old asked.

His question caught me by surprise, but it was the same thing he had asked after the barn fire. He deserved an honest answer. I thought back to the fight and the ride home afterwards. There was pain and exhaustion along with the echoing beat of my heart, and worry about Madelyn and everything she had gone through. The red light filled my memory, guiding me to safety.

I shook my head. "I wasn't."

He thought about that for a moment, then nodded. "Sleep well, Kel," he said. He left the room quietly without giving any insight into his thoughts.

I let out a slow breath. "I don't know if that was the right thing to say."

"If it's honest, it's right," Uncle Rick replied, surprising me. "The one thing I've learned about kids is that they always know if you're lying." He sat down near the fireplace and leaned his elbows on his knees. "That was brave of you to take the rap for Madelyn."

Mom took the armchair near him. I could tell by her expression that she wasn't so sure.

"She's had a rough life. I didn't want a black mark on her record to hinder her future. And the reporters here are ruthless, trust me," I told them. Exhaustion made me close my eyes. I used the strength I had left to open them again. I met Uncle Rick's gaze. "I don't want it to affect your family."

He shrugged. "We'll deal with it if it comes to that." He rose with a groan of protest. "These old bones aren't used to staying up so late. I'm going to hit the hay."

He ruffled my hair when he went past. I refrained from telling him I wasn't a puppy. He left down the hallway and I listened to the bedroom door open and close.

Mom waited in silence for a few minutes. My eyes closed, but I forced them open again. She was staring at the fire with an intense expression on her face. She didn't look at me when she asked, "Could you have avoided that knife?"

Her question caught me by surprise. I took a moment to think about it. I reviewed the fight in my mind, seeing it blow by blow. There had been two of them attacking me. I turned from the man with the knife to block a punch from the other one, then the first one sliced my side. I frowned and thought it through again. I knew better than to turn my back on the one who was armed. I had trained against weapons and taught others the same tactics. My mistake was a stupid one that almost cost my life.

I didn't know what to tell Mom. If she guessed the truth, she could force me to seek psychiatric help or make me take medication to address a supposed death wish. I refused to do either. I met her gaze and said with as much conviction as I could muster, "He was faster than me."

She studied my expression for a minute. The firelight danced against the side of her face, highlighting her right side and leaving the left in shadow. It gave me a skewed impression of her thoughts. She nodded, but I couldn't tell if she accepted the lie. "Good night, Kelson. Holler if you need anything."

Aunt Lauren despised hollering. She said it was an act of laziness and rewarded anyone who did it with extra chores. I wondered if mine could wait until I was feeling better. "I will," I told her with a weary smile.

She paused with her hand on my shoulder. "Does it hurt?"

"Nope," I lied with another smile.

She smiled back, turned the lamp off, and left through the door. I listened to her walk to Cassidy's room that had become her bedroom while she stayed at the Ashbys'.

As soon as her footsteps faded down the hall, I fumbled on the end table for the cell phone. The movement sent a wave of agony through my side so sharp, my breath caught in my throat. I leaned just a bit further, afraid I would tear my stitches, and touched the phone. I grabbed it with a jerk and pulled it back, unplugging the charging cable so I could lie down.

I hit Maddy's number on the speed dial and listened to it ring. When her voice came on asking me to leave a message, I listened to it three times just to hear her voice. I couldn't think of what to say through the fog in my brain, so I finally gave up.

I let my head fall back against the pillow and allowed one tear to squeeze through my tightly shut eyelids. My side burned as if fire ate at it from the inside. I knew I should probably take the pain meds that sat in a little cup on the end table near my head, but deep down, I felt like I deserved the pain. I gritted my teeth and refused to make a sound.

Chapter Seventeen

MONDAY CREPT BY. I was supposed to stay in bed, but I had never been able to do nothing. Thoughts about Madelyn haunted me. I missed her terribly and wished she would call. I tried her number four more times, and listened to the message over and over again just to remember the way her voice made me feel real. As soon as I was able to sit on the four-wheeler, I planned to visit her father despite his hatred for me. I needed to make sure she was all right.

Mom worked at the grocery store. She was going to take the day off, but I told her I was feeling okay and wouldn't be doing anything besides sleeping anyway. It was nice to see how much she liked her job. She used to work in an office building where her job was to sort mail and fax papers. She hated it, but it paid the bills. Now, though, she actually smiled when she got ready, and she kissed me on the head when she went out the door. Moving to Sparrow had definitely been good for her.

In my current state, I couldn't argue that the same applied to me, but at least I was making a difference. I shook my head at my thoughts and pushed up gingerly from the cot. I could only review my actions so many times without the mistakes I had made driving me crazy.

My vision swam for a minute and I closed my eyes against the lightheaded rush. When I opened them again, I felt somewhat more in control. I took a drink from the cup on the end table and ignored the pain pills beside it. I tried to fish a pair of pants from my clothes bag with my foot.

Someone had taken off my blood-soaked riding pants and jacket before I was stitched up. I knew they were worried about the risk of an infection, but public exposure wasn't one of my goals. There wasn't anyone I felt comfortable with doing such a thing, and so I decided it was better not to dwell on the fact that it had been done.

I managed to catch the drawstring on a pair of loose gray sweat pants. Bruises covered the side of my left leg where the motorcycle had fallen on it, and some mild road rash scraped along the outside. The doctor had put some sort of salve on it and it was feeling fairly pain free. I hoped the motorcycle had fared as well.

I pulled the pants on while trying to avoid leaning over. If anyone had seen me, they would have laughed hysterically as I tried to slip my foot in the hole and pull up one leg, then the other, without bending at the waist. I was grinning at my own stupidity by the time I was done.

I debated whether to put on a shirt, but the thought of trying to find one in the bag was too much. I rose and steadied myself against the mantle above the fireplace. The fire had burned to coals and the heat of it felt good against my shins. I wondered if I had a slight fever.

I kept one hand on the wall and made my way slowly toward the bathroom in the hall. Every time I put weight on my right leg, it sent pain through my side, forcing me to limp and slide my foot along as though I was a lame duck. I was glad nobody could see the

Black Rider in my state; they definitely would lose all respect.

I reached the bathroom and gave a little pathetic cheer of triumph. I was far from jumping through windows, but I was making baby steps even though the voice in the back of my mind said that a baby would have made it to the bathroom faster.

I wanted to take a shower. Dr. Carrison had cleaned the blood from my side, but I felt hot and gross after spending the morning in bed. I knew I should leave the gauze and bandages on for another day at least, so I settled for wiping my skin down with a rag and told myself I felt refreshed. I then forced myself to look in the mirror.

I stared at the stranger I had become. Hollow circles surrounded my eyes. My hair stood up in more cowlicks than usual and the right side was plastered to my face. My chest was a mess. Small circular bruises still remained from the impact of the bullets. They had turned a sickly green that faded to yellow around the edges. The bullet wound Dr. Carrison had stitched along the top of my shoulder had healed to look like a centipede sat there. I couldn't remember when he had removed the stitches.

More bruises covered my ribs and sides from the fights I had been in. I realized then why Mom had asked if I could have avoided the knife. Even as captain of the Mixed Martial Arts Club at my school in California, I had never come home with bruises like these. I debated whether I was careless or had truly let my skills slide so badly. I made a mental note to train Magnum so he could be a sparring partner. I could definitely use a refresher.

I clenched my jaw and turned around, then reluctantly looked at my back using Aunt Lauren's small hand mirror from the counter. A diagonal row of scars showed where the beam had fallen on me in the warehouse fire. I had tried to get Zoey out, but I was trapped under the beam until the firemen came. My shirt was burned through and had to be cut away; the rest was an agonizing recovery.

A memory surfaced of Jaren under a beam in the barn. He had almost suffered a similar fate.

I wondered what Madelyn saw in me. Thoughts of her made my body ache with a different kind of pain. I longed to hold her and know that she was okay. I missed her with every fiber of my being. It felt like my heart only beat at half strength when she was gone. I wondered if she felt the same way or if she had forgotten me in the chaos that had swallowed her life. She needed stability, and I wanted to give that to her so badly. The inability I had to reach her was infuriating.

I regretted not pulling on a shirt, but refused to go back to the cot. I needed to stand in sunshine before I succumbed to cabin fever and destroyed the place. I was sure Uncle Rick would be a little concerned about such thoughts.

A tin of fresh muffins sat near the oven. I grabbed one and limped painfully toward the back door. I debated pulling on some shoes, then decided it would be more agonizing than it was worth and made my way outside.

The moment I stepped past the screen door, Jake came running up to me. The black-and-white dog sniffed my hands, my sweat pants, my bare feet, and snorted at the scent of the bandages along my side.

"Thank you," I told him. "I'm sure that's sanitary." I tossed the dog a piece of muffin.

He followed me across the lawn to the wooden chair swing that sat in the shade of an ancient oak tree. I eased gingerly down onto it. Lying down, I was comfortable if I stuck one leg through the arm rest and let the other dangle so my toes touched the cool grass. I let out a breath of relief.

After a while, Jake looked up from his place curled on the grass beneath me. I opened my eyes at the sound of his dog tags jingling and found Uncle Rick watching me with an approving expression on his face.

"If I didn't have work to do, I'd be right where you are," he said. He pushed his hat back and wiped the sweat from his forehead with his handkerchief before shoving it back into his pocket.

"It's quite comfortable," I replied.

His eyes creased with humor. "Lauren and Sarah will probably kill you if they see you out here instead of restin' inside."

I shrugged. "I'm feeling about half dead. They could finish the job."

An interested expression touched his gaze. "Did you take the pain meds the doc left?"

I was tempted to lie, but he only had to go inside and look to know the truth. A part of me wondered where the inclination to lie was coming from. I had too many secrets in my life. "No."

When I didn't expound, he nodded. "I've never been one to take meds either. It always seemed like the easy way out."

That brought a small smile to my face. "Why take the easy way out?"

"Exactly," Uncle Rick replied. He gave me a good-humored smile. "But if you need them, nobody will think less of you, especially me."

He left me to think about that. I did for about two minutes until the warmth of the day and the loss of blood from my wound swept me away into a deep sleep.

$$\sim\!\!\sim\!\!\sim$$

"YOU LIVE A HARD life."

I opened my eyes at the sound of Magnum's voice.

He stood where his body blocked out the sun. It was setting gracefully behind the western mountains, bathing the rectangle of grass that made up the Ashbys' backyard in autumn hues despite the fact that it was the beginning of summer. The young aspens that marked the edge of the yard rustled peacefully in the evening breeze. A few crickets chirruped near the railroad tie garden, but it was still a bit early for most of them to start singing.

"What time is it?" I croaked out the question, then tried to swallow. My mouth was as dry as a desert.

Magnum picked up a cup someone had left on a small fold-out television tray and handed it to me. I downed it in two big gulps.

"Want more?" he asked with one eyebrow lifted.

The water hit my empty stomach and made me feel nauseated. I shook my head. "That might have been too much."

"You could have taken your time," he said, rolling his eyes.

I eased up slowly and slouched against the chair so my legs hanging down wouldn't pull against my stitches. Magnum took the seat next to me without asking. When I looked at him, I found him watching me.

"What?" I asked warily.

He grinned. "Why do you sound like I'm about to push you from this swing or something?"

I shrugged. "I can't quite remember all the details from yesterday. I seem to think you were upset at me."

He nodded. "I was. You were going to wuss out on catching the robbers."

"I had a good reason."

"Which you failed to tell me until after I got into trouble," he replied.

I glanced at him. "Sorry about that."

He grinned. "Hey, man, you saved my life. I can't exactly be mad at you after that."

"I saved your life at the fair," I pointed out. "But you were mad at me yesterday."

His eyebrows lowered. "How long you gonna hold that one against me?"

I laughed, then held my side when it gave a sharp jab of protest. "The fair? Another week, I think."

A smile broke across his face. He slouched next to me and stared at the orange-and-rose-painted horizon. The mountains caught the last of the sunlight in their dark purple embrace, throwing the world around us in golden light and soft shadow.

"Coach Farston put me in as starting quarterback," he said suddenly.

I looked at him in surprise. "That was quick."

He shrugged. "I was a backup before . . ." He frowned and glared hard at the sunset. "Before Kyle raced the train and got himself killed." He rolled his shoulders as if adjusting the weight of the memory. "Coach said I deserved a shot. I think he was happy to replace Beau. The guy's a tool."

I nodded. I had seen the jock throw a football into the air and then attempt to catch it with his mouth. It was no wonder he was missing a few teeth.

"How are you liking it?"

He nodded toward the sunset. "I'm late because Coach made me run laps for throwing too many ducks."

I thought of the coach forcing the leader of the Bullet gang to run laps. The idea was absurd, but Magnum actually seemed pleased. He looked at me and I could tell there was something else he wanted to say.

"Some of the other Bullets decided to join the team with me."

"That's great," I replied, puzzled by his expression.

He shook his head. "Except for Colt, Thompson, Uzi, and Snipe. They're saying we've lost the focus of the Bullets and they're planning to branch off and form their own gang."

His concern made sense. If the old members of his gang were causing trouble, he would probably run into them riding with me. Confronting his friends could make for a pretty awkward situation. "If we come against them, I'm expecting you to lie low. We don't need them figuring out your identity."

He gave me a grateful smile. "Sounds like a plan."

I eased down to the grass. The Ashbys' lawn was thick and in need of mowing, as Uncle Rick had reminded Cole many times. I didn't mind; it was quite comfortable to sit on. The sun had set and only hints of orange lingered on the horizon. Someone had flipped on the back-porch light, illuminating a tiny circle around the door. A shiver crept across my skin at the touch of the cooling grass on my back. I knew I should go inside, but the thought of lying on the cot for hours wasn't a pleasant one.

Magnum studied me from the chair swing. "You gonna stay out here all night?"

I shrugged and laid my head back on the grass to look at the first gleam of stars. "It's tempting."

The back door opened and I turned to see everyone come out. Cassidy and Mom were carrying cookie trays while Cole dropped a sack of chopped carrots on the steps. Jaren brought a bowl filled with potatoes cut into wedges.

"What's this?" I asked in surprise.

Uncle Rick came out last with a lighter in one hand and a bottle of lighter fluid in the other.

"We figured it'd be easier to bring dinner to you than vice versa," he answered. He gave me a stern look with a hint of humor dancing in his eyes. "But don't get used to it."

I pushed up gingerly and leaned against the chair swing. "Oh, I won't," I told him. "I'm still trying to decide whether this is real or

I'm delirious."

"You should probably take your pain meds then," he said.

"You haven't taken your medicine?" Mom asked, appalled.

Uncle Rick read the apprehensive look on my face and chuckled. "If he wants to tough it out, let him. Pain's good for a growing boy."

Mom shook her head. "If you don't need to be hurtin', why suffer?"

I stared at her. She gave me an uncomfortable look. "What?"

"You're starting to sound like a farmer," I told her.

Everyone laughed. Mom blushed and smiled at herself. "Is that a bad thing?"

"Definitely," Cassidy said, which brought more laughter from the group.

Aunt Lauren set one of the cookie sheets on the ground, then eased down next to me. Her hand rested on her stomach and she gave me a warm smile. "I'm not showing much yet, but it's amazing how much this little guy or girl is already kicking!"

"*She* likes tinfoil dinners," Cassidy said.

"It's not a she, it's a he," Cole argued.

"We don't know yet," Jaren put in calmly, "So just be prepared for either."

"What if it's twins?" their mom asked.

All three kids stared at her with shocked expressions. She laughed. "Don't worry. I'd be showing a lot more by now. I'm pretty sure we're just having one."

"Might be good to check," Uncle Rick said.

Aunt Lauren shook her head. "I want to be surprised about our baby's gender. Our midwife will let us know if she thinks we should get an ultrasound before the delivery."

Uncle Rick shook his head, but it was obvious this was a repeat of an old argument. He sighed and began pouring lighter fluid over the logs in the fire pit near the corner of the lawn.

"Can I light it? Can I light it?" Cole asked, jumping up and down.

Uncle Rick gave him a calculating look. "Normally I'd say no, but I'm worried you'll get your experience with fire elsewhere other than burning ditches."

"So I can!" Cole exclaimed.

His father grudgingly gave him the lighter. "Take it easy and light the fire in several places. We'll let it burn down before we start cooking."

"What are we cooking?" Magnum asked interestedly.

He sat on the grass next to Cassidy and watched her flatten a piece of tinfoil on one of the cookie sheets.

"Tinfoil dinners," she told him.

"Who wants to eat tinfoil?" he asked.

Cole laughed so hard, he fell over backwards.

Jaren shook his head and said, "We don't eat tinfoil. We use it to cook the food in."

Magnum gave a sheepish smile. "I knew that."

"We used to do these when we were kids," Mom said with a fond smile. I watched her load rolled balls of raw hamburger, some of the potatoes, a handful of carrots, and chopped onions onto a sheet of tinfoil. Then she sprinkled salt, pepper, and a spice mix on top. She folded everything into a square, then wrapped another sheet of tinfoil on the outside.

"Don't forget to write your name on it, Aunt Sarah," Cole said, helpfully supplying a marker. "I don't wanna get stuck with your crappy one."

"Cole!" Aunt Lauren chided.

"Well, mine's gonna be the best," he stated smugly.

Mom exchanged a look with Sarah. "That sounds a lot like us when we were his age."

"Don't remind me," Aunt Lauren said with a laugh.

Mom scooted her now-empty cookie sheet toward me. "Your turn."

Cassidy made sure I could reach everything. "I can't believe you haven't done this before," she said.

"We didn't exactly have a fire pit in our apartment," I replied.

Magnum grinned. "I guess I don't have an excuse. I'll have to go home and show Jess, Derek, and Tommy how to make these."

"I could help," Cassidy said.

Magnum stared at her, then glanced at me. I pretended to be busy piling potatoes and carrots on top of the hamburger on my tinfoil.

Silence stretched on for a few uncomfortable moments until Mom thought of something to say. "The ladies at the store showed me a report on the Black Rider. Apparently even though the robbers took out the security cameras before they hit the gas station, the store owner had installed a hidden camera in case they showed up."

I glanced at her as Cassidy helped me carefully crease the edges of my tinfoil square so that nothing would fall out. "What did the report say?" It was the first time Mom had voluntarily brought up the Black Rider. I figured I could count that as progress.

She pushed her hair out of her face with her arm as she wiped her hands clean on a dish towel. "Apparently it was quite the fight. The report from the *Bulletin* said that an imposter showed up dressed like the Black Rider and they beat him up pretty good before the real one appeared."

Everyone looked at Magnum; his black eye made it painfully obvious who the second Rider had been. He shrugged sheepishly. "I had to try."

Uncle Rick nodded. "I'm happy to know Kelson has somebody in his corner when it comes to taking on guys like this. You have nothing to be ashamed of."

Magnum dropped his eyes and nodded. A hint of pride showed in his expression as Cassidy wrote his name on his tinfoil dinner. He took it to the fire and dropped it by the others.

Mom nodded. "It's brave of you to do that. I'm glad you guys have each other."

Magnum cleared his throat. "This is getting a little too mushy. You guys have any marshmallows?"

Cassidy jumped up and ran for the house. Cole raced right behind her. We could hear the ensuing tussle in the kitchen.

"Just what that boy needs—more sugar," Uncle Rick remarked.

"We'll just make him run laps around the house before bed," Aunt Lauren answered. They both chuckled at the thought even though I knew they would never do it. Aunt Lauren leaned against her husband and slipped her hand through his. He positioned himself so he could support her and traced his fingers along her arm. It wasn't often that I saw them so affectionate with each other. The sight made me miss Madelyn all the more.

Cassidy ran back out with a bag of marshmallows. Cole followed slowly behind, obviously upset that a girl had beat him.

She tossed the bag at Magnum. He caught it and followed her to the fire where they proceeded to slide them on roasting sticks. Cole grabbed a handful from the bag and stuck as many marshmallows as he could fit onto one stick before holding it over the fire.

"This is nice," Aunt Lauren said with a contented sigh.

Uncle Rick nodded. "It's been way too long since we ate outside."

"Thank you for doing this," I said, touched by all the effort they put into it so I could stay outside. A cool evening breeze ran across my skin and I shivered.

Mom dropped a long-sleeved shirt on my lap and said, "Last thing you need is to catch a cold," she said with a worried smile. I hadn't even heard her leave to get it.

I pulled the shirt over my head, and then she helped me work my arms through the sleeves. It was embarrassing to have my mother dress me, but the warmth of the shirt was greatly welcome. "I think it'll take more than a cold to kill me," I said.

"That's for sure," Cole replied, hurrying back over with a dozen smoldering marshmallows on his stick. "If jumping through a window, getting shot, flying off a roof, or getting stuck with a knife didn't do it, a cold won't."

"Cole," Aunt Lauren said with a shake of her head.

Cole shrugged and shoved a marshmallow in his mouth. "What?" he asked around the sticky mouthful. "It's the truth."

"Just the same," Mom replied calmly, "I'd rather not take the risk."

"I think they're done," Jaren called from beside the fire after a few more minutes had passed. He pulled one tinfoil dinner onto the grass with a pair of barbecue tongs and opened it carefully to reveal the steaming interior. The wonderful scent of cooked meat, potatoes, onions, and carrots filled the air.

"I'm getting mine!" Cole yelled. He scrambled to his feet and tossed his full marshmallow stick to the grass, already forgotten.

"I'll get yours," Uncle Rick said to his wife. He carried one of the cookie trays to the fire and loaded a few of the tinfoil packages onto it. He set his and Aunt Lauren's on one tray, then handed me the other one.

Mom sat next to me and proceeded to open hers with a fork so she didn't get burned. I followed her example and did the same. My mouth was watering from the aromas by the time I had the folds undone. I breathed deeply and smiled.

"Bon appetit," Aunt Lauren said. "I think this is exactly what the baby ordered for dinner."

"So it's a boy," Cole said.

"Girls like tinfoil dinners too," Cassidy pointed out.

"Yeah, but meat and potatoes are a man's food," Cole said.

Magnum snorted. "What are the women supposed to eat?"

Cole grinned around his fork. "Donuts."

"That's all?" the Bullet leader asked, humor shining in his eyes.

Cole nodded. "Then they'll be slow and fat and can stop chasing me at school."

"Do they catch you?" Magnum asked curiously.

The blush that stole across the young boy's cheeks was enough of an answer to send everyone laughing.

"And here I thought you were fast," Jaren said.

"I am fast," Cole replied indignantly. "They're just faster."

Magnum laughed so hard that he choked on a piece of potato; Cassidy patted his back until he stopped coughing. I doubted it helped, but I noticed he didn't stop her. I glanced at Uncle Rick to see if he was aware of what was going on. The way he pointedly avoided looking at the pair said enough. I made a mental note to talk to Magnum about that later.

"This is amazing," I said. I ate quickly, astonished at my appetite. Jake settled at my feet and caught the pieces of hamburger I tossed to him. For some reason, it meant a lot to me that the dog preferred my company. I saw Uncle Rick noting the same thing; he gave me an approving nod.

Aunt Lauren slid her dinner to me when I was done. "You need to keep up your strength to heal," she said. She rubbed her stomach. "Besides, my eyes are always bigger than my stomach. I think the baby's taking up most of the room."

I looked at Uncle Rick. He waved his fork at me. "You'd better eat it or I'm going to, and I don't need more food." He patted his stomach meaningfully.

I grinned and finished Aunt Lauren's tinfoil dinner. Exhaustion filled my limbs when I was done. I settled back on the grass and listened to the others talking quietly around the fire. Mom brought out blankets to chase away the night chill. I rested under a big white-and-red patchwork quilt that looked warmer than all the rest. I knew it wasn't an accident; warmth filled me at my mom's kindness.

I wasn't sure when I fell asleep, but the stars were shining bright overhead when Mom touched my shoulder. "Time to go inside," she said softly.

A glance showed that Magnum had already gone and Cassidy and the boys were in the house. Uncle Rick bent and took my arm, pulling me carefully to my feet. He helped me inside even though I didn't ask for assistance. I think he knew how much I hated asking; the farmer had my same sense of pride, whether it was misplaced or not.

I lay back on the cot and smiled when Mom settled the blanket over me. "I'm a little old to be tucked in," I said.

She shook her head. "I'm not too old to be your mother, so you're going to have to put up with it once in a while."

I laughed, then held my side until the throbbing stopped. Mom picked up one of the pain pills from the end table and handed it to me with a cup of water. "Take it, for me," she said. "I hate to see you hurting."

I gave in and put the pill in my mouth. She watched as I took several swallows from the cup, and then she set it back on the end table.

"Have a good night," she said, kissing me on the forehead.

"You too," I replied.

I waited until she was gone and the lights were out before I slipped the pill from under my tongue and tossed it in the fireplace.

Chapter Eighteen

MY CELL PHONE BEEPED urgently from the end table. I reached for it with a lazy groan. Last night had worn me out more than I thought, and I spent the morning sleeping in until ten o'clock, eating a plate of pancakes, then sleeping again through lunchtime. It was the laziest I ever remembered being, but the rest felt good.

Magnum's name showed on the screen. I pushed the answer button. "Hello?" I said groggily.

"Kelson, you've gotta get over here," Magnum said in a hushed voice filled with panic.

I sat up quickly, then winced at the protest in my side. "What's going on?" I demanded.

"The Brown Hawk gang stormed the pep rally at school. They're looking for me," Magnum said in a quick whisper.

I pushed the speaker phone button and set the cell phone on the end table while I pulled on my freshly cleaned riding pants as quickly as possible. "Where are you?" I asked.

"The entire student body is in the gymnasium. They have the doors barricaded and they said they'll shoot anyone who pulls out a cell phone. They have Principal Dawson and the teachers in the middle of the floor at gunpoint."

"Hang up so you don't get shot. I'll call the sheriff."

"Hurry," Magnum said. "They're acting crazy and saying they'll hurt someone if the Black Rider doesn't show himself."

I grabbed my vest and jacket, wincing as I pulled them on. I rushed to the mudroom and picked up my shoes without slowing. I hurried outside as fast as the pain in my angry side would let me. I hadn't seen the motorcycle since I wrecked it. I could only hope it was in working condition.

I found it hidden behind the barn where hay had been stacked to form a convenient hiding place. The left side was scratched, but other than that, it appeared to be fine. I hopped on one foot and pulled on a shoe, ignoring the way my side protested at the process. I slipped on the other one, then stomped it on the ground to settle my foot inside. The force caused a pain so sharp that I had to lean against the barn to catch my breath.

"Come on," I growled to myself. "They're in trouble."

I pulled out my phone and called Jagger, grateful he at least had a landline. He was surprised to hear from me, but listened carefully and said he would be ready when I reached the junkyard.

I jumped on the motorcycle, glad it started right up. I fastened my helmet, heedless of the pain when I raised my arms. I was pretty sure I would be feeling a lot worse by the time the day was over.

Jagger was as good as his word. He met me in front of the shack and handed over a backpack of supplies.

"Take care a yurself," he said, concern bright in his eyes. "I phoned the sheriff. He said they'd be there when ya arrived."

"Thanks, Jagger. It's going to be all right."

He nodded, but it was obvious by his expression that he was unconvinced. "Ya got yur vest?"

"Always," I said, forcing a smile.

He nodded and I drove out of the junkyard.

WHEN I REACHED THE school, police cars, fire engines, and two ambulances were already out front. The sheriff waved me down as soon as he spotted me. Deputies crowded around us.

"We're waiting for SWAT to show up. We have all the exits covered, and a team is standing by," Sheriff Bowley told me. His face was pale, but he was calm and in control. "Jagger said it was the Brown Hawk gang."

I nodded. "That's what Magnum told me. They're looking for the Black Rider."

His expression tightened. "This has gotten out of hand."

"Tell me about it," I replied. "Has anyone been in contact since Magnum's call?"

"Mr. Monroe got a call out right after we heard from Jagger, but they took his phone away and told us they would shoot anyone else who tried, so we would be better off not trying to call in." His expression said there was more he didn't want to tell me.

"What else did they say?" I pressed.

He let out a breath through his teeth. "That they would let everyone go if we sent in the Black Rider."

"I'm going in."

Sheriff Bowley shook his head. "We're waiting for SWAT before we begin negotiations."

My gaze was hidden beneath the tinted visor, so I used Uncle Rick's steel-laced tone. "If I can save lives or stall the gang, it's worth it."

He shook his head. "They're armed. You could get shot."

"I've been shot," I replied. "Better me than anyone else."

"I'm not going to let you do that."

I revved the motorcycle. "I'm driving through the glass if you don't open that door," I said in a deadly calm voice.

"I can't do that," he said.

I lowered my head and rolled the throttle, then released the clutch. The bike sped toward the two glass doors that made up the main entrance to the gymnasium. Two deputies stood in the way. At the last minute, one of them pulled a door open and let me through.

I paused just inside the hallway and grabbed a gun from my backpack. My heart began to pound harder at the weight of the weapon. I pulled off my right glove and shoved it in my pocket. The gauze around my left palm made it necessary to keep the other glove on.

Shouts and screams of fear sounded from the gymnasium doors at the end of the hallway. My heart raced at the thought of Cassidy and the other students in trouble. I shoved the gun into the waist of my pants and gunned the motorcycle.

I hit the gymnasium doors without slowing. They flew open with a splintering crash. My motorcycle roared across the polished wooden floor. Time slowed to the pace of my heartbeat. I saw the frantic faces of the two gang members who had been guarding the doors. The sound of my motorcycle was loud in the gym, echoing against the brick walls and bouncing back with the sound of a jet engine.

Gang members turned, their faces reflecting their shock. Several lifted weapons and aimed them in my direction. I ripped the gun from my waist and, holding in the clutch with my left, fired with my right hand.

Members of the Brown Hawk gang scattered. Several had the presence of mind to return fire; luckily I was a moving target and most of the bullets whizzed past me. One struck the headlight of my motorcycle, shattering it. Another clipped the side of my helmet.

Brown Hawk members surrounded the teachers and Principal Dawson in the middle of the gymnasium. The principal was sporting a bruised face and his usually pressed suit was ripped. Several of the teachers were in a similar condition. Anger flared in my chest at the way they had been treated.

I gunned the motorcycle toward the group. Before the Brown Hawks could react, I shot two of them in the shoulder. A Brown Hawk built like a bear aimed a gun at my head. I jumped off the motorcycle and slammed a fist into his face before my feet hit the ground. My momentum knocked him back several feet before he slumped unconscious to the ground. My side ached from the force; I held a hand to it in the hopes of keeping the stitches from tearing.

My motorcycle slid on its side to the far wall. Gang members rushed me from both sides. For a split second, my promise to Madelyn surfaced. I wouldn't cause her more pain. I would do my best to get back to her.

I ducked a punch and hit one attacker in the stomach, then spun around and caught another on the side of his head with my elbow. I chopped an arm hard enough to send a gun flying, then bashed the man in the face with my own gun. I turned and shot, catching one Brown Hawk in the shoulder and another in the leg. Both fell screaming to the ground. I fought to catch my breath at the pain screaming in my side, but there wasn't time to rest.

"Run," I shouted to the teachers and principal. With their captors running for cover, they took off toward the bleachers, intent on protecting their students.

I ran for the motorcycle. Several Brown Hawk members stood in my way. I clipped two with lucky shots, sending them sprawling to the floor. Another dropped to one knee and shot. I hit him in the shoulder and he fell back with a cry of pain. The bullet he got off tugged at my jacket on its way past.

The sound of the rubber bullets Jagger had loaded into my gun echoed strangely in my helmet as they hit their targets. A part of me that was detached from the danger was grateful I wasn't using lethal ammunition, though Jagger had assured me the rubber bullets would kill just as easily if I wasn't careful with my aim.

I ran past students crouched in fear on the bleachers that lined the north side of the gymnasium. The football team was in uniform and shielded the cheerleaders behind them. The Brown Hawk gang had surprised the school in the middle of a pep rally. My heart clenched at the sight of boyfriends hiding their girlfriends behind them, protecting them with their bodies. The teachers reached them and began pulling students to hide underneath the bleachers. Principal Dawson directed the students where to find shelter.

I pulled the motorcycle upright. The movement sent a sharp, angry pain through my side. I blew out a breath and turned back. A teacher ran past me. I grabbed his arm and realized it was Mr. Monroe, my chemistry teacher who had braved the threats of the gang and called the police in the first place.

"Get the students out through that door," I said, indicating the one I had smashed. "I'll keep them busy."

"I—I'll try," he said.

Several gang members hid behind the bleachers on the opposite side from the students. One cried out in pain and fell over, then another. I fought back a grim smile at the sight of Bullet members in football gear beating them down. One Brown Hawk grappled with Magnum, trying to drive a thumb into his eye as he held the Bullet leader in a headlock. I took careful aim; the bullet struck the gang member in the thigh. He fell to the ground screaming. Magnum gave me a thumbs-up.

Two more Brown Hawks had taken cover behind the podium near the door. A knee showed. It was a small target and I wasn't sure of the bullet's accuracy. I aimed, let out a slow breath, and squeezed the trigger steadily as Jagger had taught me. The gang member jumped with a scream of agony. His move forced the other member into the open. He froze and stared at me, knowing he couldn't reach cover before I shot him. He dropped to the ground and put his hands behind his head.

Under Mr. Monroe's supervision, students began to flee the gym. Teachers shielded them as they ran, placing themselves between the students and the danger. From my vantage point, I could see them rush down the hall. Deputies opened the doors as soon as they drew near. Sheriff Bowley's team rushed in. Soon, the Brown Hawk members would be overrun.

I surveyed the room. My heart slowed at the sight of two Brown Hawks taking aim at the students. One stood on the bleachers while the other was partially hidden at the end. I pulled the trigger twice.

The first bullet struck the one on the bleachers hard enough to spin him around. The other hit a bleacher close to the second Brown Hawk and bounced off. He ducked out of sight. I revved the motorcycle and sped down the length of the bleachers. I reached the end in time to see the man pick up a folding chair and throw it.

I dropped the gun and grabbed the brake, holding up an arm to block the chair. It hit my shoulder and side. I spun the motorcycle on its back tire and kicked the man in the chin hard enough to snap his neck back and send him to the floor. Magnum, Mauser, and Saw ran out to make sure he stayed down.

"You better get outta here," Magnum said. He pointed toward the entrance. Deputies were rushing in. Two grabbed the gang members by the doors and handcuffed them. The one I had shot in the knee still howled in pain. Other deputies helped the students outside and protected the teachers as they made their way through the broken doors.

I saluted Magnum and gunned the motorcycle to the middle of the gym floor, then spun it in a tight circle. I doubted the principal would mind the rubber I left given the circumstances. I waited until the students were clear, then sped through the doors. I passed several deputies in the hallway and was grateful they knew not to shoot me. A surprised deputy at the doors pulled them open before I hit the glass. I flew down the sidewalk and across the grass, then jumped the curb and raced through the parking lot.

I smiled at the sight of SWAT trucks speeding toward the school. I waved when I passed them, regardless of the stupidity of such an action. I was just glad someone was on their way to help the sheriff with the rest of the madness.

Chapter Nineteen

WHEN I REACHED THE Ashbys', everyone was in a state of panic. I was swarmed the second I stopped in the driveway.

"Where have you been?" Mom demanded. "I've been worried sick! You can't just disappear like that."

"We kept trying to reach your cell phone," Aunt Lauren said.

Uncle Rick regarded me with a solemn expression that said I'd better have a good explanation for making everyone worry.

I ducked my head to pull off my helmet with the least amount of stress to my throbbing side. Mom gave a frustrated huff and pulled the helmet off for me; she was about to throw it to the ground when Uncle Rick caught it out of her hands.

"What's this?" he asked, pointing to the bullet mark along the left side.

I could feel the dampness through my jacket and knew I had torn stitches. The thought of getting them redone made me nauseated. I didn't have Madelyn to run to when I needed her. I wondered how she was doing. I missed her so much it hurt.

"What is this?" Uncle Rick yelled.

I went with the truth. "A bullet hit it," I said.

"What?" Mom gasped.

Aunt Lauren's hand flew to her mouth. "Where were you?"

Uncle Rick watched me carefully. "At the school," I told them. "The Brown Hawk gang had everyone held hostage in the gym. Magnum called me, so I went to help."

I climbed off the bike amid their stares.

"Go call the school," Uncle Rick told Aunt Lauren. She took off for the house. "Were you shot?" he asked me quietly.

I shook my head. "But I think I need to go to the hospital this time. I'm sure I tore some stitches."

"Kelson," Mom said with more worry than reprimand.

Uncle Rick checked me over quickly with the proficiency of a farmer used to surveying his cattle for ailments. He unzipped my jacket and looked at the blood soaking through my shirt. "Did you tear them all?" he asked, more to himself than to me.

Mom helped him gently lift the edge of the vest, and then he said a string of words I had never heard together. Aunt Lauren would have been appalled.

I cracked a smile. "What does that mean?"

His eyebrows creased. "That you're an idiot and should let the cops handle things once in a while."

"They are now," I replied. "And SWAT showed up as I was leaving."

"Let me get some towels to help slow the bleeding, then we'll head to the hospital," Uncle Rick said, hurrying toward the house faster than I had ever seen him move.

"Kelson, I'm tired of this," Mom said. I looked up at the tone of her voice. Her eyebrows were pinched together and she shook her head. "I can't stand seeing you get hurt anymore. I'm tired of you running off and worrying if you're going to get yourself killed! You aren't careful and you don't think when you get into these situations." Tears shone in her eyes, tempering her anger.

"I do think, Mom," I protested. One side of me said she was just concerned as a mother should be, but the other was hurt at the fact that she doubted me. "I think of Maddy and what it would do to her if I was killed."

Her face washed with white. I flinched at the pain I saw on her face. "Mom, I just—"

"Kelson, get in the truck," Uncle Rick said, jogging back to us. He pressed a towel against my side, set another one on top, and opened the door to his new Dodge Ram.

"You sure you want me to get blood all over your new truck?" I asked.

He rolled his eyes. "Just get in."

Mom followed me inside and pulled the door shut without a word. Aunt Lauren appeared back outside and Uncle Rick hurried to her. Mom unrolled the window so we could listen.

"Cassidy is okay. She called before I got to the phone. The police say the situation is under control and all the gang members are arrested. The kids are safe. They're sending the buses home— where are you taking Kelson?" she asked in surprise.

"He needs to go to the hospital before he bleeds out in my truck," Uncle Rick explained.

"What should I do?" Aunt Lauren asked in a voice close to tears.

"Wait here for the kids. Call Sarah's cell phone when they get home so I know everyone's really all right," Uncle Rick told her.

He kissed his wife quickly and climbed in the driver's seat. The diesel engine rumbled to life.

"Wait!" Aunt Lauren called. She waved something in the air. I squinted and recognized my helmet. A quick check showed I was still in my Black Rider outfit. We had almost blown my cover.

"Good thinking," Uncle Rick said, accepting the helmet and handing it to Mom. She stared at the bullet gouge across the side like it truly had taken my life.

"I'm all right, Mom," I said gently.

She shook her head with tears in her eyes. "You're not," she said. "And I don't know what to do about it."

Chapter Twenty

"AS MUCH AS I like to redo my handiwork, this is pushing it," Dr. Carrison said.

My side was numb, re-stitched, and wrapped. "Thanks again," I replied. My voice cracked from my dry throat. My head felt strangely light, as though it were filled with helium. I knew I was in shock. The emotions of the last few days hammered against me. I put a hand to my head in an effort to slow my thoughts.

"Drink some water," Dr. Carrison said with a kind smile. "You'll feel better. It's been quite the day."

I complied and sipped from a plastic cup on a side table, then rested my head back against the flat pillow on the bed. Besides the doctor, no one had been allowed inside the room after I took my helmet off. I felt like the silence was too much, but if someone talked about anything that had happened in the last few days, I was going to lose it. I had never felt so close to a mental breakdown before.

Dr. Carrison checked my vitals. "Everything looks fine. I'd like you to stay here for a bit until I decide you're fit to go home."

The way he emphasized the last few words caught my attention.

I gave a small smile. "If you think like that, I might be here a while."

He nodded with a touch of truth in his eyes. "You just might." He gave a kind smile. "If you're feeling up to it, I have a visitor who is very anxious to see you."

I didn't know who it would be. I didn't feel able to talk to anyone. I couldn't decide on my emotional state; my heart hammered in my chest. Whenever I thought of the school in danger, I couldn't quite catch my breath. I felt like the students were still under threat despite the fact that the school had been emptied and the gang arrested. I couldn't find my center of calm.

Dr. Carrison read the look on my face. "Trust me. This is one visitor who will help."

He stepped outside, and my heart stopped entirely when Madelyn entered.

Tears filled my eyes to match those running down Madelyn's cheeks. She ran to the bed and ducked under my arm, resting against my uninjured side as sobs tore from her. "I know," I whispered, touching her cheek. I curled around her, holding her tight with every last bit of strength I possessed. I let the emotions flood from me, the fear, anger, frustration, and helpless fury that filled me when Magnum had told me about the situation at the school.

Every bit of loss I felt at Madelyn's absence rushed away with her embrace. Her hands tangled in my hospital gown, pulling me closer as she cried. "I thought about you," I said, my voice shaking. "I thought about you when I drove through those doors. I knew you would want me to save them if I could."

She nodded against my chest. "When I heard, I didn't know what to do. Dad was at Aunt Masey's when Cassidy called, and he drove me straight here. He knew I couldn't stay away."

"I'm so glad you didn't," I said. I wondered when the tears

would stop rolling down my cheeks. My chest was tight and my arms shook as I held Madelyn.

She took a shuddering breath. "Dad wants me to move in with Aunt Masey."

I shook my head before she stopped speaking. "You can't move. You can't leave Sparrow. I'm in Sparrow—*we're* in Sparrow." I took a breath, trying to think. "I love you and I know you love me. We'll make it work. You can live at the Ashbys or something."

"I know," she said, looking up at me with tear-filled eyes. "I told him I couldn't go, but he's insisting that it'd be better for me to get away from the house for a while."

I swallowed against the knot in my throat, but it refused to go away. I wanted to cry, to shout, to hit something, but I just held her, both of us trapped by our circumstances.

Whenever I closed my eyes, I saw gunfire, bullets hitting my chest at the fair and flying past my head at the school. I felt the weight of the gun in my hands. I fired at headlights and cans. I heard the echo of rubber bullets against the wooden gymnasium floor. Screams of fear sounded over and over again.

I closed my eyes tight, trying to shut them out. Madelyn was going to leave me. The phrase repeated itself over and over in my mind.

"I don't want to go," she sobbed. I held her closer, lost in the sound of her crying.

Dr. Carrison left us alone. Eventually we both cried ourselves out and could only lay there numb and trying to cope with everything that had been thrown at us. I couldn't lose Madelyn. I wouldn't.

"If you go, I'll go too. I'll visit you every night."

She sniffed, but a hint of light showed in her eyes. "She lives in Warrell. It's four hours away."

"That's just a short bike ride," I said, winning a small smile from her. I sighed and forced myself to ask. "When?"

She closed her eyes. "I'm going to school Monday to gather all my things."

I rested my chin on her head, taking a deep breath of her vanilla scent. "I'll help you."

She shook her head. "You'll be resting; at least you should be."

"I'll be there," I replied.

A tap sounded on the door. We both looked up to see Mr. West standing in the doorway. His eyes tightened slightly at the sight of Madelyn lying in my arms on the bed, but he didn't say anything.

"Time to go," he said quietly.

Madelyn kissed me lightly on the cheek as she rose. "I love you," she whispered quietly enough that her dad couldn't hear. I listened to her footsteps fade down the hallway and felt empty inside.

"HEY, DUDE," MAGNUM SAID when he walked through the door. He made himself comfortable on the chair next to the bed and looked around. "Nice crib."

I forced down the sorrow I felt at Madelyn's departure and smiled. "Thanks. I hired a decorator."

"Yeah," he replied. "Because your taste is crap."

I motioned toward the beeping monitor near the bed. "It adds a nice ambiance."

He lifted an eyebrow. "I'm surprised you even know a word like that."

I shrugged. "I wasn't raised on a farm."

"Oh, the *ambiance* wasn't good enough for you?"

I laughed again and winced at the pain. "You'd better leave.

Your sense of humor is killing me."

"I don't have a sense of humor," he replied dryly, then he grinned.

"How'd you get in here? I thought they only let in family."

"I told them I was your estranged brother," he said.

I couldn't help laughing again despite the pain. "And they didn't think it was weird that you were visiting me if you were estranged?"

He shrugged. "I think they got stuck on the word. I don't know what it means—I just threw it in there because it sounded important."

Exhausted, I rested my head on the pillow and turned to look at him. "Thanks for coming."

A furrow formed between his eyebrows. "I shouldn't have called you. I'm not sure what I thought you could do." He jerked his head in the direction of the school. "Definitely not that."

"What, too dramatic?"

A begrudging smile touched his lips. "Yes, but it was effective."

"Think the principal will charge me for the doors?"

He laughed. "And for cleaning the court. You made a mess with those tires." He sobered. "But man, you were a good shot."

"I had a good teacher," I replied.

He shook his head. "I handed you an Uzi and about let you kill us all."

I chuckled. "Not you, idiot. Jagger."

He laughed. "You mean the redneck with the ammunition warehouse beneath his junkyard? Sure, learn from him instead of your best friend."

"You're my best friend?" I asked with enough sarcastic doubt that he laughed again.

"I don't see Martin lining up to shake your hand, although he would if he knew who you were."

"It was close," I said, thinking of the factory. "I owe you for that."

He shrugged. "I think you evened it out when you shot the guy who had me in a headlock. Although you could've hit me if you were two inches off."

"I took a chance," I said nonchalantly.

He let out an incredulous laugh. "I hope it was more than just luck!"

I gave him a serious look. "Magnum, if there was any doubt I couldn't hit him, I wouldn't have shot, trust me."

"I do," he replied with enough emotion that both of us grew uncomfortable. He cleared his throat. "I, uh," he paused and took a breath, then said, "I think I'm going to use my free time to concentrate on football."

I let his words sink in. "You mean you don't want to be the Black Rider's sidekick anymore?"

His hands curled into fists; at my grin, he realized I was giving him a hard time and he took a calming breath before he nodded. "You have a death wish, man. I don't think I could keep up with you. Will you be all right riding without a *partner*?" he asked, stressing the last word.

I nodded. "I'll be fine. I don't have a death wish," I said, but we were both unconvinced. I held out a hand. "It's been great riding with you."

He shook my hand firmly. "You too. And it's not like this'll be the last time we see each other. I still have to pick on you at school."

"Maybe I should sign up for karate so I can explain it when I beat you down."

He chuckled. "Unfortunately, Sparrow doesn't have a karate instructor. The best you could do is yoga. You could yoga me to death."

"That sounds pleasant."

He stood up, then sighed and grabbed something from his jacket. He held out a bunch of very wilted flowers, some of which were missing petals. "Jessica said to give these to you."

I stared at him. "Your sister knows I'm the Black Rider?"

He shook his head. "I told her you had the flu and she said they would make you feel better." He looked very uncomfortable holding the flowers. When I didn't take them, he set them on a side table and wiped his hand on his pants. "Don't ask me why girls do what they do. I just know she'd kill me if I didn't give them to you."

"We don't want the toughest member of the Fisher family on your case."

He grimaced. "Shut up."

"Please tell her thank you."

He stalked out without looking back.

Chapter Twenty-one

THE SHERIFF WAS THE last person I expected to see, but he walked in with an apologetic smile. "Your mom said you were taking visitors."

I sat up, holding my side. "I thought you'd still be at the school," I said, shaking his hand.

He shrugged and sat down on the chair Magnum had vacated. "The FBI pretty much has the place closed down. Sounds like they'll be taking pictures and collecting evidence for the rest of the night."

"How'd you know I was here?" I asked curiously.

He studied the wall for a minute. "I saw the blood on the gas station door. After you left the school, I called your cell and then the Ashby house. When no one answered, I figured you either got shot or messed up whatever happened at the gas station." He grimaced. "Although, when I called Dr. Carrison, he was very tight-lipped about everything. It seems you have more friends around here than I do."

I shook my head. "I only have a few, and I think I just lost another one."

He glanced at the door. "You mean Magnum? He mentioned he wanted to trade his motorcycle for another CBR. Think I can get him to take a scooter?"

I chuckled at the thought. "He might lose a bit of cred with the Bullets."

"Oh, I don't know about that. He could wear one of those half helmets and get passed by tractors."

We both grinned at the thought. "He thinks I have a death wish," I said. I lifted the edge of my shirt and showed him the bandages around my side. "Magnum called me right after your help with Mitch West. He said he found the robbers and I told him we should call the cops. He called me out for being a coward and said he was going to take them on himself, so I had to go."

"Naturally," the sheriff said, though his sarcasm was good-natured.

"There was a pretty entertaining knife fight, and I made the stupid mistake of turning my back on an armed assailant to take down an unarmed one."

He nodded. "Happens sometimes in the heat of the moment. That's why kids aren't supposed to be vigilantes."

"I know better," I said.

He shrugged. "Just like I knew not to let you in that gymnasium, yet here we are." A smile raised his mustache. "That was pretty smart, using those rubber bullets."

"Jagger's idea. I told him I didn't want to hurt anyone, but it was going to be dangerous. He said he had just the thing."

He nodded. "I need to commend him for that." He ran a hand across his beard, then gave a small sigh. "I came here for another reason."

I wondered how many times I would hear that. Tension tightened my shoulders.

The sheriff continued. "Bustin' up gang wars, getting stabbed in a knife fight, and now single-handedly taking down school shooters? I think you've done enough for a dozen lifetimes, Kelson."

The tension tightened. "Are you telling me to give up being the Black Rider?" I couldn't hide the loss that filled my voice. Somehow, I felt like the Black Rider was the true part of me, not the coward who was beat up by bullies and fumbled the simplest farm jobs. If I gave up being the Black Rider, I didn't know if I could accept what was left.

The sheriff slammed a hand down on the table, catching me by surprise. "Dang it, Kelson," he barked. "It's driving me crazy. I should be giving you a medal, not telling you to lie low because the FBI wants to take the Black Rider in."

I stared at him. "Why?"

"A million reasons," he explained. "You're a vigilante who took on a terrorist group at a school."

"But I used rubber bullets and I was trying to save the students," I protested.

He nodded. "It's still a very serious situation, and they weren't satisfied when I told them I didn't know who you were."

"What if they followed you here?" I expected to see FBI agents walking through the door at any moment.

He shook his head. "They're busy right now, but I'd recommend getting home as soon as possible." He shook his head. "Just lie low for real this time. No Black Rider stuff for a while. You're a good kid and I don't want you taken in for this."

"Thanks for the warning," I said, my mind reeling from what he had told me. I let out a slow breath. "I appreciate the visit."

He rose and shook my hand. "I'm glad you're open to the suggestion. You're not without friends, no matter what happens to the Black Rider," he reassured me.

"Thanks."

Mom met me out in the parking lot in her little green car. I eased onto the seat, then leaned my head back against the rest as she drove slowly down the road.

"I'm sorry, Mom," I said after a few minutes of silence.

She let out a quiet breath and glanced at me. I was still wearing my black helmet and gear, but we were far enough from the hospital that it no longer mattered. I eased the helmet off my head and held it in my hands.

"Sometimes I feel like I lost you when we lost Zoey," she said quietly. She glanced at me again as if she immediately regretted the statement.

"I think you're right," I replied, staring at my reflection in the helmet's visor.

She sat in surprised silence for a few minutes. When she broke it, her voice was gentle. "It hurt when you said you thought of Maddy and what it would do to her if you were killed. I was foolish to hope you'd think of me."

I opened my mouth to protest, but she held up her hand, her look asking me to wait. I obeyed and kept silent.

She continued, "I was wrong to think I would be first on your mind after all we've been through. I'm just grateful that you care about her enough to think before you do something dangerous." Her eyes glittered in the passing streetlight, showing tears she refused to let fall.

I rubbed my eyes. "Do you know what I kept thinking when Dr. Carrison stitched me up at the Ashbys'?"

She shook her head silently.

I clenched my hands around the helmet. "It was, how many times would my mom have to worry about losing me?" I rubbed a thumb over the groove the bullet had cut into the black paint. "I know I'm not the easiest son to have."

She cracked a smile. "You are the easiest son," she said. She gave the helmet a wry look. "It's the Black Rider I'm not so sure of."

I chuckled and leaned my head against the seat. "Don't worry. The sheriff mentioned I may have to give it up anyway." At her questioning look, I frowned at the night outside the window. "It seems the FBI wants to bring the Black Rider in for shooting a gun in the school."

Her mouth fell open. "You saved those students' lives."

"I know, but I definitely crossed some lines."

"You risked your life," she said, her voice rising.

I held up my hands in surprise at her reaction and fought back a laugh. "Mom, I thought that's what you wanted."

"Not like this," she protested. "You deserve better than this."

Her sentiments echoed mine, but I didn't say anything. I merely smiled and closed my eyes. The hum of the tires lulled me into a dreamless daze. We pulled up to the Ashby house that was blissfully quiet due to the late hour.

When we got inside, I collapsed on the cot. In the time it took Mom to let Aunt Lauren and Uncle Rick know we were home, I was half asleep. Mom came back to the living room and kissed me on the forehead, smoothing my hair back the way she used to when I was a child.

I forced my eyes open. "Hey, Mom."

She gave me a warm smile. "Get some sleep, Kel. You need it."

I closed my eyes and was out before she left the room.

FOOTSTEPS SOUNDED ON THE carpet. I didn't know how

much time had passed. I opened my eyes and saw Cassidy looking in the door as though uncertain whether she should enter. When she saw I was awake, she rushed to the bed.

Tears filled her eyes before she spoke. "I was there, Kel. You saved us from them. I was so scared."

She buried her face in her hands as she cried. I patted her arm uncertainly, not knowing what else to do. "They're gone now," I said. The words sounded pathetic compared to what she was feeling. I wondered if they needed to treat all the students for post-traumatic stress. The annoying voice in the back of my mind said I probably could use it too.

"How do you stay so brave?" she asked without looking at me. The light of the slowly burning fire in the fireplace reflected in her tears.

"I was scared to death," I told her honestly.

She looked up at me and sniffed. "Really?"

I nodded. "I was afraid they'd shoot someone or hit a student trying to get me."

"It was close," she said, wiping her eyes.

"Too close. I think going in might not have been a good idea," I told her ruefully.

She shook her head. "They said they were going to start shooting students if the Black Rider didn't step forward. When no one spoke up, they made all the teachers stand in the middle of the gym and said they were going to shoot them one by one while we watched."

Her words made a knot form in my stomach. I had almost ridden in on a mass teacher slaughter. "It would have been because of me."

She shook her head and defiance sparked in her eyes. "You didn't make them come to the school with guns—or try to set up

Sparrow as a drug trading center, for that matter." The seriousness in her gaze gripped my heart like a fist. "You saved us from their selfishness. Don't ever forget that, because the students at Sparrow High won't."

I blinked back tears that burned in my eyes. I refused to cry, but the stark honesty in my cousin's words meant everything to me.

I COULDN'T SLEEP AFTER Cassidy left. Thoughts of Madelyn leaving kept circling through my head. I finally rose and made my way to the four-wheeler. I had to sit on it for a minute to wait for my head to clear. Going from nearly bleeding to death, stitches at the Ashbys' house, riding through the gymnasium like a madman and fighting off a gang out for blood, then getting the stitches redone definitely didn't leave me with much to work with as far as mental clarity.

Jake ran up to the four-wheeler as I pulled out of the driveway. If anyone in the house heard, no one tried to stop me.

I drove to the edge of the Wests' property, then sat on the four-wheeler wondering how I was going to climb up the tree to Madelyn's room. Just walking to the house looked exhausting, but thoughts of Madelyn gave me no choice.

I set a hand on the tree and was about to put a leg up when a voice spoke from beneath the shadowed branches.

"I think climbing trees might be outside of doctor's orders," Madelyn said.

Giving a silent prayer of thanks for not having to climb, I turned and peered through the leaves. The expression on Madelyn's face made everything stand still.

"What are you doing here?" she asked, her voice breathless and full at the same time.

"I couldn't sleep without seeing you again," I answered honestly.

She took my hand as if she needed to reassure herself that I was real. "I hoped you would come," she admitted, lowering her lashes to peer up at me through them. "I knew it was foolish after everything you've been through, but I hoped anyway."

Her words gripped my heart. "How long would you have waited here?"

"All night," she answered softly.

Without a word, I led her across the lawn to the four-wheeler. Jake sat down by where Buck was still chained to his dog house. Neither animal made a sound, as if they knew how important this night was to us.

Madelyn climbed on behind me and I drove us along the path carved by our footsteps. The long grass rustled against the four-wheeler, brushing our legs in passing. I drove along the fields to the trees that hide our pond from prying eyes. I shut off the engine and leaned back, enjoying the feeling of Madelyn's arms gently encircling my waist. A breeze toyed with our hair and sent a few dried leaves spiraling into the night sky. In the distance, a coyote barked.

"Come with me, my Maddy," I said, climbing off the four-wheeler and offering her my hand.

"Your Maddy," she said with a smile. "I like that."

I led her beneath the twisted limbs of the branches that reached out over the pond and helped her sit gently on our little grassy knoll dappled in starlight and swaying leaf shadows.

I sat down beside her and could only stare at the beauty of the girl next to me. She reached up a hand and touched my face. "You look so tired."

I shook my head. "Just tired of being away from you. Monday

is going to kill me."

"Me too," she said softly.

I settled back on the grass and she laid her head on my shoulder. One hand with gentle fingers splayed across my stomach. My skin heated beneath her touch.

"I was so worried," she said quietly after a few minutes.

"I'm sorry I scared you." I weaved a strand of her long dark hair between my fingers. "You've been through enough without having to worry about me."

A smile showed in her voice when she replied, "I'll always worry about you."

I gave a small chuckle. "At least you're thinking of me."

She turned so her chin rested on my chest and her eyes stared into mine. "I always think about you, Kelson Brady."

"Really?" I said, my eyebrows raised. "What do you think about?"

A small blush stole across her cheeks, but she kept her gaze locked on mine. "How much I miss being held in your arms. How safe I feel when I'm with you." She lowered her eyelashes. "How I love kissing you."

Heat flared through me. I pulled her closer and brushed her lips with mine. She sighed against my mouth, closing the space between us. I tasted her kiss, memorizing the way her skin felt against mine, the way her fingers toyed with the hair at the back of my neck, and the way her breath rose and fell with mine.

We kissed under the light of the stars, silent witnesses to two souls intertwined with one love. I held her close and promised to myself that I would never let her go, not really. No matter how far away she was, I would always remember the softness of her cheek under my fingers, the ruby shine of her lips, the golden and green of her penetrating eyes. She undid everything inside of me and laid me bare and helpless as I had never been before, and I loved her for it. She was my one and only, my world.

⁓

A SMILE SPREAD ACROSS her face when she saw me on the bus. "I can't believe you're here," she said.

"I'm not going to miss any chance to see you," I replied.

She smiled again and I knew we were both thinking about our visit to the pond.

"I'll visit you even if I have to borrow Uncle Rick's truck," I promised.

"I'll call you every night," she said, blinking back tears.

I held her close. "Don't cry," I whispered in her hair. "Don't cry. It'll all be all right. This will pass and we'll be together again, I promise."

She nodded and leaned her head against my shoulder. It was the last time I would enjoy the bus ride from the Ashby house to Sparrow High.

I was disappointed that Ms. Narrow, the round, cheerful school secretary, had Madelyn's transcripts and information ready at the office. I had anticipated going with her to each class to collect her work. Instead, it was over too soon.

Masey pulled up in front of the school before the first bell rang. It caused a little commotion with the school buses, but they negotiated around her as if eccentric ladies in red Cadillacs often clogged the bus lane.

Madelyn leaned against me, as reluctant to leave as I was to let her go. Aunt Masey gave two honks of her horn and waved cheerfully, unaware of the hearts that would break as soon as Madelyn stepped into her car.

"Promise me this isn't forever," I whispered into her long

brown hair. She had worn it down, a fact that wasn't lost on me.

"It's not," she said, her voice trembling. "Forever is for us to live together." Her arms tightened around me. "Just promise me you'll take care of yourself while I'm gone."

"I'm not promising anything," I said with a smile, reminded of a similar conversation we'd had before I jumped my motorcycle through the window of the livestock building at the fair.

She looked up at me with an answering smile. "Then at least promise to think of me before you do anything rash."

"I will."

It was too tempting to kiss her. We were on school grounds where public displays of affection were highly discouraged, but I couldn't help myself. I leaned down and kissed her soundly on the lips, determined to give her some reason to return.

When we parted, her special smile touched her eyes, making them glow in green and gold. "I'll be back, Kelson," she promised.

"I'll be waiting, Maddy."

I watched with a heavy heart as she climbed into the car and her aunt slowly drove away. I figured at that pace, they would travel the four-hour distance in about two days.

———— ⌇⌇ ————

MS. NARROW TOOK PITY on me and gave me an excuse slip to take to my first class. I sat in the back row and listened to Mrs. Carol talk about Shakespeare; for the first time, I truly commiserated with Romeo. I had never been able to understand why he was willing to face death for the girl he loved; to me, the thought had seemed absurd, but now I understood. Now, the thought of being away from Madelyn truly tore me in two.

Mrs. Carol quoted, "'My bounty is as boundless as the sea, my love as deep; the more I give to thee, the more I have, for both are infinite.'"

I buried my head in my arms and let the rest of class flow by me in a numb wave.

I fell asleep during second-period music history, only to be awakened by the dull tone of the speaker. "Mrs. Franklin?"

"Yes," she asked, a bit annoyed to be interrupted.

"Please send Kelson Brady to the office."

"Gladly," she said. Her tone told me my sleeping hadn't gone unnoticed.

I picked up my book and wrinkled notebook, then walked from class to the sound of whispers and giggles. Foreboding rose in my chest as I entered the office and met the cheerful grin of Ms. Narrow.

"Good morning again, Mr. Brady," she said, adjusting her hot-pink cat-eye glasses.

"Morning," I replied noncommittally. My side ached and I was worried about what the principal wanted, but the secretary's smile was infectious. "It's a beautiful day," I said.

Her smile widened. "It sure is! Summer will be here before long!"

The thought cheered me. "I'm looking forward to it."

"Me too," she said, then her smile faltered. "Not that I don't like being here. I love Sparrow High. It's just—"

I took pity on her and gave her another smile. "It's just nice to have a change once in a while."

A relieved answering smile touched her eyes. "Exactly." She waved a set of hot-pink nails toward the principal's office. "Principal Dawson is waiting for you."

"Thanks." I tried and failed to sound thrilled by the prospect.

"Don't worry," she reassured me. "For a nice boy like you, it can't be something horrible."

I wasn't so sure, but walked obediently back toward his office anyway.

The principal had traded his red politician tie for a blue one of equal expense. His black suit looked as if it was being worn for the first time, and the toes of his black shoes that showed beneath the desk were polished so they shone. He was leaning back in his chair studying a book of trees. When he looked up and noticed me, he sat up and set the book on the corner of the desk, then ran his thumb and forefinger along his impressive mustache before he motioned for me to take a seat.

"I've been expecting you," he said.

I didn't know what to reply. The summons to his office made it obvious he was expecting me. I wondered if he just liked the ominous sound of the words. I took a seat on the edge of one of the uncomfortable hard-backed chairs.

He linked his fingers together and sat forward with just the appropriate angle of intimidating yet authoritative friendliness. "You've been absent a few days."

"I had the flu," I said evenly.

His eyes narrowed slightly. He picked up a file on the opposite corner of the desk from his tree book and opened it. "You've missed quite a few days of school since you moved here, Mr. Brady."

I kept my face carefully expressionless. "I have a weak immune system."

He continued to study my file. "Unfortunately, your grades have also suffered from the absences. You've missed several tests in key classes, and failed to turn in a few important assignments." He gave a dramatic sigh as if he cared and looked up at me. "You're going to have to take summer school in order to graduate this year."

His words made my heart sink into my stomach.

The principal's eyes tightened and he sat forward. "Unless you have a good reason for the absences."

I watched him carefully, unsure what he was getting at.

When I didn't say anything, a small smile pulled the corners of his lips but didn't reach his eyes. "I was asked by the FBI to help identify the Black Rider. They seem to think he's a student at this school, so I pulled the list of students who were absent during the pep rally last week." He watched me like a cat with a mouse. "You were on that list."

I gave him an incredulous smile despite the knot that had tightened to a brick in my stomach. "You think I might be the Black Rider?" I forced a laugh. "The one and only time I was on a motorcycle, I wrecked it into Magnum's truck."

His brow creased slightly. "You mean Magnum, the leader of the Bullets?"

I was about to ask him if he knew of any other Magnum, but kept silent with the thought that sarcasm might not be the best choice at the moment.

When I nodded, he let out a breath. "That really doesn't prove anything. Why were you absent the day of the shooting?"

"I had the flu," I repeated in a carefully expressionless tone.

Silence fell between us. He watched me as though waiting for any movement that would give away the lie. I held perfectly still. I wasn't a good liar, but I had to be. For a second, I debated telling him the truth. If being the Black Rider kept me from summer school, it might be worth it.

I opened my mouth, then I remembered it was the FBI who was asking him to find out my identity. Sheriff Bowley said they would take the Black Rider in for firing a gun in school despite the fact that I was doing it to defend my fellow students. I couldn't let them know who I was. Things were finally going somewhat all right; I couldn't screw up now.

"The flu?" Principal Dawson pressed.

I nodded without saying anything.

His lips pressed together, and then he picked up his phone. "I'm going to have to verify that."

He flipped the file open to the last page and dialed a phone number. My hands clenched into fists as I waited nervously.

"Hello, Mrs. Ashby?"

Principal Dawson waited, then said in a warm voice that would have made a badger smile, "This is Principal Dawson. It is a pleasure talking to you today. Do you mind if I take a moment of your time?"

I wished I could hear Aunt Lauren's reply on the other end. Instead, I had to be content with one side of the conversation, the side I really didn't want to hear.

"No, no, everything is fine," Principal Dawson continued. "I'm just having a chat with your nephew. I had a quick question for you." He paused and his eyes met mine. "Could you tell me the reason Kelson was absent last Tuesday?"

I held my breath as I met his gaze squarely.

"Uh-huh," he said with doubt in his voice. He paused, then said, "Are you sure about that?"

Aunt Lauren's voice rose to the point where I could hear her shouting. The principal held the phone away from his ear and gave me a wide-eyed look, then quickly said, "I apologize, Mrs. Ashby. I didn't mean to give you the impression that I doubted your integrity, or Kelson's. Of course I feel horrible about him having the flu. I'm glad that he's feeling better and I'm going to ask him to return to class now. Thank you for your time. Good-bye."

He hung up the phone quickly and stared at it for a moment, then looked up at me. "She confirmed you had the flu," he said in a voice that tweaked only slightly at the end.

"Is that all she said?" I asked innocently.

He cleared his throat and tugged at his tie uncomfortably, messing up the careful knot. "She wasn't, uh, happy when I asked her if she was sure about that."

I fought back a smile. "Well, she's pregnant."

"Ah," he said in relief, as if that explained everything. "Well, please let her know when you get home that I didn't mean any offense."

"I will. Am I okay to go?"

He nodded, but when I rose, a strange look crossed his face. For a moment, he didn't look like a sure candidate for principal of the year; instead, he appeared lost, and oddly, a bit scared.

"Kelson, I'm sorry for all this." He waved an arm to indicate the desk and chair. "I didn't mean for the way it came across."

I stood still, entirely unsure what to say.

He rubbed his forehead, then ran a hand down his mustache in an unconscious motion. "I've never been as terrified as I was the day that gang attacked the school." He looked up at me, his expression stark and bare. "They were going to shoot the students and teachers. I tried to protect them, but there were so many guns."

I crossed behind the desk where I was sure no student had walked before and set a hand on his shoulder. "It's all right, Principal Dawson. I heard you did a wonderful job."

He shook his head. "I could have done more."

I thought of the way he placed himself between the teachers and students as they hurried out the door. There was fear on his face, but also intensity. He wasn't going to let anyone get hurt if he could help it.

I lowered my voice, hoping he could hear the truth in my words. "No one was hurt, so you did a good job. You protected the teachers and students. They look to you for guidance and you were a good leader. That's the most anyone could do in a situation like that."

He nodded, his eyes on his desk. He picked up my file. "I was hoping to thank the Black Rider for what he did."

I let out a quiet breath. "Maybe you'll find him someday."

He kept his eyes on the manila folder. "The students are holding a candlelight ceremony tonight to honor the Black Rider and to remember those who weren't lucky enough to have a Black Rider at their school during other shootings."

That was news to me. I felt stunned that the students would do such a thing. I didn't know how to reply.

The intercom buzzed, shattering the stillness that had settled around us.

Principal Dawson blinked, then pushed the button. "Yes, Ms. Narrow?"

"Mrs. Jethro from the PTA is on line two. She wants to speak to you about the 2k fundraiser."

The principal covered the receiver with one hand. "That'll be all, Mr. Brady. Have a great day."

"Same to you," I said, surprised but grateful to have our conversation ended so abruptly.

When I stepped from the room, my shoulders sagged in relief. I made my way past Mrs. Narrow, who waved at me and wished me a fabulous morning. I walked into the nearest bathroom and let my books fall to the floor. I leaned against the wall and let out a sigh.

That was too close. Thank goodness Aunt Lauren told him I had the flu even though we hadn't even talked about it. I made a mental note to give her a hug when I got home. Between Martin, the FBI, and now Principal Dawson, there were quite a few people on my tail. The sheriff's advice to lie low hit home a lot heavier. If I wasn't careful, any wrong move would blow my cover sky high.

Chapter Twenty-two

I COULDN'T STAND THE thought of riding the bus home without Madelyn at my side. I wandered to the football field instead and watched Magnum throw the ball. He looked truly in his element as he hit a wide receiver square on the numbers. The player ran to the end zone and spiked the ball, then proceeded to do a ridiculous celebration dance that involved arm waving and hip thrusting.

The coach proceeded to rant about focusing energy on something more important than dancing after every single catch. Magnum noticed me and jogged to the fence that separated the bleachers from the field. His coach's rant turned into something about use of time and threatening the player with laps until the sun set. Apparently Magnum had listened to the tirade before.

He pulled off his helmet and leaned against the fence. "Miss the bus?"

I shook my head. "Tired of the noise."

He chuckled. "Thought listening to Coach Farston would be nice for a change?"

I grinned. "His language is more colorful."

Magnum laughed. "It definitely is. I'll give you a ride home after practice."

"Thanks."

He gave me a searching look. "You goin' to the candlelight ceremony tonight?"

I rubbed my forehead. "I'm not sure. I just found out about it today from Principal Dawson."

His eyebrows rose. "Why were you talking to the principal?"

I sighed. "It's a long story."

"I think you should go," he said.

I shook my head. "I didn't do it for the glory."

His brow furrowed. "But it's the second time you've done something that saved a ton of lives. Let them thank you."

I didn't feel comfortable about, especially with the FBI breathing down my neck, but I could tell it meant a lot to him. "You're a Black Rider too."

"Was," he corrected with a smile. "And you were the one who made the difference that day. I really think you should go."

"I'll think about it."

He nodded in acceptance, even though it wasn't really an answer.

"Heads up!" someone yelled.

A football flew across the fence and bounced to the bleachers a few feet from me. I walked down and picked it up.

"Our kicker has problems with direction," Magnum said, rolling his eyes.

"That's a pretty bad problem," I said.

I was about to chuck the ball back to him when another person yelled, "Throw it."

I looked up to see Coach Farston watching me with an expectant expression on his face. I glanced at Magnum; he nodded encouragingly.

I took a deep breath and held the ball the way I had seen Magnum do it, then I pulled my arm back and threw it as hard as I could. The ball flew end over end in the worst duck I had ever seen. It landed about ten feet over the fence. Any hopes I might have harbored about becoming some surprise football star were dashed along with the dust that puffed up at the ball's rough landing. I fought back a wry smile.

Coach Farston looked from the ball back to me with a mixture of disgust and humor on his face. "Maybe you can be the mascot," he said.

"WHAT'RE YA DOIN' 'ERE?" Jagger demanded from the door of the shack as Magnum's truck pulled out of the junkyard. "Yur suppose ta be restin'."

"I can only rest so long before I go crazy. There's nothing to do at the Ashbys' and the sheriff warned me against riding. I'm stuck," I said rougher than I intended. Surprise showed on his face at my tone. I took a calming breath and ran a hand through my hair to push it out of my eyes. "Sorry. It's been a tough day, but I shouldn't take it out on you. I just need something to do."

He stepped down from the low porch and gave me a careful look-over. Mick ran around both of us, but he didn't bark. I took it as a sign the little dog had accepted that I was a part of his junkyard. The thought warmed me even though I couldn't explain why.

Jagger shook his head. "Sorry, boy. Ya look like you could use another year a sleep. I hafta send ya home." He gave me a sympathetic pat on the shoulder. "I'd keep ya if I could, but I promised Lauren and I know better than ta git on her bad side."

I thought of the scolding Principal Dawson had taken and nodded. "I understand. Thanks, though."

Mick followed me to the back of the shack. I opened the door to the lean-to and looked at the pair of motorcycles. The headlight was shattered on my Er-6n. I pulled a piece of glass free and let it fall to the ground. I felt as though I had mistreated the bike, especially since I left it in the shed in case the search got a little too close to home.

It was more tempting that I cared to think about to jump on the motorcycle and drive south away from Sparrow, away from the school, the principal, the farm, and away from Madelyn's house where bad memories warred with the good. For the first time, I understood Madelyn's wish to be a goose, to fly with the flock and leave my home with the knowledge that there was a more welcoming place on the horizon. I wanted to leave it all behind.

I turned away from the bike and climbed gingerly onto the four-wheeler. I waved at Jagger when I drove past the shack, then took the road toward the Ashby house that I was reluctantly beginning to think of as home. I pulled into the driveway, but couldn't bring myself to enter the house. Jake ran up and licked my hand welcomingly. I patted his head, then watched him run across the lawn and through a fence in pursuit of some unknown objective.

The sun was setting behind the Ashby home, casting the lawn and fields around me in hues of gold and yellow. I closed my eyes and filled my lungs with the scent of alfalfa and Aunt Lauren's sunflowers that swayed against the house. I wanted to find peace, but it flitted at the edge of my mind, teasing me but not sinking in to rest my weary soul.

Instead, I was filled with a need to fight, to protect my loved ones, to defend Sparrow; unfortunately, the sheriff's orders to lie low had stifled my ability to do so. I wanted to hold Madelyn in my arms, but she was gone, and it felt like she took my sanity with her. My hands clenched into fists. I needed to hit something.

I crossed to the side of the house and the hay bales that had served as a hideout for my motorcycle. A pair of Uncle Rick's thick work gloves sat on the stack. I pulled them on, then punched one of the bales. It stung, but the gloves kept my knuckles from getting torn apart by the dry alfalfa. I gritted my teeth and hit the bale again.

A small smile touched my lips. I faced the bales squarely and punched with a slow rhythm, easing my body into the motion. Left right, left right, left left right, right right left. The rhythm increased as my body warmed up. My side ached, but not enough to slow me down. I breathed with each hit, remembering my training. My muscles loosened. I turned into each punch, causing the hay to flatten under my fists. My shoes turned on the crab grass as I rotated, giving more power into each blow.

By the time I was done, sweat soaked my shirt and my side ached, but a smile crossed my face. I leaned against the hay bale to catch my breath. I hadn't hit long, but my strength was still lagging. I tipped my head against the bale and felt the cool evening breeze brush past my face.

For a brief moment, I enjoyed the silence that settled through my thoughts. My mind was no longer harried by concern about the FBI searching for the Black Rider and the guilt I felt at avoiding them, or my worry for Madelyn being so far away and the way my heart ached at the distance. For the moment, exhausted, I could finally breathe.

"Finished harrying my hay?" Uncle Rick's tone was even.

I opened my eyes and looked at him. "It had it coming."

He nodded. "I'm sure it did." His eyes creased slightly under his straw cowboy hat. "Lauren wants to talk to you."

I pulled off the gloves and left them where I had found them. Uncle Rick followed me into the house. We both kicked off our shoes and made a half-hearted attempt to push them under the bench where Aunt Lauren liked them. He hung his hat near the door, then trailed me into the kitchen reluctantly as though he wasn't happy with the conversation that would follow.

Aunt Lauren's face lit up when she saw me. Her happy expression chased away my trepidation. "Kelson, I'm so glad you're here!"

I smiled and took a seat at the table, worried that anything I said would remind them it was me they were talking to, not one of their sons.

"We're planning a surprise party for Cassidy," Aunt Lauren continued.

That explained the look on Uncle Rick's face. He was in denial that his little girl was about to turn sixteen. A party would make it a fact. I fought back a smile. "She'll be excited."

Aunt Lauren nodded with all the enthusiasm of a six-year-old girl. "We want to keep it a secret, but I need you to invite all her friends. The problem is her birthday is Wednesday, so it's short notice and I'm worried about getting invitations to everyone in time."

Reluctance filled me at the thought of sneaking around delivering invitations to Cassidy's friends. They were nice girls, but several had made it clear I would be on their hit list as soon as their parents would let them date. Seeking them out definitely wouldn't be a good idea. A thought occurred to me. "Why don't we let Sandy text them. You know she'll keep the secret." I doubted that last part, but it was definitely better than Aunt Lauren's idea.

Her smile widened. "That's a great idea! I'm going to call her mother." She disappeared into the hallway and I heard her dial.

The silence that filled the kitchen wasn't as comfortable as it had been outside. I could feel Uncle Rick brooding even without turning around. I tried to think of a subject to get his mind off the impending party. "I'd like to take a turn at the next irrigation shift," I said, surprising myself.

Uncle Rick grunted. I turned to find him watching me. "You think you can handle it?"

I shrugged. "The way Jaren and Cole grumble, they'll be glad to have another person step in."

"Guess you can't mess it up as much as Cole did last week." A reluctant smile spread across his face. "You should have seen Monte's horse when it flooded his corral. By the time we showed up, his prize stallion had rolled so much in the muck, he looked like a dun mule. Monte wasn't thrilled."

"You should have made Cole clean the horse."

Both of us chuckled at the thought of Cole trying to scrub the huge Clydesdale clean. He could barely reach its flank.

"It's done," Aunt Lauren said with a huge smile. "Sandy will text all Cassidy's friends and I don't even have to make invitations. It's perfect."

I took a chance. "Can I invite Madelyn to the party?"

"Of course," Aunt Lauren replied with a warm smile. She surprised me by pulling me into a hug. "Thanks so much, Kelson!"

She hurried into the next room and left us both staring after her.

"She's always been prone to greater shows of affection when she's pregnant," Uncle Rick said uncomfortably.

I heard Mom's car pull in. "I'll go help carry groceries."

"You'll do nothing of the sort," he shot back. When I looked at him, he pointed to the living room. "You better rest that side if you haven't already torn all the stitches again."

"I was careful," I protested.

He shrugged. "Nonetheless, Sarah will tan my hide if she thinks I'm wearin' you out." He gave me a shrewd look. "Besides, if I'm not mistaken, it's time for you to head to that candlelight ceremony."

I was surprised Uncle Rick knew about it.

He smiled at my look. "Cass is already there. She took Jaren and Cole with her because they wouldn't stop buggin' me about it. Lauren and I will be along shortly with your mom." His voice lowered. "You know you need to be there."

"Be where?" Mom asked, coming in with a paper bag of groceries in each arm.

"The candlelight ceremony," Uncle Rick explained.

"Of course you should be there," Mom said as Uncle Rick took her groceries and set them on the counter.

I stared at her. "You hate the Black Rider."

She shook her head, ruffling my hair on her way back to the car. "You're the Black Rider, and I love you. I just hate it when being the Black Rider puts you in danger." She paused at the screen door. "The ceremony won't put you in danger."

"That's what you think," I said under my breath when the door shut behind her.

"Why is that?"

My heart sank. I had already forgotten Uncle Rick was behind me. I definitely needed some sleep. I debated whether to tell him, but having someone who knew both sides might be helpful. I let out the breath I had been unconsciously holding. "The FBI wants to take the Black Rider in."

Instead of looking surprised, Uncle Rick nodded. "Jagger mentioned something of the sort. Said he heard it at the bar."

"So you don't think I should go?" I asked.

He shook his head. "I think it means more to the people of Sparrow that you're there."

"But—"

He cut me off with a raised hand. "And if the FBI shows up, I have a feeling your bike can get out of there a heck of a lot faster than they can. Right?"

His eyes lit up as though he wished he was the one tearing through town on a motorcycle. I couldn't help but smile. "Right." He nodded. "Great. We'll see you there."

———————

I SAT ON A low rise overlooking the school. The front of the gymnasium had been turned into a memorial of sorts. The two buildings on either side of the gymnasium stood forward, forming three sides of the square. The fountain made the fourth, boxing in a beautiful place for the ceremony that was completely packed with students and teachers.

Lit candles lined the sidewalks, the fountain, the doorway, and had been set in graceful patterns all the way to the parking lot. Students said words too soft for me to hear, then lit the candle they carried with a bigger one at the front of the fountain. The sight of all the candles along with the reverent students and teachers was breathtaking. My heart hammered in my chest.

My phone buzzed in my pocket. *GET DOWN HERE,* Magnum's text demanded.

I was about to put it back in my pocket when it buzzed again. I wished with all my heart it would be from Madelyn. I hadn't heard from her since her aunt picked her up, and not for the lack of trying. I had called her four times and sent three texts, but hadn't heard anything back.

A begrudging smile stole across my face when I saw what Magnum wrote. *Keldon's scared of a little ceremony.*

I'm stalling, I wrote back.

Put on your helmet and pretend to be a man.

I rolled my eyes and wrote, *Thanks for the vote of confidence.*

He responded, *Do it, Black Rider.*

I stared at his text for a minute, then slid the phone in my pocket and climbed on the motorcycle. I didn't want to destroy the reverence of the scene below, so instead of turning it on, I shifted it to neutral and coasted slowly down the hill.

The glow of the candles reflected gently off the buildings, creating an atmosphere of gold and shadows. The faces that showed within the light looked serene. I tried to place them with the chaos of students who filled the halls every day. The fact that the ceremony was for me made it feel surreal, as though I rode into a dream.

I slowed to a stop on the other side of the fountain. A few seconds later, students began to notice me. Shoulders were nudged and fingers pointed. A quiet stir rushed through the crowd. I saw Magnum near the student building. He and Cassidy stood near each other. My heart lifted at the sight of Mom, Aunt Lauren, and Uncle Rick just beyond.

Aunt Lauren was trying to take a candle from Cole; it looked as if he had already scorched his sleeve. Mom held her candle in both hands; her smile was proud and filled me with warmth when she saw me. Magnum lifted a hand. I nodded at him.

The crowd around him followed his action, raising their candle in the air like a salute. A wave of lifting candles flowed through the students, parents, siblings, teachers, and spouses. Principal Dawson left his place near the fountain and walked toward me, his own candle carried carefully in his palm.

I climbed off the motorcycle to meet him. He held out his hand and I shook it, aware of how differently he regarded me compared to the student in his office who kept missing class.

"Thank you," he said with a depth of sincerity that shone in his eyes. "It means a lot that you're here."

"This," I gestured to the crowd, "Means the world to me. You didn't have to do it."

"The students started it," he said, then he concluded, "But I supported it completely. You saved lives, many, many lives." His voice lowered. "And I know you risked a lot coming here tonight."

"How could I not?"

A camera flashed. We both looked over to see Martin scribbling notes on a pad of paper, his camera hanging around his neck.

Principal Dawson gave me a wry smile. "Guess that'll be in the papers."

"Nothing goes unnoticed," I replied, thinking of the truck driver between me and Magnum on my motorcycle.

He chuckled and I wondered if he thought of the same image. "You've done this town and school a great service. At least now you know it's been appreciated."

"I was glad to do it."

He shook my hand again and I climbed back on the motorcycle. I had pushed my luck just appearing; the worst I could do was outstay my welcome and risk the FBI showing up.

I raised a hand to the audience. A cheer went up, a rushing wave that turned into a roar echoing between the buildings. I started the motorcycle and drove off into the night with the sound caught in my helmet and a smile on my face.

***

EVERYONE WAS STILL AT the ceremony when I reached the Ashbys'. I collapsed exhausted into my cot and texted Madelyn. When she didn't respond, I tried to call her, but there was no answer. Worry weighed heavily in my chest. She had promised to call, yet I hadn't heard from her since she drove away with Masey.

I missed her so much, I couldn't think of anything else. The light from the low fire in the fireplace pounded against my eyelids. Doubt toyed with the edges of my heart, questioning whether she loved me as much as I did her. If she did, how could she possibly go so long without contacting me?

The rational part of my mind said maybe her phone had died or gotten lost, but surely her aunt would have one she could borrow. I fell asleep with myriad questions flooding through my mind that left my dreams troubled and my heart aching.

Chapter Twenty-three

THE NEXT DAY, MAGNUM slammed his shoulder into the locker next to mine and leaned over. "You've got to get me into Cassidy's party."

I stared at him in surprise, then looked up the hall to see if anyone was watching us. "You're supposed to be a bully, remember?" I said in a low voice.

He stood up and grabbed me by the front of my shirt, then forced me against the locker he had been leaning against. "Give me your lunch money, Keldon."

I fought back a laugh. "Lunch money? What is this, elementary school?"

He rolled his eyes. "I've been out of practice. So get me into the party."

"You're two years older than Cassidy. Uncle Rick would kill you, and then kill me for inviting you."

He shook his head. "Get me in as your friend. I'm sure you're inviting Madelyn." When I hesitated, he grinned. "See, it'll work."

"I'll think about it." I tried to pry my shirt from his fist. "Let me go, Bazooka," I said loudly, then dropped my voice. "That would be a good sidekick name."

His expression darkened. "I'm not a sidekick," he growled. He raised a hand to push me harder against the locker at the same time that my shoe slipped on the linoleum floor. His fist slammed against my nose, forcing my head back against the locker with a loud bang before I fell to a sitting position on the floor.

Magnum stared at me as blood began to run down my face. I held my nose and felt laughter rolling in my chest. Students stopped and stared. A few members of the Bullets who appeared slapped each other high fives and patted Magnum on the back.

"What's going on here?" a familiar voice asked. Magnum's eyes widened.

Principal Dawson pushed through the crowd that surrounded us. His eyes narrowed slightly when he noticed me, and then he turned to Magnum. "Did you do this?" he asked the Bullet leader with a voice that was full of camaraderie instead of accusation.

Magnum looked back at me with a look of helpless shock.

I failed to keep the grin from my face and hid it with my hands as I cupped my bleeding nose. "I slipped, Principal Dawson. Magnum was just helping me to the bathroom."

The principal nodded as if he had expected as much. "Carry on," he said with a nod. He walked away and I heard him mutter to himself, "And to think I thought that boy could be the Black Rider."

Magnum grabbed my shoulder, hefted me to my feet, and steered me toward the restrooms. Students gave way in a wide swath as the Bullet leader walked through. When the door shut behind us and the way was clear, I collapsed against the wall laughing.

"What is your deal?" Magnum demanded. "You're bleeding all over the place!"

I couldn't explain to myself why I was laughing, let alone him. The whole situation just struck me as hilarious.

"You're insane," he said, shoving a handful of paper towels at me. I grabbed them and held the pile against my nose. It throbbed, but I didn't care. "I guess that clears me from the FBI."

"What are you talking about?" Magnum demanded. He ran another handful of paper towels under the faucet, then handed them to me as well.

I let the laughter die away and used the rags to wipe the blood from my nose. I met Magnum's gaze in the mirror. "The other day the principal asked if I was the Black Rider because I missed school the day of the attack."

His eyes widened. "What did you say?"

"I told him I had the flu, and Aunt Lauren backed me up when he called her."

"He called her?" he repeated incredulously.

I nodded. "Guess he was getting close." I indicated my nose. "Now he thinks I'm a wimp."

"You are a wimp," Magnum grumbled, grabbing another handful of paper towels.

"I beat you up plenty of times," I retorted.

"You throw a football worse than a girl," he said.

We glared at each other in the mirror for a few seconds, then we both started to laugh. "You looked like an idiot," he said. "I mean, you actually ran into my fist."

"I tripped," I protested, but the thought brought a smile to my face. I had been captain of the MMA club in my California school, yet I bloodied my nose by slipping into someone's fist. My club members would be proud.

Magnum shook his head, but he couldn't keep from smiling either. "I guess no one will think you're the Black Rider now."

I TOOK MY USUAL seat on the bus and was sinking into melancholy at Madelyn's absence when Cassidy surprised me by breaking the rules to sit next to me. The bus driver had his rules laminated and taped to the back of his seat. Seniors sat in the last four rows, the rest of the high schoolers took the next four, then the middle school, followed by the elementary closest to the driver. He was very strict about the consequences of breaking his rules, which usually resulted in a glare fierce enough to send the miscreant back to the appropriate seat.

This time, however, when I looked at the driver in the mirror, he merely rolled his eyes and returned his attention to the road.

"I brought him some of Mom's raspberry preserves for Christmas," Cassidy explained at my questioning look.

I sat back and propped my knees on the seat in front of me much the same way Madelyn had done when I first noticed her.

"Kel, you've got to get Magnum to come to my party," Cassidy said before I could ask why she was there.

I let my head fall back against the seat. "You too?" I glanced at her. "You're not supposed to know about the party."

"Like Sandy can keep a secret," she said. "Besides, it's gonna be the biggest party of the school year. Everyone wants to be there."

"That'll make your dad happy," I said, looking out the window. Every student who showed up would drive the fact deeper that his little girl was growing up. A part of me agreed that Cassidy was too little to be sixteen.

"Smile," she said, looking at my reflection in the window. "The world's not such a gloomy place. I'll bet you can invite Madelyn. In fact, I would love for her to be there, so you'd better."

"I'm planning on it," I said quietly.

"Then will you invite Magnum?" The pleading in her voice made it worse.

I shook my head without looking at her. "The last thing your dad needs to see on your sixteenth birthday is you with a boy two years older than you, not to mention the leader of the Bullets, the biggest bully in Sparrow. I won't do it."

She was quiet for a moment, but when I didn't budge, she pushed my shoulder. "You're such a jerk, Kelson." She stood up and stormed back to sit by Sandy. I could hear her heavily vocalized disappointment from my seat. I set my forehead against the window and watched the world rush by in a blur.

I HELPED UNCLE RICK pitch hay to the cows, the one task he felt I could complete without either screwing it up or messing up my healing knife wound. I gritted my teeth against the pull of the stitches as I used the pitchfork, determined not to let him know it hurt. I levered alfalfa from the bed of the truck to the cows strung out in a long line to eat the piles of hay I made in the field.

When the last forkful was pitched, Uncle Rick drove slowly across the uneven ground and paused by the gate long enough for me to fasten the wire across the pole, then climb gingerly back on the bed. Jake rode beside me and panted happily as the truck pulled onto the road and headed back toward the house.

I set a hand on the hood of the truck and rode with my eyes closed, standing with my face in the wind and the truck bed swaying beneath my feet. I remembered seeing Cassidy ride the same way my first time to the farm. I now understood the peace of the familiar sun setting against my eyelids, the evening breeze rushing through my hair and trying to sweep the straw cowboy hat from my head, and the scent of alfalfa fields and sunflowers coloring the air.

When we pulled into the driveway, I was surprised to see Magnum's truck there. He waved and Uncle Rick waved back before going into the house.

"About time you got here," Magnum said. "I stopped by the junkyard and Jagger said you needed to go over there. He wouldn't say why."

I climbed into Magnum's truck and he turned back the way he had come. The tension inside the vehicle was palpable. I finally sighed and leaned my head against the window. "Cass hates me because of you."

I could feel Magnum's complete attention on me, but didn't look at him. "Why?" he asked in a voice that was touched with hope and worry at the same time.

"Because she asked me to invite you to her party and I told her I wouldn't do it."

I wondered if he would stop and demand for me to leave his truck or punch me without warning. I doubted either of us or the truck would hold up in a brawl inside the tiny cab.

Instead, he waited in silence. I looked over to see a smile on his face as he looked out the front window.

"Why are you so happy?" I asked.

"She wants me there," he said.

I rolled my eyes. "But I told her no."

He shrugged. "It doesn't matter. She wants me there." He looked at me with more excitement and happiness in his expression that I had ever seen. "She likes me."

"She's sixteen tomorrow."

He shrugged again. "Doesn't matter. She's two years younger than me. You think it makes a difference now, but I've heard that when we get older, those two years don't matter at all."

I knew he was right. My mom and dad had been four years apart, and it didn't matter. What mattered was the finances that tore through their marriage and my dad left without looking back. Aunt

Lauren was definitely younger than Uncle Rick, but the look in her eyes when they were together showed there was still love between them.

It wasn't the age difference so much as the fact that we were talking about Magnum. I had seen him shove kids into lockers because he thought they were new students and needed to fear him. I had seen him terrorize the drama department by throwing paint all over their sets. I had seen him conspire with gang leaders to establish Sparrow as a center for drug trade.

I had also seen him confront the same gang leaders to protect the town when the situation escalated out of control. I was there when he almost got killed trying to pull over a semitruck loaded with stolen goods. He had single-handedly attempted to take down the trio of gas station robbers who evaded our sheriff.

I ran a hand through my hair and rested my head back against the seat. He had saved my life by guiding me home on the motorcycle that night. With the blood loss from the knife wound, I shouldn't have ridden and I was too stubborn and worried about the sheriff's warning to go to the hospital. The red light of his bike was the only thing that helped me survive the trip to the Ashbys'. Without him, I would have wrecked and probably bled to death unnoticed on the side of some farm road.

"I want you to come to the party," I said quietly.

He turned and stared at me. "What?"

I met his gaze. "You're a good guy, Magnum. I wouldn't mind it if you dated my cousin." His eyes widened and a smile spread across his face. I lifted a hand. "Granted, that doesn't mean Uncle Rick won't kill you, so take it slow."

"I will," he said quickly. "Don't worry." He surprised me by holding out a hand. "Thanks, Kelson."

I shook it uncertainly. "It's not like I have any say in this."

He shrugged. "Just the same, I wouldn't date her if you said no."

"Seriously?" I studied him.

He nodded. "Bro code, man. It just wouldn't be cool."

I sat back. "Thanks."

He pulled into the junkyard and we both fell silent at the sight of the sheriff's truck and another vehicle in front of Jagger's shack. The mood thickened when we saw them wheeling the motorcycles inside the second truck. Jagger and the sheriff watched together from the porch.

"What's going on?" Magnum asked quietly.

"I'm not sure," I said as he stopped. "But I'm going to find out."

The sheriff smiled and pushed his hat back at the sight of us. "Hello, boys."

"What's the deal, Sheriff?" I asked, not in the mood to play around.

"How's your side?" he countered.

"Healing," I replied. "What's going on? Why are you taking our bikes?"

His deputy who loaded the motorcycles paused at my tone, but the sheriff waved for him to continue. "Well, the FBI is getting a bit too close in their investigation. I know you spoke to Principal Dawson and that'll help for a brief while, but they're becoming too familiar with the Black Rider's movements. We have word that they're planning to raid the factory on Thursday because they heard the Black Rider races students there."

"So we're finished?" Magnum asked.

The sheriff tipped his hat in the Bullet leader's direction. "Hello, Magnum. Pleasure to see you again."

I could tell Magnum was becoming as frustrated by the sheriff's evasive charade as I was. I cut in before Magnum could reply with something that would put us both in hot water. "I'm not worried about the FBI," I said. "I'll turn myself in when Sparrow is safe."

Everyone stared at me. I met the sheriff's gaze. "But I'm not done here. With the Brown Hawk gang terrorizing the school, there's no saying if the Verdos will be close behind. I want to be ready."

He nodded. "We figured as much, so Deputy Addison and I got a little creative."

"What do you mean?" Magnum demanded.

The sheriff refused to let the Bullet leader's tone bother him. He waved a hand nonchalantly toward the loaded motorcycles and the deputy who now watched us with interest. "We figured if we gave the FBI your motorcycles, that would give you a break for a while."

"While we do what?" Magnum asked.

"Ride in style," the deputy piped in. An embarrassed grin spread across his face at the sheriff's look. "Sorry, couldn't help myself." He held out a hand. "I've been a fan of the Black Rider for quite some time."

I shook his hand and noted the questioning look on his face. "What?"

His grin turned sheepish. "I guess with everything you've done, I thought you'd be older."

Magnum sputtered a laugh behind me, but I took the deputy's words seriously. "Wisdom and recklessness sometimes look the same."

His eyes widened in surprise. He took his hat off and ran a hand through his dark brown hair before pushing the hat back on and exchanging a glance with the sheriff. "You were right."

"About what?" Magnum asked.

"He's a sharp one," the man said. Magnum gave a huff of

disappointment.

"Yeah, but at this rate he won't live to see nineteen," Sheriff Bowley countered.

"Ha!" Magnum said, then his face took on a slightly disturbed look as though he realized what the sheriff had just said.

The words hit too close to home. "You said something about riding in style?" I pressed.

"I's wonderin' when ya'd remember tha' part," Jagger said from the porch. He pointed his crowbar cane toward the back of the shed. "Go see fur yurself."

Magnum and I exchanged a look. Then we walked around the shack to the back. We tried to keep calm and collected, but we were eager to see what waited for us. By the time we reached the lean-to, we were at a run and jostling each other to get there first. I could hear the sheriff and deputy laughing behind us.

Magnum and I stopped and stared at what the lean-to revealed. My heart rose in my throat and I found it hard to swallow. It was a strange reaction to the motorcycles in front of us, but I found myself looking at the exact make and model of motorcycle I had left in California.

I reached out a hand and touched the headlight of a new CBR painted black to match the Er-6ns we had just let go. The paint glowed in the light of Jagger's rigged porch lights instead of the dull sheen of flat black we were used to.

"This is more like it," Magnum said. He walked into the lean-to and grabbed the helmet hanging from the back footrest. "Come on, Black Rider. Let's try them out."

The name propelled me forward. I climbed onto the other motorcycle and picked up the helmet. It shone like the bike, the dark gleam of water illuminated by the midnight moon. I pulled the gloves and riding gear from my backpack and saw Magnum do the same. When we were ready, we grinned at each other before lowering our dark-tinted visors. I turned the key and pressed the starter. The engine rumbled to life. I smiled at the memories that came flooding back.

I used to lead the pack, our little rag-tag group of riders on bullet bikes, converted dirt bikes, and a few old-school Harleys. Zoey rode on the back of Jeff's motorcycle, her pink helmet bright compared to the fierce reds and blacks of the guys. We left all our cares behind as we followed the winding path along the coast. The ocean sometimes lapped at the shore feet below the road, and other times jutted up with waves of spray that caught the setting sunlight in rainbow hues. The hum of the motorcycles told of power and speed. We could go anywhere and do anything. We felt unstoppable.

"Ready?" Magnum asked, bringing me back.

I let out a slow breath and nodded. I eased the bike forward and smiled when it moved faster than I intended; it felt as if I rode a horse chomping eagerly at the bit. I laughed even though I was the only one who could hear it above the sound of the engine.

Uncle Rick would be proud of the farm boy he had turned me into; the California kid of my past would never have compared a motorcycle to an animal. My experience back then had been limited to a few wild birds and the random mouse that fell into my garbage can and Zoey made me set free behind the apartment building.

"Now I believe you're the Black Rider," Deputy Addison said.

Sheriff Bowley had his arms crossed in front of his chest and nodded appreciatively. "Those should keep you busy for a while."

"Bu' not outta trouble," Jagger commented. "Ya wearin' the vests?"

"Always."

He gave me his usual salute. "Take care a yurselves."

"Will do," I said. "Thanks, Sheriff, Deputy."

They both nodded. The sheriff stepped back with a proud look on his face as though he was personally responsible for the Black Rider. I revved the engine and shot out into the rapidly falling darkness. The headlight of Magnum's motorcycle reflected in my rearview mirror. He pushed the bike, attempting to surge ahead. I shifted and sped forward, keeping in front of him as we sped along the roads at speeds well over sheriff-approved levels.

I grinned beneath the helmet. Every bike was born different. Each had its own personality brought not just by mechanics and framework, but also by something that felt like a soul instilled in the machine itself. My last bike was tame compared to this one. The beast beneath me roared and ate up the road hungrily. It lunged with a roll of the throttle, and protested when I slowed. The bike I rode was born angry, and I liked it.

Chapter Twenty-four

MANGUM MOTIONED THAT HE needed to go home. I followed him back to the junkyard and waited as he traded his motorcycle for his truck. When he left, I headed into town and, on a whim, parked in front of the pizza house.

When I pushed the door open and walked inside wearing my Black Rider outfit, all talking ceased from the students and employees inside the tiny restaurant. I felt every eye on me as I made my way to the counter.

"Wh—what can I get you?" a skinny blond-haired boy asked. He held up a notepad as though jotting down my order was the most important thing in his life.

"A large ham and pineapple, and a large pepperoni," I replied, trying not to smile even though he couldn't see through my visor.

"Th—that would b—be one large ham and p—pineapple, and one large pe—pepperoni," the boy repeated.

I nodded. "How much?"

"It's on the house." A big man with a used-to-be-white apron tied around his generous belly strode to the counter. He wiped a few remnants of shredded cheese from his fingers and held out a hand.

"It's an honor to have you visit my establishment, Black Rider."

"Thank you, sir," I replied, shaking his hand and trying not to sound as taken aback as I felt.

"After all you've done, anything you want here is on the house," he said.

"Can that apply to us as well?"

I turned to see a few players from the basketball team and Thompson, the tall, skinny boy from the Bullet gang. Apparently Magnum wasn't the only one searching for a new outlet. The boys had been eating a pizza at a corner booth, but they ambled up as they spoke.

"Ben, if I gave you the same deal, you'd eat this place out of business," the owner said with a deep chuckle. "Nice try, though." He looked back at me. "Thanks again. Your pizzas will be out soon." He disappeared behind the giant oven.

"Thank you," I replied. I leaned against the counter and studied the basketball players who watched me curiously.

"Didn't take you for the pizza type," Ben said.

I shrugged. "Is there another type?"

He grinned. I noticed Thompson watching me warily from the back of the group. I tipped my head toward him. "Glad to see you found a new hobby."

"Beats beatin' on you," he replied.

The air thickened with tension, but it broke when the laugh I tried to hold in rolled out despite my efforts. "As I recall, I gave you a couple of good punches."

A begrudging smile touched his lips that looked unused to such an expression. "You could say that."

"Were you the one who took my uniform?" a boy demanded from the table the basketball players had just vacated.

It took me a minute to recognize him as the boy I swiped

the mascot outfit from at the football game. I wondered just how incriminating admitting it would be.

"Were you the one pretending to be the mascot?" Thompson pressed.

I glanced around the room. My heart sank when I saw Martin in the corner with a full pizza in front of him. His complete attention was on our conversation along with the rest of the room. I knew whatever I said would end up in the next *Bulldog Bulletin*.

"Were you?" the mascot boy asked. I heard a note of desperation in his voice and wondered just how much trouble I had given him. The least I could do was clear his name.

I nodded. "Sorry about the knife." I gestured toward Thompson. "The Bullets didn't exactly fight fair."

"That's the name of the game," Thompson said with a grin. He rubbed a hand over his shaved head. "But those paws hurt."

"I don't know how you move in that thing," I told the boy who wore the mascot costume. "It's like fighting in a giant pillow."

Several people in the room laughed. The mascot joined them. "You're not supposed to fight in it," he said with a chuckle.

"I don't know," another basketball player said. "I saw you getting violent with the hawk from Fairfield last week."

The boy's cheeks turned red, but he looked at me. "Just taking a few notes from the Black Rider."

I laughed and held up my gloved hands. "I will not take the blame for a mascot throw-down."

"I could lend you the costume again if the other team's giving us a hard time," the boy said.

"I might consider that," I replied. Everyone laughed.

"Black Rider, your pizza's up," the owner said from behind the counter. I pulled a twenty from my pocket and tried to hand it to him, but he waved it away. "Keep it. I mean what I say. You eat free here whenever you want."

"Thank you very much," I replied, touched. "I really appreciate it."

His eyes narrowed slightly and he looked around the room. "Keep an eye out for the feds. They've been askin' around."

I nodded. "So I heard. Thanks for the warning."

Ben held open the door and I stepped into the night with two boxes of pizza and a smile that wouldn't leave my face. I was almost to my motorcycle when I heard footsteps behind me.

"You got a new bike," Martin said.

I breathed a silent sigh and turned around. "Changing things up a bit."

He nodded. "I hope it throws them off your trail for a while. I heard they're getting pretty close."

"Where'd you hear that?" I asked, curious.

He grinned. "I have my sources."

"That's a very reporterish thing to say." I set the pizzas on the tank of the motorcycle, wondering for the first time how I planned to carry them.

Martin ran a hand through his hair and straightened his glasses. I was tempted to leave, but I could tell he was working up the courage to ask me something, so I waited. "Could you do me a favor?" he finally said in a tentative voice far different from the bravado he usually exuded.

"What do you need?" I asked warily.

"Could—" He stopped and swallowed as if he was losing his nerve. When I waited, he took a deep breath and said quickly, "Could you come to the football game tomorrow and let me take a picture to show your support of Sparrow High?"

I shook my head. "That would be a bad idea. The FBI is getting a little too close. I don't want to risk them waiting for me."

He held up a hand. "Just for a few minutes. Come take a picture, and then you can leave. It'd just be great for the *Bulletin*."

I remembered how he always made the Black Rider look good, even to the point of embellishing my accomplishments. Martin may have been a journalist through and through, but he had never thrown dirt on the Black Rider's name. I nodded. "Okay. I'll be there."

He stared at me as if amazed I had agreed. "You mean it?" he squeaked.

I nodded. "I owe you my gratitude for your stories, even if they do get a little extravagant."

He straightened his glasses and grinned. "I'm pleased that you read them. It's all for the sake of good journalism," he said. "And I really don't go that far. You do most of it yourself."

I climbed onto the motorcycle without a word and started the engine. Without a better idea, I kept the pizza boxes balanced on the tank and my legs. I gave Martin a salute Jagger would have been proud of, then pulled slowly from the parking lot.

By the time I arrived at Magnum's door, I vowed never to order pizza while riding a motorcycle again. I shoved my outfit in my backpack and hid the bike behind his house, then carried the somewhat tattered boxes to the rickety porch. The steps squeaked as I made my way to the door. I was surprised when Magnum was the one who answered, but the look on his face made it all worthwhile.

"Am I glad to see you," he said. "Derek and Tommy have eaten pretty much everything in sight. I'm beginning to think they're part goat." He opened the door wide so I could enter.

Jessica sat at the stained coffee table with an open math book lit by the glow of a lamp without a shade. She glanced up, then a smile spread across her face. "Feelin' better?"

I remembered Magnum's visit to the hospital. "Thanks for the flowers."

A blush touched her cheeks, making her hair look even redder. "You're welcome." She rose and hurried from the room without looking back.

I grinned and followed Magnum to the kitchen. The second I opened a box, footsteps ran down the hall.

"Pizza, pizza!" Tommy shouted.

"I call a box to myself," Derek yelled.

They collided against the table, a whirlwind of red hair, dirty elbows, and swinging fists. Magnum pulled them both apart while I held the pizza boxes over my head.

"Settle down or you won't get any of it," he barked.

That sobered them up. They stood eyeing the boxes I set on the plastic table. "Everyone gets two slices, then we'll go from there," Magnum said. He handed out paper plates and I set the slices on them. Both brothers took the plates and rushed off to the living room.

"Jessica," Magnum called.

"I'll eat later," she shouted from the back of the house.

He set the plate on the counter and shook his head. "Usually she's the one fighting for pizza first. Girls." He grabbed a slice and took a big bite, then gestured toward the boxes. "Thanks for those."

I shrugged. "After that ride, I would have been too tired to make anything for dinner."

He nodded gratefully and took another slice. "You call Maddy yet?"

I hesitated, then shook my head.

"What's stopping you?" he asked, surprised.

I avoided meeting his gaze and leaned against the counter. "I've tried, but she won't answer."

"Try again," he said. "It's as easy as that." He pulled a cell phone from his pocket and tossed it to me. "Don't even pretend you don't know her number by heart."

He slid two more slices of pizza onto his plate and wandered into the living room to give me some privacy.

I studied the phone for a few minutes, then sighed. I set his phone on the table and slipped mine out of my pocket where I had been hoping it would ring all day. I dreaded the sound of her voicemail, empty tones with empty promises because she didn't call back. I closed my eyes and hit the speed dial. The phone rang four times and my heart sank. Just before the voicemail answered, there was a pause.

"Kelson?" The sound of Madelyn's voice made my heart pound. I didn't know what to say. All the doubts that had been flooding my mind at her silence made it impossible to come up with a single word. I swallowed dryly, hoping she wouldn't hang up. "Kelson, I'm so sorry."

The heartache in her voice ate at me, freeing me from the chaos of my thoughts. "Don't be sorry."

"I should have answered," she said, the misery in her voice making it crack. "I just didn't know what to say."

"You've never had problems talking to me."

"I know. It's just being here all by myself makes all the memories come back so real." Her voice choked off, then she said, "I would have killed him if you hadn't stopped me."

I wanted to hold her. My arms ached to wrap around her and press her close against my chest, letting her know she was safe. The distance between us felt insurmountable even though we spoke as if we were in the same room. "You're not a killer," I replied.

"I would have been, Kel. If you hadn't been there, I would have cracked his skull with that bat." Her voice quieted even as it became thicker with pain. "And I don't think I would have regretted it. I'm not a good person, Kelson."

"Yes, you are," I said firmly. "He did horrible things to you, terrible things. No one should have gone through what you did, especially a young girl trapped at home because of her mother's condition. You were a victim, Maddy. It wasn't your fault." I put every ounce of conviction into my voice, willing her to believe the truth. "I almost killed him the first time I beat him behind the bar. Magnum stopped me. I wanted to kill him."

Her voice was barely a whisper when she said, "I wish you would have."

I told her the truth. "Me too." It would have saved her from the fear, the heartache, and the regret and guilt she carried with her if I had ended his miserable life that day behind the bar. Perhaps the Black Rider would be no more; perhaps I would be in jail for murder, but I wouldn't hear the anguish in Madelyn's voice and know the guilt she would carry for the rest of her life.

"I miss you so much," she said.

My heart leaped at her words despite the pain with which she said them. "I miss you too." I took a breath to slow my heart. "It's been difficult here."

She let out a small breath. "I got your text about the candlelight ceremony. I'm glad you went."

I shook my head even though she couldn't see me. "I didn't know if I should."

She let out a whisper of a fond laugh. "One of these days you need to take the credit you deserve. Sparrow loves you."

"Yours is the only love I care about."

She fell silent for a moment. My heart clenched with doubt, worried things had changed. I shouldn't have pushed it; I would rather wait forever hoping there was still love than know with a certainty I had lost it.

Time stood still until she said, "I love you with all my heart,

Kel. Whenever I feel like I'm falling apart, I think of that night we laid on the grass by the pond. I felt so safe in your arms, so loved. I don't know why you care about me so much." She sniffed quietly. "Especially after everything with Uncle Mitch, but I care about you so much, you're all I think about." Her voice took on a wry twist that made me smile. "And all I talk about, according to Aunt Masey."

I took a deep breath, letting it fill up my lungs as full as they would go. When I let it out, I felt the tension ease from my shoulders and release the grip on my heart. She loved me. No matter what, Madelyn was mine and I was hers.

"I can't tell you how good it feels to hear you say that. I guess I worried you were enjoying the distance without me," I admitted.

"If I could come home to you, I would," she said.

My heart soared with her words. When Zoey died, my sense of home had died with her. Even though I had a place at the Ashbys' and my mom was there, it was missing that feeling of belonging, of warmth and comfort and all the things that made up a true home. Whenever I thought of Madelyn, I felt those things; it was only until she phrased it that way that I realized she was truly my sense of home.

When I was with her, I was more myself than I had been since I left California. She broke down my walls and accepted who I was without them. I felt better about who I was when I was around her, and she made me see things about myself I never knew existed. Madelyn was my safe place, my soul mate, my home. I missed her with all of my heart. "I need to see you again," I said.

"I don't think Dad would bring me back just to visit." Her wish to do so hung heavily in her voice.

"I wish there was something you could come back for." I had my head in my hand while my elbow rested on my knee. Something sharp struck me in the shoulder. I jerked back and looked at Magnum in surprise.

"Cassidy's party, idiot!" he said in a loud whisper.

I almost laughed out loud. Somehow in the midst of Maddy's confession about how she felt regarding Mitch and the confirmation of her continued love, I had forgotten entirely about Cassidy's party. I grinned at Magnum and said into the phone, "The Ashbys are throwing a party to celebrate Cassidy's sixteenth birthday on Wednesday. She would love for you to be there. Think your dad would go for it?"

My words hung in the air a moment, then she said with excitement in her voice, "I think he would! He knows we're friends. I'll ask him and let you know as soon as I can."

After we said good-bye, I hung up and looked out the tattered kitchen blinds at the night beyond.

"A smile like that means she'll be there," Magnum ventured.

I turned to find him leaning against the door frame with his arms crossed and a smug expression on his face.

"She's going to try," I said. "Thanks."

He shrugged. "It's the least I can do to repay you for the pizza."

He followed me to the motorcycle. I pulled on my helmet. "Guess I'll be seeing you at the game tomorrow. Martin saw me at the pizza house and made me agree to take a picture showing school support."

Magnum snorted. "I'll bet he doesn't sleep tonight because he's up writing an epic article about it even though it hasn't happened yet."

"I'll bet you're right," I said. I stared the motorcycle. "Don't lose the game or it'll ruin his article."

He laughed. "Don't worry. We've got Meadowland beat already."

I chuckled as I pulled out of the driveway and into the night.

There was something nameless and wonderful about riding the roads on a machine able to do anything I asked of it. The Er-6n was great, but it had been an older model and already driven hard before I owned it. The CBR was new and had been fitted with all the latest equipment. It responded immediately to every touch. I wanted to race it at the factory and see how it held up against the others.

Chapter Twenty-five

EVERYONE WAS EXCITED ABOUT the game. Banners that proclaimed the Bulldogs would destroy the Meadowland Meadow Larks lined the hallways. As far as mascots went, we already had them beat, according to pictures of a bulldog on steroids beating up a little bird much like old Tom and Jerry cartoons. Apparently violence didn't matter as long as it was painted on poster paper in our black and yellow school colors.

The thought of showing up to the game dressed as the Black Rider made me nervous. I nodded at the deputy stationed at the back door as I made my way back from the gym. Deputies at the school were a familiar sight since the Brown Hawk gang's attack. I was just glad he was one of Sheriff Bowley's men instead of an FBI agent.

A shoulder slammed against mine.

"Watch where you're going, Keldon."

I fought back a smile. "Sorry, I didn't see you walking there."

Magnum glared at me with a few members of the original Bullet gang following behind.

"What are you gonna do to him?"

We both looked over at the angry voice. Uzi, Colt, and Snipe stood glaring at Magnum. I wished I knew their real names so I didn't have to think of them in terms of Bullets, because by the way they were looking, they had disbanded completely from Magnum's leadership.

"Your beatings are pathetic, unless you want to show him what a real beat-down feels like," Uzi said. He toyed with one of the rings in his eyebrow and studied me like I was fresh meat.

A crowd began to form around us. I met Magnum's gaze and lifted a shoulder just enough that he would notice it. His eyes widened slightly.

"I wouldn't mind showing him who's really boss around here," Uzi said, taking a step toward me.

"We all know who's really boss," Magnum growled.

Uzi met his eyes. "I don't think we do."

Things were quickly spiraling out of control. We were out of sight of the deputy, but enough noise would probably draw his attention.

"I'm outta here," I said. I attempted to push past Uzi, but he and Colt grabbed my shoulders.

"No, you don't," Colt said. He had painted his Mohawk blue instead of the usual red. I wondered if it was his attempt to show his separation from his old gang. Snipe, the girl who used to have green hair, had done the same. The three of them glared at me. "You're always getting in the way."

"You have no idea," I muttered under my breath.

"What was that?" Uzi demanded.

When I didn't answer, he punched me in the stomach.

I could have avoided the blow; it wouldn't have taken more than a sidestep. I would have caught his fist and punched him under the ribs, then followed it with a jab to the stomach and a haymaker to the jaw. In less than a minute, Uzi would have been sprawled on the hallway floor, but that would have blown my cover.

Instead, I breathed with the blow, lessening the impact as I doubled over in what wasn't completely mock pain. I saw him shift his feet and knew he intended to elbow me in the head. I dropped to my knees before he could do it and head-butted him in the groin. It wasn't one of my usual moves, but it was effective and looked like an accident.

Uzi fell to the floor in much the same way I had imagined. Colt and Snipe stared at him in shock. I stumbled back to my feet. "Sorry about that," I said. I pushed through the crowd and made it to my next classroom. I was the first one in there because everyone who should have been seated was out in the hallway. I stretched and felt the slight pain in my stomach ease.

"That was smooth. I used to think those things were by accident."

I looked up to see Magnum standing in the doorway. "You've given me lots of practice."

He rolled his eyes. "Thanks, anyway."

"Forget about them," I recommended. "Concentrate on the game. They don't matter."

He nodded. "That cop from the back door showed up and scattered everyone anyway. It might give us a few days."

"We might need to brush up on your fighting skills. What do you say we meet at the junkyard tonight after the game?"

He looked relieved. "I'll be there. If we win, there'll be a party, but I can meet you after that."

"When we win," I said.

He grinned and nodded. "When we win." He glanced down the hall. "I'd better go."

I ignored the looks of pity from my classmates who filed in just before the bell rang. Even the teacher gave me the compassionate smile one reserved for a victim. I sank further in my chair and tried to concentrate on statistics, but found myself imagining how I would have preferred the fight to go instead.

———◦◦◦———

FAKING SICK TO GET out of going to the game wasn't an option this time. When I showed up at the game as the Black Rider, they would just be upset, so I had to let them know.

"You're sure it's a good idea?" Mom asked.

"I made a promise," I said. "I'll leave right afterwards."

"It could be dangerous," Aunt Lauren said.

Uncle Rick shrugged. "It might be good for the team to know the Black Rider supports them."

Aunt Lauren and Mom stared at him. He set his nice black going-out cowboy hat on his head and straightened his tie. Football games and church were the only occasions Uncle Rick dressed up, and he wore the same clothes to both. Aunt Lauren wore a yellow and black Bulldogs sweatshirt that enunciated her growing belly, while Mom settled for a yellow Tee-shirt from her last job in California.

She smoothed the shirt in an effort to get out the wrinkles from being packed. "I don't understand why the Black Rider has to show up to a football game. It just doesn't make sense to me. What if the FBI is there?"

"It's a fast motorcycle," I said, trying to make her smile.

She shook her head. "Not if they shoot out your tires."

"That'd be cool!" Cole piped in.

"They don't do that," Uncle Rick said calmly. "It'd put too many people in danger. Let him have his time in the sun. He's earned it."

The way Uncle Rick put it made me second-guess my decision. I wasn't thinking of the glory; I was just doing it because I promised Martin and I owed him one. I wondered how the rest of the school would see it. "I'll stay," I said quietly.

A spark flashed in Uncle Rick's eyes that I had never seen before. He crossed to me and said in a low voice, "Son, you've put your life on the line for this town more than once and given the folks here exactly what they needed—a hero. You go to the game and get your picture taken. It's important to you, and it's important to the town. Be proud of what you've done, and let Sparrow know you're still here for her."

My heart clenched even as warmth spread through me at his words. I glanced at Mom. She threw up her arms with a sigh. "Rick's right. You've handled things just fine without me interfering. I shouldn't start now."

On impulse, I hugged her. "Thanks, Mom," I said even though we both knew she was worried.

"Just take care of yourself." She hugged me back. "I'm proud of you and I know you deserve it. I just want you to be safe."

"I will," I promised.

A surge of anticipation flooded my limbs as I watched them drive away. I drove the four-wheeler to Jagger's and traded it for my new CBR. Mick barked at me from the back porch, but Jagger was nowhere to be seen.

"Protect the junk," I told the dog. He snapped at a fly and his teeth gave a tiny click when they closed on air. "Exactly," I said with a laugh. I started the engine and felt the excitement that filled me roll into a steady thrum with the growl of the motor. I pulled out of the junkyard and headed to the game.

IT WAS IMMEDIATELY APPARENT that Martin had let it leak that I would be at the game. A huge crowd stood in front of the small football stadium. Most of the town was there because in Sparrow, football was a religion; you had better have a good reason if you missed a game, and then everyone would fill you in with enough highlights, it felt as if you had been there.

The crowd shouted and cheered when I drove through the parking lot and along the sidewalk to where Martin waited by the ticket booth. I wondered if every stand inside the stadium was empty. The clapping grew louder when I turned off the engine. I spotted Cassidy standing with Sandy and several of their other friends near one side. She gave me a wave with an ironic smile. I lifted a hand in return. The cheer that followed was deafening.

I leaned over to Martin. "A little much, don't you think?" I shouted.

"I'm just glad you kept your promise. I almost had a mutiny," he yelled back. He motioned to a photographer with a camera bearing a lens as long as the CBR's muffler. I recognized him from his picture at the back of the *Bulldog Bulletin*. He wore a yellow baseball hat backwards and clicked away with the camera as though I were a runway model. I should have come up with some more poses. The thought made me grin wryly inside the helmet.

The audience drew closer as students attempted to get in the picture. "Why is everyone out here?" I asked Martin. "The game should have started."

He shook his head. "Apparently Magnum hasn't shown up yet." He rolled his eyes. "That's what happens when you put the leader of the Bullets in as starting quarterback."

My stomach twisted. "They don't hold a game for the quarterback; where's the backup?"

"They're refusing to play until he shows up."

That had me concerned. "They'll throw the game."

He nodded. "Too much riding on one person, I'd say."

I barely heard him as I searched the crowd quickly for anyone I could ask for information. Thompson's shaved head stood out above the students, parents, and teachers. He looked relieved to see me and was heading through the audience with two other members of the Bullets. I climbed off the motorcycle and the crowd moved out of my way. I closed the distance between us.

"What's going on?" I asked quietly.

Thompson bent his head in an effort to ensure only I heard. "Magnum was taken by the Verdos. They jumped him after school."

I gritted my teeth. "How do you know?"

Behind us, members of the crowd began taking pictures with my motorcycle. The photographer clicked away, happy to have willing subjects.

"They called me and said to tell you they'd be calling, so to keep your phone handy."

I swore quietly. The Verdos wouldn't play around. Magnum was in real danger. I put a hand over the rectangular form of the cell phone in my jacket and felt my heart hammering underneath.

"You've got to get him away from them," Pistol, a short, scrawny member of the Bullets said.

"I will," I promised.

I let out a breath and made my way back to the motorcycle and Martin standing proudly beside it.

"Something came up," I told him. "I've gotta go."

His eyebrows drew together. "Does this have anything to do with Magnum's absence?"

I hesitated, then nodded. At least they would know somebody was trying to help.

He stepped back from the motorcycle and motioned for the

crowd to clear away. "Be careful," he called over his shoulder.

I waved at the audience and revved the engine. People cleared the sidewalk. I caught Mom's worried look from where the Ashbys waited. I hoped I could keep my promise to her that I would be safe. I sped across the parking lot searching for a place to wait for the phone call.

Chapter Twenty-six

I PARKED THE MOTORCYCLE behind a billboard near the fairgrounds and tried to wait patiently. Ironically, it was the same sign I had hidden my bike behind during the gang's first attack at the livestock building. Tall grass baked brown by the persistent sun brushed against the tattered billboard that proclaimed, "Sparrow Fairgrounds." It had a picture of a girl with blonde pigtails leading a big Holstein cow. The picture was faded and wood showed through in several places as though it had been many years since anyone touched it up.

The phone rang and I pulled off my helmet to answer it. My heart thundered in my chest.

"Hello?"

"The elusive Black Rider." The voice chuckled without humor. "We have a friend of yours."

I glared at nothing in particular. "Let him go."

"We will, for the right price," he said.

"Name it."

"You."

My blood ran cold at his tone. He was silent for a minute, then said, "Did you hear me? We will trade the Bullet leader for the Black Rider." A dangerous tone entered his voice. "But if you don't come alone, we'll put a bullet through his head. If you don't show up, we'll make sure he suffers before he dies. After all you put us through, it's the least we could do."

I had no doubt he would follow through with the threat. I kept my voice carefully calm. "How do I know he's still alive?"

"Talk to him yourself," the man said.

There was a fumbling sound, then, "Kelson, don't you dare try to rescue me. It's not worth—"

A sharp crack sounded, followed by a cry of pain.

Magnum never would have used my real name if he wasn't in a horrible situation. My heart pounded in my chest. I heard the leader take the phone back. "Where do I find you?"

He gave a few directions, then hung up before I could say anything else. I stared at the phone in my hand, hearing Magnum's cry of pain again and again. He was tough. I had never heard him make such a sound before. My stomach twisted and I felt sick. I rose and was about to climb back on the motorcycle when the phone rang again.

"What?" I demanded without looking at the caller ID.

"Kelson?"

Relief filled me at the sound of Madelyn's voice. I closed my eyes and leaned against the motorcycle. "Maddy."

"What's wrong?" she asked.

I rubbed my eyes. "It's bad. Really bad."

"Tell me what's going on."

I quickly repeated everything that happened. The Verdos had given me until sundown. A plan formed in my mind as I spoke to Madelyn.

"Promise me you'll call Sheriff Bowley," she said.

It sounded like she was close to tears. "I will."

"Really, Kelson? You can't do this alone. It's too dangerous."

"I know," I replied. I looked up at the sky. "I've got to go."

"I don't want you to."

"I'll call the sheriff," I promised. "I'll be as careful as I can."

I heard her breathe out quietly. "Call me as soon as you get back. Please take care of yourself."

A lump formed in my throat at her words. "I will," I promised.

I hung up and slid the phone in my jacket, then jumped on the motorcycle. I broke the speed limit by double on my way to the junkyard. I wasn't about to meet the Verdos empty-handed.

"I'M STILL NA' SURE 'bout this," Jagger said.

I wrapped Magnum's black jacket around a concussion grenade and packed it inside his helmet. Using the chin strap, I fastened the helmet carefully to the seat of the CBR. "Me neither," I admitted. "But I'm out of time. If the address leads to an abandoned gas station like you said, they're in the middle of nowhere and able to see me coming."

"Ya promised Maddy."

I tried to remember why I had told him that. I blew out a breath. "Fine. Just give me a head start before you call the sheriff. I don't want to jeopardize Magnum."

He nodded and checked one last thing on my vest before handing me my jacket to wear over it. "Watch the bumps."

I gave him a grim smile as I slipped carefully into the jacket, then pulled on my helmet. "See you soon."

"I hope so," he replied.

He gave me a salute I returned before heading back to the road.

The hum of my tires on the pavement cleared my thoughts.

The only thing that mattered was freeing Magnum. There was no certainty that he would even be alive when I got there. The threat in the Verdos' voice was real. He wouldn't hesitate to carve his hatred for me into Magnum's skin.

The sun slowly met the mountains as the gas station grew larger. It was in the middle of nowhere, a good business venture gone to pot when the bottom fell out of the economy and people stopped traveling down the lonely road. As I neared, a tumbleweed blew past the two dusty pumps. The gas station's windows had been boarded up, and the door to the car-repair side of the station was propped halfway open by a rock. Four cars sat at the rear of the station—two beefed-up Camaros, a red Corvette, and a Shelby Mustang with the top down. I hoped a windstorm filled it with dust.

I circled the gas station once and found a place near the main door that stood in a conspicuous circle of moonlight. I quickly unbuckled Magnum's helmet and left it on the ground. I wasn't sure what I would find inside the gas station. I could only hope Magnum was safe.

I ducked my head and drove the motorcycle straight through the sliding door that once let cars in to be repaired. The crooked metal gave way with a loud crash. I braked to a halt in the middle of the repair shop and met the stunned gazes of the Verdos members.

"Now that's an entrance I'd expect from the Black Rider," said a man whose voice matched the person on the phone.

I studied him carefully. He wore a green bandana around his head. Dreadlocked black hair stuck out from beneath it. A scar circled his neck as though someone had tried to cut his throat, and instead of hiding it, he enunciated it with a thick black tattoo that looked like a chain.

My gaze drifted from him to the men who were getting over their shock and toying with various weapons. Four men stood to the right of their leader, and five to the left. Ten armed men total. It was more than I had ever taken on alone. Each wore a green bandana either on the head or around a limb. Two clubs, three pistols, a shotgun, a chain, and three knives made up their visible arsenal.

Behind them, Magnum was handcuffed to a chair. One of his eyes was bruised and his lip was split; blood trickled down to stain the yellow and black jersey he had worn to school in preparation for the game. He shook his head, his face pale. "Kelson, get out of here!" he said in a voice weaker than I was used to hearing.

"Let him go," I growled.

The leader leveled a pistol at my chest. "What's to keep me from just shooting you both?"

"Besides your word?" I asked wryly. At his smug smile, I unzipped my jacket and let it fall from my shoulders to the floor. Several gasps sounded as the Verdos took in the array of grenades Jagger had helped me strap to the vest. "One shot, and this place will become a giant hole in the ground."

Magnum looked like he was ready to cry. I had never seen the Bullet leader at such a loss. He hung his head as though ashamed I had gone to such an extent to try to save him. I hoped it wasn't in vain.

The Verdos leader lifted his gun to my helmet. "I'll bet that's not bulletproof."

I shook my head slowly. "No, but there's enough C-4 packed in here to leave pieces of us all tiny enough that even your mother wouldn't be able to identify you." I held my breath and hoped they didn't know C-4 wouldn't explode with a gunshot, only a detonator, as Jagger had argued when I came up with the idea he quickly threw aside.

The leader lowered his gun slightly. "Then what do you propose?"

I climbed off the motorcycle carefully. "Let Magnum leave and I'll take off the vest."

"No!" Magnum protested.

The leader's eyes narrowed slightly. He looked behind him at Magnum, then motioned toward one of his men.

"I'm not leaving!" Magnum shouted. He struggled as the man unlocked his handcuffs. Two others grabbed him under the arms and pulled him toward the motorcycle. He kicked and tried to get away, but it was obvious he didn't have the energy to put up a real fight.

I grabbed his shoulder and put my visor close to his face. "Listen to me," I said in a tone I hoped left no room for argument. "Get on the bike and leave. I made a promise, and I'm keeping my word. The Black Rider's life for yours."

He shook his head before I was through talking. "No. I'm not going."

The sound of a gun cocking caught both of our attentions. "He might be wearing explosives," the leader said, "but you're not." He pressed the gun to Magnum's forehead. "Get on the bike."

Magnum looked from me to the Verdos leader. His eyes were wide with fear and anguish. Both of us knew he had no choice.

"Ride," I said quietly.

He climbed onto the motorcycle and started the engine in motions that told of habit instead of conscious thought. He turned the bike slowly to face the wreckage I had made of the door. The entire time, his gaze was on me. His eyes shone in the light of the camp lanterns the Verdos had brought before he drove slowly out of the gas station.

The Verdos leader listened to the engine fade away, then turned back to me. "Now the vest."

"All right." I willed my hands not to shake. I couldn't deny that there was stress involved with wearing two dozen grenades strapped to my chest and back. Each bump in the road had raged war with my heart. Driving through the gas station door had been a little reckless. I undid the straps carefully, and breathed a sigh of relief when it was undone. I gingerly shrugged out of the vest and lowered it to the floor. Tension hung thick in the air. The Verdos members backed to the opposite side of the room.

"And the helmet," the leader pressed.

I had hoped I could keep it on, but like he said, it wouldn't stop bullets. It wasn't full of C-4, but he didn't know that.

I undid the strap and slowly pulled it off as if afraid it would detonate at any moment. Complete silence filled the room as though every person held their breath. I eased the helmet off my head. The second it was clear, I threw it at the Verdos leader. He caught it with a shocked expression. I followed the helmet and threw a right haymaker that connected with his jaw and spun him all the way around before he hit the floor. His gun slid out of his hand and underneath a broken-down cabinet.

I turned before the others could react, knocked the shotgun away from a man who looked like an NFL linebacker, and chopped him in the throat. When he lifted his hands, I hit him twice in the belly, then swept his legs out from under him. He fell to the floor hard enough to shake it.

The other two men with guns were my first targets. I wouldn't make the same mistake of disregarding the most dangerous weapons. A man swung a club at me as a skinny dark-skinned boy lifted a gun. I stepped swiftly to the side to avoid the club, elbowed the man in the side of the head, then used his body as a shield between me and the skinny boy.

I shoved the man forward and when the boy lifted his arm to avoid shooting his companion, I wrenched the gun from his grasp and clubbed him in the head with the butt. I spun and tried to hit the man with the club as well. He raised the bat to block the blow and the gun went flying out of my grasp. I kneed the man in the groin, then again in the face when he doubled over.

A hiss sounded in the air. I wrenched the bat from the man and raised it in time to catch the end of the chain before it lashed against my face. I jerked the bat forward and drove my fist straight into the man's face. His head whiplashed back with the force of the blow and he collapsed without moving.

The slight click of a gun's safety warned me and I dropped to the ground an instant before the bullet smashed through the air. I rolled to the left, picking up the club as I did so. I threw it and jumped back to my feet to avoid a knife. It sliced across the back of my T-shirt, missing me by millimeters. I dove forward, grappling for the last gun. The shooter was built like Rambo. I wouldn't win the weapon out of force. He bent the gun slowly in my direction. His finger tightened on the trigger.

"Let him go."

Everyone started at the voice that shouted through the broken door. I grinned at the sight of Magnum in the Black Rider jacket and helmet I had left in the parking lot.

"There's two of them?" a man near the door swore.

I poked the man with the gun hard in the eye. He let out a string of curses and dropped the gun to clutch his face. I grabbed for the weapon, but a club smashed into my back. I let my body fall forward with the blow, then rolled to the right. The club slammed into the cement where my head had been.

Before the man could swing again, Magnum tackled him around the waist. They crashed into a work table, sending it to the ground in splinters. Instinct warned me to move. I sprang to the right just as a knife tip pricked the back of my shoulder. I spun around and grabbed the man's knife hand, attempting to punch him in the face with my right as I did so. He blocked the blow with one arm, driving his own fist into my cheekbone.

I staggered back, seeing stars. I blocked a kick for my stomach, caught the man's leg, and drove a chop into his groin. He fell to the ground with an unmanly scream. Near the wall, Magnum slammed a fist into a man's face. His head rebounded off the wall and Magnum hit him again.

My brain said we could hold our own against them if we kept them from the guns. Two were underneath the cabinet, while another was unaccounted for. I dodged a sweep of a knife, my eyes searching the ground for the last gun. Out of the corner of my eye, I saw a hand reach down for it. I turned ready to stop him when a two-by-four beam slammed into my face, dropping me straight to the ground.

Pain exploded in my vision. Something wet began to drip down my face as a circle of cold metal was pressed hard against my forehead.

"Whoa!" Magnum said. "Take it easy."

"Think you can mess with us?" the Verdos leader demanded. His eyes burned with anger and hatred as he looked from one of us to the other, his green bandana skewed to one side.

The man with the two-by-four shoved Magnum against the wall and pressed the beam tight against his throat. One of Magnum's hands fought to keep the wood from cutting off his air while the other fumbled for his pocket.

A siren sounded in the distance, followed closely by at least four more. A surge of hope ran through my chest. Sheriff Bowley knew I was in trouble and was making as much noise as possible in an attempt to distract them and save my life.

"The cops? Really?" the Verdos leader yelled. Spit flew from his lips and he pressed the barrel of the gun harder into my head. It felt like my skull would break. "At least I can take one of you down first," he muttered.

His finger tightened on the trigger with agonizing slowness. I stared into his demented gaze, wishing all the while I looked at Madelyn instead. I missed her face. I would never see it again.

A tear leaked from the corner of my eye, whether from pain or the hopelessness of the situation, I didn't know. The Verdos' gaze sharpened and he let out a laugh. "I'll be the first and last to see the Black Rider cry." His eyes narrowed. "Say good-bye, Rider."

Before he could pull the trigger, I threw both legs up and wrapped them around his throat, pulling his arm back until his elbow was in full extension. I jerked the arm down and heard his elbow snap. A scream of agony tore from his lips and the gun fell from his hand.

The man with the two-by-four turned, ready to slam it down on my head, when a chink of metal on cement sounded. I shut my eyes and covered my ears. A percussion rocked the air and was followed by a flash so sharp my eyes burned despite the fact that they were closed. My ears rang and my head pounded as bad as it did when I'd had a concussion. I couldn't remember where I was or what I was doing.

I forced my eyes open and saw a man rolling in agony next to me. He had a green bandana in his hand and his eyes were open, but he acted like he couldn't see. My gaze focused on the green bandana. I suddenly remembered Magnum and the Verdos. A gun had been pressed to my head.

I searched for it wildly, my vision still spattered with spots and shadows. The other Verdos sprawled around me, moaning and rolling on the floor. Their leader held his arm with cries of agony. Magnum leaned against the wall as he struggled to stay standing. The sirens surrounded the gas station. I spotted the gun next to my helmet. I staggered to my feet and grabbed both, sliding my helmet back over my head.

"Kelson! Magnum!" Sheriff Bowley called. Panic was evident in his voice.

"We're okay," I shouted. The sound made my head pound. Magnum helped me to my feet. I leaned against the wall, trying to stay upright. Blood dripped in my eye. I pushed the visor of my helmet up and searched for the source. My fingers found a deep gash through my eyebrow from the two-by-four. I pulled the visor back down just before the sheriff and a dozen other deputies appeared around the doorway I had battered down with my motorcycle.

The sheriff's gaze swept the bodies quickly; relief flooded his face when he saw us near the far wall. "Thank goodness," he said. He motioned to his men; they swarmed through the doors and began handcuffing the gang members.

The Verdos leader pushed up to his knees, cradling his broken arm. I pointed the gun at his head. "If you move, I will pull the trigger."

Magnum shoved the man with the two-by-four onto the floor next to him. The sheriff crossed to me and pushed the leader to his stomach, then proceeded to slap handcuffs around his wrists. When he was done, he shoved his hat back and looked up at me. "I almost believed you'd do it."

I let out a breath and held out the gun. He took it with a half smile as he stood. "Thought I'd find you both dead."

I rubbed the back of my neck. "Would have been if it wasn't for Magnum chucking that flash grenade when he did."

"It was close," Magnum echoed, shaking his head.

I took a step forward, then had to reach back to the wall for support. Magnum grabbed my arm to steady me. The stun grenade and being hit in the face with a beam didn't bode well for my equilibrium.

The sheriff's face creased with worry. "Did you get shot?"

I put a hand to my helmet. "Got hit in the head is all. Shook me up a bit."

"Met a two-by-four that didn't like him," Magnum said.

Sheriff Bowley nodded. "Let's get you guys out of here."

He steered us out of the gas station and into the welcome embrace of night. Stars glittered down like shattered glass. Deputy Addison left the other deputies he was talking to and crossed to meet us.

"Get the Black Rider checked out at the hospital before he goes home," the sheriff told his deputy.

"I'm fine," I protested. "I'm not going to the hospital again."

Deputy Addison chuckled. "You can barely walk straight."

I shook my head. "I'm fine."

"Good luck arguing with him," Magnum said. "He's stubborn as a mule."

Sheriff Bowley sighed. "Go get checked at the ambulance. If they feel you need to go to the hospital, I don't want an argument."

A thought struck me before he walked away. "Sheriff?" He turned back with an expectant expression. "There's a vest in there with grenades strapped to it. Tell your men to take care."

His brows knit together. "How do we disarm it?"

"Call Jagger," I replied. "He'll know what to do."

"I should've guessed as much," the sheriff said.

I followed the deputy to the ambulance. Magnum walked next to me like a silent shadow, brooding in the dark evening. "Grab some butterfly bandages," I told him. He stared at me like I was crazy. "I'll meet you at the deputy's car. The fewer people who know who we are, the better. It'll be safer for them and us."

"The sheriff said—" Deputy Addison began, but I shook my head.

"I have the right to refuse medical treatment." I shrugged. "I'm just skipping the middleman."

"By middleman, you meant EMT," Magnum put in. "The one with real medical training."

I grinned beneath my helmet. "You know that hasn't stopped me before."

He stalked off toward the ambulance, muttering things beneath his own helmet.

Deputy Addison opened the door and I sat on the seat. My head spun and I was grateful to be done moving. After a few minutes, the crunch of Magnum's footsteps on gravel sounded around the car, then he opened the other door and sat down. He took off his helmet and threw it on the floor. "That wasn't easy," he growled. "They don't like parting with their medical supplies."

I glanced at him. "What did you tell them?"

He let out a huff at my humored tone. "That the Black Rider needs to see a psychiatrist."

I chuckled. "You're probably right."

He rolled his eyes. "Luckily, it seems anything the Black Rider asks for is given to him." He nudged the helmet on the ground with his foot. "This thing comes in handy. I think I've actually missed it."

Deputy Addison started the car and pulled away from the gas station.

"Take off your helmet," Magnum said in a resigned tone.

I eased it off and he flicked on the door light. By the look on his face, I was glad I couldn't see what I looked like.

"Don't know how I let you talk me into this stuff," Magnum said. He grabbed several alcohol swabs and began cleaning the wound far more gently than I would have given him credit for.

After a couple of seconds of enduring the grimace on his face, I grabbed the swabs from him and used the helmet visor as a mirror to scrub the dried blood away myself to save him from doing it. I grimaced at the reflection. The skin above my eyebrow was extremely tender and bruises were already beginning to form along my forehead and around my right eye where the beam had hit. I probed my jaw and found it sore as well from the punch I had taken.

"You look like you got kicked by a cow," Magnum muttered.

Deputy Addison grinned in the rearview mirror. "At least you've got your cover story."

I nodded. "It's no secret Uncle Rick's Holsteins hold a grudge."

"The Black Rider's worst enemies," Magnum said with a laugh. The deputy chuckled.

When the wound was clean, Magnum drew the butterfly bandages tight, pulling it closed. "You should probably get stitches," he said, spreading gauze across the wound.

"Then I'd have to get them taken out again."

"You'll probably be back at the hospital before then," Magnum reasoned coldly. He tore a piece of white tape and used it to hold the gauze in place. The silence that filled the car was palpable. When he tore the second piece of tape, it sounded louder than the concussion grenade had. He finally let out his breath in a heavy sigh. "Why did you make me leave?"

"I needed you to save my life," I said. I met his angry gaze. "Somebody had to chuck that grenade."

"I almost didn't notice it," he replied. He rubbed his split lip, then winced as though he had just remembered it was there. He tore one of the alcohol swabs open and used it to clean his chin. "You got lucky," he said with a wince.

I nodded. "All the same, thanks."

He rolled his eyes and took the helmet from me. He tore another swab open and began scrubbing the blood from inside the helmet.

Deputy Addison met my eyes in the mirror. "Be nice of the Black Rider to give us a bit more warning before he goes off on his adventures. Might get the both of you a little less beat up."

I watched Magnum carefully clean the helmet. "I think it's time for the Black Rider to take a break."

"I'll believe it when I see it," the deputy said amiably.

"I'm serious." The deputy and Magnum fell silent at my tone. I studied the seat in front of me to avoid looking at either of them. "It's time to give in. The Verdos are incarcerated, the Brown Hawk gang won't be bothering anyone for a long time, and Sparrow's sheriff department can handle the rest." I rubbed the fresh bandages on my forehead. "I think it's time I call it quits."

Deputy Addison broke the silence that followed. "Can't say I'll miss seeing you beat up. You deserve a break." He met my gaze in the mirror and I read the stark remorse on his face. "Do what you need to. The town is in your debt."

Magnum didn't say anything. He merely continued cleaning the helmet, replacing dirty swabs until they no longer came out colored dull brown from the dried blood.

I closed my eyes and listened to the quiet hum of the car over the road. I missed the growl of my motorcycle. Thoughts of Madelyn kept surfacing in my mind. I needed to call her, but didn't want to do it with the deputy and Magnum listening. I missed her smile and the feeling of her fingers entwined in mine. Cassidy's party couldn't get here fast enough.

WHEN WE PULLED INTO the Ashbys' driveway, Mom was the first one to the car. Everyone else crowded behind her. Apparently the sheriff had called. My stomach clenched at the concern on Mom's face. I tried to act as though nothing had happened as I climbed out.

Mom took one look at my face and tears filled her eyes. "I'm so glad you're back safe," she said, putting a hand on my cheek. "I was so worried."

I pulled her to the side, anxious to reassure her. "It's all right, Mom. I'm fine and Magnum's safe. The gang who kidnapped him has been arrested. Nothing like this should happen again." I took a deep breath. "And I'm done. This was the Black Rider's last ride."

She nodded as though she wanted to believe me, but doubt showed in her eyes. "I just hate seeing you hurt."

"He gave out worse than he got, trust me," Magnum said, following me from the car. Cassidy ran forward, then stopped herself just behind Uncle Rick. Her father didn't appear to notice how badly she wanted to make sure Magnum was all right. Magnum's gaze held hers, then shifted quickly away before anyone saw.

"That's for sure," Deputy Addison said. "The shape those guys were in, they'll think twice about messing with Sparrow again if they ever get out of jail, which is doubtful." He held out his hand to my mom. "I'm Deputy Addison. I don't think we've met."

"Sarah Brady," Mom replied with a small smile. "You say the gang is under control?"

"Sheriff Bowley is taking care of them as we speak," he reassured her.

All I could think about was calling Madelyn. The phone felt heavy in my pocket. I cleared my throat. "I'm going to go lie down."

Mom gave me a worried smile, her brows pinched together. "I'll go make sure your bed is ready." She hurried toward the house and Aunt Lauren followed.

Magnum lifted an eyebrow as if he guessed my intentions. "I'll get the deputy to give me a lift back to the gas station and hide the bike at the junkyard." He held out a hand. "Try to get some rest, Kelson."

"You too," I told him. "Thanks for the help."

His brow creased. "Thanks for saving my life."

I shrugged. "Gotta keep you humble somehow."

He laughed and turned back to the car. I noticed Cassidy fidgeting. Knowing how much she liked Magnum, I could only guess how much self-control it took to pretend she wasn't interested in his well-being. I caught Uncle Rick's attention. "Mind if I talk to you about something?" I asked him.

He looked surprised, but nodded and turned to Deputy Addison with a hand out. "Thanks for everything, Deputy."

Deputy Addison shook it. "Anytime, Mr. Ashby. Happy to help. Your nephew is a brave boy and a fine example to this town."

"I'm proud of him," Uncle Rick said. He followed me toward the house with Cole and Jaren close behind us. I glanced back and Cassidy mouthed a quick "thank you" before she hurried to Magnum's side.

I smothered a grin

"Did your brains almost fall out?" Cole asked, breaking my attention from them.

I grinned at him as he walked backwards beside me. "Almost."

"Cole," Jaren chided behind us. "If he only got bandages, his skull wasn't cracked so his brain couldn't fall out."

"Thanks for that," Uncle Rick replied dryly. He held open the screen door and waited for me to pass through.

I racked my mind for something to ask him so he wouldn't see through my diversion for Cassidy. I walked through the kitchen and sat on the cot freshly made with new blankets. The scent of laundry detergent wafted into the air. Aunt Lauren set a pitcher of water on the end table with enough water in it to quench a football team, then hurried back to the kitchen.

Mom smiled at my look. "In case you get thirsty tonight. You shouldn't be walking around with your head in that condition." She set a cup with pain medicine in it next to the water. "Take that if you get a headache."

I already had one, but I didn't tell her. "Thanks, Mom. You're the best," I said.

Mom smiled down at me, her smile tightening as she took in the bruises on my face again. "Get some rest, sweetheart."

"I will," I told her.

She turned to go, then shook her head. "You can't sleep with your shoes on," she chided with a kind smile.

I fought back a chuckle as she slid my sneakers off and pulled the blanket over me. A memory flashed through my mind of Zoey doing the same thing when I was sick enough to keep both of us home from school for a week while she cared for me. "Thanks, Mom," I said, trying to keep the emotion from my voice. "I appreciate it."

Cassidy came hurrying in. She practically floated across the living room with her mother close behind. Aunt Lauren had one hand on her stomach and the other reaching to entwine Uncle Rick's fingers.

"Are they gone?" Uncle Rick asked. Something to his tone caught my attention. He never asked what I needed to talk to him about. I wondered if he suspected something.

"The deputy took Magnum home," Cassidy replied as casually as she could, but it was impossible to miss the sparkle in her eyes when she said Magnum's name. She knelt next to the cot. "How are you feeling?"

"I'll survive," I told her.

"Good. Have to get you feeling better in time for my party," she replied, ruffling my hair because she knew I hated it. At her mother's dismayed look, she gave an abashed smile. "You can't tell Sandy if you want to keep something a secret, but I'm so excited! I wanted to tell you I knew, but you wanted to keep it a secret and if you knew I knew, it would ruin the surprise. But I think all this time you already knew I knew and didn't want to tell me because if I knew you knew I knew, we couldn't pretend that nobody knew I knew."

Aunt Lauren laughed and gave her daughter a hug. "If you don't stop talking like that, I think Kelson's headache is going to get worse."

Cassidy threw me an apologetic look. "Sorry. I'm just excited for the party."

"Me too," I said. "I'll try my best to feel better for it." Her grateful smile warmed my heart. "And I invited Magnum," I told her. "I hope you don't mind." Uncle Rick gave a noncommittal snort.

Cassidy's eyes widened and she looked like she wanted to hug me, but she also couldn't give away to her parents just how much having Magnum there meant to her. She gave me a wide smile. "Is Madelyn going to make it?"

"I need to call her," I said, hoping the urgency I felt didn't come across as desperate.

Cassidy gave me a knowing smile. "We should let you rest."

Mom smoothed the blankets and looked like she didn't want to leave. Aunt Lauren looped her arm through her sister's. "Let's let Kelson call his girl." She threw me a warm smile. "I'm sure she's anxious to hear from him."

Mom gave in and let her sister lead her from the room. Cassidy followed close behind. Uncle Rick paused at the doorway. "You look tired. I think we'll put off that talk until tomorrow, if you don't mind."

"Not at all," I replied in relief. Maybe by then I could think of something for us to talk about.

My phone was out of my pocket before his footsteps sounded up the stairs. Madelyn answered on the first ring.

"Are you all right?" she asked, skipping hello entirely.

"I'm fine." I rubbed my forehead, then winced at the bandages. "Mostly. But Magnum's okay and the gang is under arrest."

"I was so worried," she said. "I told Aunt Massey I wasn't hungry and stayed in my room with the phone plugged in just so the battery wouldn't die and I would miss your call. I was afraid you were hurt and no one knew where you were, and I couldn't stand the thought of you being in the middle of nowhere at the mercy of an armed gang." Her voice broke at the end.

"It's all right," I said gently. "I'm fine, really. Everything is under control now and I'm back at the Ashbys'."

"I'm so glad you're home," she said.

I shook my head, quickly reminding myself of my headache. "It's not home if you're not here."

"I'll be there tomorrow," she promised. "I can't wait to see you again."

The thought made me happier than any other. "I can't wait to see you," I told her. My chest tightened at the thought of how close I had come to never seeing her again. I felt the barrel of the gun against my forehead and closed my eyes. "It's so good to talk to you again."

She was silent for a moment, then said, "Things were worse than you're telling me."

"A bit," I admitted.

"I love you, Kelson," she said as though she knew how very much I needed to hear those words.

"I love you, my Maddy," I replied.

"Sleep tight. I'll see you tomorrow."

I said good-bye with a smile on my face. Firelight danced in front of my eyelids and I fell asleep with the thought that I had gotten off much luckier than I should have.

Chapter Twenty-seven

"GOTTA WATCH OUT FOR those cows," Ryan, a boy from
Cassidy's Spanish class, said with a laugh.

"Thanks for the advice," I replied dryly. My face ached, so I
held a cold can of Pepsi to it. I searched the crowd that danced and
mingled in the Ashbys' backyard, anxious for any sign of Madelyn.

My gaze landed on Magnum and Cassidy dancing near the
center of the mass. Cassidy had a pink plastic crown on her head
that said "Sixteen and Loving It". She laughed at something
Magnum said, her eyes bright and matching the exact color of the
new dress she wore because as Cassidy put it, "You can't go to your
own birthday party wearing something everyone has seen, so thank
goodness I knew about the party!"

I wasn't sure Aunt Lauren agreed, but at the moment, everyone
seemed happy. Well, almost everyone. I caught Uncle Rick scowling
near the halfway rebuilt barn. His gaze drifted around the crowd,
but it kept finding its way back to his daughter dancing and having a
good time with the well-known leader of the Bullets.

"A cow, huh?"

My heart jumped and I turned at the sound of Madelyn's voice.

Her eyes held mine with so many emotions that I didn't know what to say. I wanted to hold her, kiss her, laugh, and cry at the same time. The look on her face said she was feeling the same thing.

I took her upper arms gently, pulling her closer. "Cows don't like me," I said quietly.

"I don't know how anyone couldn't like you," she replied in a soft voice that gripped my heart.

"Oh, they manage, believe me," I reassured her.

She buried her head against my chest. "I'm so happy you're all right," she said quietly enough that no one around us could overhear.

I wrapped my arms around her, holding her tight like I had wanted to do for days. I took a deep breath of her hair, happy to be surrounded by her vanilla scent once more.

My eyes found Mom across the back lawn. She smiled at me, looking beautiful in a new green-and-cream-colored dress Aunt Lauren had helped her picked out. She served small plates of finger foods to Cassidy's guests and laughed with her sister, looking happier than she had in a very long time.

We paused by the refreshments table to get punch, then I led Madelyn to the porch swing. She sat down and looked at me. Little worry lines creased at the corners of her eyes when she took in my bruised face. She reached out a hand and brushed her fingers across my cheek. "Looks like it hurts," she said softly.

Unfortunately, it looked a lot worse than it had yesterday. A black bruise circled my right eye and I still had a bandage across my forehead to keep the new butterfly bandages Mom had put across the gash in place. My cheekbone was colored a lovely shade of deep purple. At least the ache had faded to a dull pain I could almost ignore.

"It doesn't hurt as long as I'm near you." It was a cheesy line, but her answering smile chased the worry from her face.

"I'll just have to stay around," she replied. "I mean, it's not that you look horrible, it just looks like it hurts. I wish I could have done something. I felt so helpless waiting for your call and I was so worried something happened to you. I barely slept after talking to you last night, and I couldn't wait to get over here. I kept telling Dad to drive faster." She closed her mouth as though she realized she was babbling. A million emotions flooded through her eyes; she finally threw her arms around me and hugged me tightly. "I was so worried," she said.

"I know," I told her. "I shouldn't have said anything."

She shook her head and sat back to look at me. "I want to know. Never keep something like that from me."

I caught a lock of dark brown hair that drifted down her cheek. "I won't," I promised. I let out a small breath. "It doesn't matter anymore."

Her forehead creased. "Why is that?"

"I'm going to turn myself in as the Black Rider." I couldn't help the way my chest tightened at the thought, but I had made up my mind. "The Verdos and Black Hawk gangs won't bother Sparrow anymore, and the Bullets are disbanded, as far as their leader is concerned." I watched Magnum lead Cassidy to the refreshment table made of two card tables pulled together and spread with a yellow-and-white checkered tablecloth.

"You can't be serious."

I turned at Madelyn's tone. "What's not to believe? Sparrow doesn't need the Black Rider anymore."

She shook her head. "I'm not so sure about that." When I opened my mouth to question her, she set a hand gently on my cheek. "And I'm not so sure you're ready for that, either."

I watched the crowd of students I had fought to keep safe.

Letting go of the Black Rider felt like abandoning a piece of myself that might be more of me than I dared to admit.

"Everyone needs a hero," she said softly.

"I'm just not sure I should be that hero," I replied. I looked at her. "The Black Rider's a costume, a black helmet and motorcycle. They don't need him." I couldn't voice the loss I felt at the thought.

"They do," she insisted.

I shook my head. "The FBI will be waiting at the factory tomorrow. The Black Rider will be there."

She slipped her hand into mine. "I don't think it's the right decision."

My throat tightened and I turned my face into her hair. "I think it's the only decision."

"What if you don't tell them? Just let the Black Rider disappear," she suggested, her expression urging me to listen.

I shook my head. "I can't. There's a lot I need to account for. The FBI has questions about the shootings."

"But Sparrow needs the Black Rider."

As much as her words lifted my heart, I couldn't let myself accept them. "I think Sparrow will be fine without me."

She looked up at me, the gold in her eyes bright in the light of the bulbs Uncle Rick and Jaren had strung over the backyard. She reached up a hand and gently traced the bruises on my face with her fingers. I closed my eyes at her touch, feeling how much she cared for me with every light brush of her skin against mine.

I tipped my face down and my lips met hers. I smoothed her long hair, happy she had worn it down the way I liked it. One of her hands slipped behind my ear, toying with my hair as she kissed me. I breathed in her scent, surrounded by her touch and the way her gentle strength and belief in me filled me with surety. I would give up being the Black Rider for her so she didn't have to worry any longer.

A throat cleared pointedly. I looked over, surprised I had forgotten our surroundings. Most of the crowd ignored our porch swing completely, but Cole stood impatiently in front of us. "About time," he said.

"Did you need something?" I asked, my words a bit short. Madelyn rubbed a hand soothingly down my arm. I let out a breath. "Sorry, Cole. What's going on?"

"I asked you like thirty times if you were ready to get Dad's present to Cass."

Madelyn's appearance had caused me to forget all about Uncle Rick's plan. I stood up. "Wait here just a minute. It'll be worth it," I reassured Madelyn.

She smiled at the excitement on both of our faces. "I'll be right here."

I took a few steps, then looked back to make sure she was still waiting. Butterflies rolled through my stomach at the sight of Madelyn sitting on the porch swing wearing a summer dress covered in yellow and pink flowers, her bare feet swinging gently above her discarded sandals. The sight was worth giving up everything for.

"Come on," Cole urged.

I jogged with him toward the barn. Uncle Rick tossed me a set of keys when we passed where he pretended to help Aunt Lauren serve punch and cookies. Uncle Rick had assigned himself the job of ensuring that nobody spiked the punch at his daughter's birthday party. Aunt Lauren gave us an enthusiastic wave.

Cole and I entered the back of the partially rebuilt barn where shadows and tarps hid Uncle Rick's present from prying eyes. He had worked hard to keep Cassidy occupied in the fields so she wouldn't wander in by accident. I grinned when Cole pulled the tarps away to reveal a little light-blue truck with balloons tied to a windshield wiper.

In most families, a truck would be a strange present for a sixteen-year-old girl, but Cassidy was no ordinary girl. She was a farm girl who loved her life with every breath. Uncle Rick said he knew the truck was hers the instant he saw it. He chuckled and told me that because it was a truck, it would also be a write-off for the farm.

I started the engine and Cole jumped in the back. Two seconds later, Jake flew inside the barn and leaped into the back to join him. I grinned and pulled the truck slowly toward the party.

Uncle Rick and Aunt Lauren were talking to Cassidy near the refreshments. They purposely had her back to the barn. Magnum hovered nearby, trying to be casual but obviously wanting to be near Cassidy. He looked up and a smile spread across his face when he saw the truck. Uncle Rick glanced back, then said something to Jaren. He stopped the music. Everyone paused as Uncle Rick spoke quietly to Cassidy. She turned and her eyes widened.

Cassidy let out a shriek of delight I heard from inside the truck as I shifted it into park. She threw her arms around her dad, then her mom. Friends and family cheered and clapped, and an enthusiastic rendition of "Happy Birthday" spread through the crowd.

I climbed out of the truck and tossed the keys to Cassidy. She caught them and laughed at the little blue cowboy hat keychain I had fastened on them. She gave me a tight hug. "Thank you so much!" she squealed.

"I had nothing to do with it," I protested. "It was all your dad."

He beamed at us both and slipped an arm around his wife. "Take it for a spin," he told his daughter.

She let out another squeal, grabbed Sandy's hand, and the two girls crowded inside. I made my way back to where Madelyn still waited on the swing.

"That was wonderful," she said, squeezing my hand when I sat down next to her.

"It's fun to see her so happy."

"I don't think she'll stop until she gets to California," she said with a laugh.

I lifted an arm and she ducked under it, resting her head against my chest. "I'm glad you're here," I said.

"Me too," she replied.

I moved the swing gently with my legs, content to stay there the entire night.

It took a lot of persuading to get Cassidy to leave her truck to blow out the birthday candles. Afterwards, she gave everyone who had shown up to the birthday party a ride. When things wound down and students started going home, I noticed Magnum standing near the trees in the corner of the yard, looking forlorn.

"Will you come with me for a sec? There's something I have to do."

Madelyn gave me a sleepy smile and followed me across the yard to where Cassidy was thanking her dad and mom again for the truck. I had lost count after her thirtieth time. "Um, Cass? I think we have a problem," I said.

Everyone looked at me. I gave my aunt and uncle an innocent smile and motioned toward Magnum. "Magnum's ride hasn't shown up and he needs to get home to make dinner for his sister and brothers." I hoped showing his responsible side would help things out a little.

Magnum looked up at the mention of his name. He watched me warily from across the yard, uncertain what I was doing.

Cassidy caught my look and excitement sparked in her eyes. "I could give him a ride in my new truck! He hasn't had a turn yet."

Uncle Rick gave the Bullet leader a steady look, studying him from head to toe. Magnum shifted from one foot to the other under the scrutiny.

"I don't know how I feel about that," Uncle Rick said.

"I'll go with them," Sandy offered before Cassidy could protest. "They could drop me off at my place."

Aunt Lauren patted Uncle Rick's arm. "They'll be okay."

He let out a loud sigh. "All right, but no dillydallying around. I want you to drop them both off and head straight back."

"I will," Cassidy reassured him, unable to keep the grin from her face. Sandy grabbed her hand and they giggled as they ran to Magnum.

"I'm not sure how I feel about your involvement in all this, Kelson," Uncle Rick said.

"No one knows him better than I do," I replied. "He's a good guy."

He studied me for a minute, then nodded. "Okay, but if anything happens, it's on your head."

"Think he saved my life just to throw it on the chopping block?" I asked Madelyn as we made our way back to the swing.

"Hopefully not," she replied with a sweet smile. "That was nice of you."

I shrugged. "At least he's scared of Uncle Rick."

"Fear of my dad didn't keep you from sneaking into my yard," she reminded me when we sat down.

The thought bothered me. "Think I need to go warn him to be careful?" I asked, starting to rise.

She pulled me back. "Slow down, Buck. You can't go rushing into things."

That made me stop. "Did you just call me your dog's name?"

She laughed. "Yeah. Haven't you seen the way he charges through the fields? He's been sprayed by skunks so many times, we keep tomato juice in stock in our storage room."

"I'm not sure I see the connection," I said stubbornly.

She laughed at my chagrined look. "Time will tell if they're going to work out. You gave them a chance—now don't ruin it for them by charging in to break it up. Let them see what they'll make of it."

I gave her a suspicious glance. "You sound older than you are."

She laughed again, a light, musical sound that chased away my lingering stubbornness. "I read a lot of Jane Austen."

At her insistence, I had opened *Pride and Prejudice* once. By the end of the first page, I swore never to read anything about marriage and women again, much to Madelyn's amusement. Her eyes sparkled at the reference. "Great," I muttered.

She grinned and pillowed her head on my lap. I moved the swing slowly, smoothing her hair as she fell into a light sleep. I tipped my head against the back of the swing and studied the stars. They were so bright in the country. Even the lights strung across the yard were dim in comparison. The pale moon glowed half full near the horizon.

Mom was helping Aunt Lauren gather up plates while Jaren and Uncle Rick stacked chairs to be taken back to the church in the morning. Cole teased Jake with bits of ham from the finger sandwiches. The last of the partiers had returned home either with their friends or rides from family members who took pieces of cake home in gratitude. The grass was flattened by the ghost of footsteps, a silent reminder of the laughter and revelry that had taken place.

I watched it all with a feeling of satisfaction. I knew I should help, but I couldn't bring myself to wake Madelyn or move from my designated position as her pillow. Mom must have guessed what I was thinking because she waved at me, indicated that I should stay put. I smiled and closed my eyes. My breathing slowed to the rhythm of the swing.

Chapter Twenty-eight

I LEFT SCHOOL EARLY and had Magnum drop me off at the junkyard without telling him my plan. Jagger was in town having lunch at the bar where Sally worked, an event that was becoming more of a tradition as time wore on despite his continued protests that he wasn't attracted to her.

I sprayed polish on a rag and ran it along the CBR's sides, causing the paint to gleam in the sunlight. I wiped dust from the chrome and made sure the mirrors were clean. Something inside whispered that I was stalling. I pulled the helmet from the peg in the lean-to and strapped it on, grateful for Magnum's careful cleaning. I zipped a vest underneath my riding jacket by habit, and pulled on my gloves.

I turned the key and pressed the starter. A reluctant smile touched my lips when the engine growled to life. I rolled the throttle a few times just to hear it roar. I glanced back one last time at the shack, then pulled out of the junkyard.

The trip to the factory felt shorter than usual. When I got there, I found the place strangely empty. Maybe I had been quicker at the junkyard than I thought. I crossed the pavement to the starting line, then on a whim, drove the path of the race for old time's sake. I took the corners slower than usual, enjoying the way my motorcycle responded to the slightest touch of throttle or lean. At one point, I thought I heard the rumble of another motorcycle, but none appeared.

When I rounded the last corner, my heart slowed at the sight of six black SUVs lined up where the students usually parked.

Two dozen FBI agents in sharp suits waited for me. I slowed, but didn't stop. I would take whatever punishment they felt I deserved; despite my preparations, though, giving up the Black Rider felt wrong. Even if the town of Sparrow didn't need him, I did because my blood boiled at the sight of people who got away with mistreating others. Riding toward the waiting agents felt like betraying the good I had been able to do in Sparrow. I wanted to protect Madelyn and my family from the worry I caused, but I wondered if Sparrow would be all right without me.

I stopped at the starting line and faced the agents on my motorcycle. It was the exact spot where I had landed when I jumped off the warehouse.

An agent on the right stepped forward. "Time to turn yourself in, Black Rider." He adjusted his sunglasses and waited as though expecting me to climb off my motorcycle and walk to one of their vehicles without a fight.

I almost did just that. I reached for the key to my CBR, and then a sound touched my ears. Another followed, then a third. Soon, the rumbles of more engines than I could count flooded the factory. I looked over my shoulder in time to see street motorcycles, dirt bikes, four-wheelers, three-wheelers, and even a few riding lawn mowers roll through the wide doors of one of the warehouses.

My breath caught in my throat. Each machine was painted black, and the riders wore black helmets and black clothes. They

sped toward me in a pack, a black mass that rumbled like the
thundering hooves of a hundred stallions. I could feel the cement
moving beneath my feet. It felt as though the very air pulsed with
their presence. I held my breath when they neared, and smiled at the
part that grew straight down the middle before they overtook me.

The majority of riders passed me, turned the corner, and circled
back around the warehouse to create a swarm of riders the FBI
agents would never be able to sort through. I laughed and wanted to
cry at the same time. I shook my head, astonished and at a loss as to
what I should do.

One very familiar rider pulled up next to me. Magnum had a
girl riding with him that I recognized even with her helmet on. She
slid the visor up. "Hey, Black Rider."

I grinned at Madelyn even though she couldn't see it through
my visor. I held out a hand and she crossed to my motorcycle.

"What's all this?" I asked.

"You might be ready to give up the Black Rider," she shouted
above the roar of the engines, "but Sparrow isn't."

My heart sped up at her words, pounding hope and truth
through my veins. She wrapped her arms around my waist. "What
now?" I asked Magnum.

He grinned. "Ride," he said before sliding his visor shut.

Madelyn's arms tightened. I revved the engine and drove into
the pack of waiting students. We watched as the lead FBI agent
reached into his jacket for a cell phone and punched in a single
number. A few terse words were exchanged. His jaw clenched. He
pocketed the phone and motioned for his companions to retreat to
their vehicles.

The students' answering roar was louder than the engines. In a
mass, we drove one giant loop around the factory, then sped across
the dusty road to the waiting town beyond.

Look for the next book in the series,

SMALL TOWN
SUPERHERO
III

A QUICK THANK YOU

I JUST WANT TO say "thank you" to the many people who helped make this book possible. Thank you to my husband for patiently reading each draft, for finding plot holes, and for adding depth to scenes and helping them come alive. I couldn't do this without you!

Thank you to my children—my beautiful daughter, Myree, and my twin sons, Ashton and Aiden. Your adventures, laughter, and love fill every corner of my life. I love every moment I'm with you. You are truly amazing and can accomplish anything you put your mind to. Thank you for your patience while I write, and for only destroying one computer in the process (the result of a sippy cup disaster). I hope someday you will lose yourself within these pages and fall in love with the world of Sparrow.

Thank you to those who have read drafts and given me valuable feedback. Thank you most of all to Tristi Pinkston, my editor, for catching the typos and helping my books be the best they possibly can. Thank you to Stonehouse Ink for giving an indie author a chance. I appreciate your patience, your open-mindedness, and your refreshing approach to the book industry!

Thank you to my family for being patient with my runaway imagination. I love you!

Thank you most of all to my readers. I am so grateful for your time, for your reviews, and for the e-mails I receive. I used to escape into books when I was younger and I always wanted to give the same escape back to others. I hope you found the Superhero series enjoyable and heartfelt. This was written for you.

With love,

Cheree

ABOUT THE AUTHOR

CHEREE ALSOP IS THE mother of a beautiful, talented daughter and amazing twin sons who fill every day with light and laughter. She married her best friend, Michael, who changes lives each day in his chiropractic clinic. Cheree is currently working as an independent author and mother. She enjoys reading, riding her motorcycle on warm nights, and playing with her twins while planning her next book. She is also a bass player for her husband's garage band.

Cheree and Michael live in Utah, where they rock out, enjoy the outdoors, plan great adventures, and never stop dreaming.

Check out Cheree's other books at www.chereealsop.com